# CUT ME
# FREE

J. R. JOHANSSON

# CUT ME
# FREE

FARRAR STRAUS GIROUX · NEW YORK

Farrar Straus Giroux Books for Young Readers
175 Fifth Avenue, New York 10010

Printed in the United States of America
Designed by Andrew Arnold
First edition, 2015
1  3  5  7  9  10  8  6  4  2

macteenbooks.com

Library of Congress Cataloging-in-Publication Data
Johansson, J. R., 1978–
   Cut me free / J. R. Johansson.
       pages cm
   Summary: "A seventeen-year-old barely escapes her abusive parents and creates a new
identity that is quickly compromised when her attempt to save a young girl attracts a
deadly stalker"—Provided by publisher.
   ISBN 978-0-374-30023-4 (hardback)
   ISBN 978-0-374-30024-1 (e-book)
   [1. Child abuse—Fiction.   2. Emotional problems—Fiction.   3. Stalking—Fiction.
4. Identity—Fiction.   5. Family—Fiction.   6. Mystery and detective stories.]   I. Title.

PZ7.J62142Cut 2014
[Fic]—dc23

                                                                    2014023371


Farrar Straus Giroux Books for Young Readers may be purchased for business or promotional
use. For information on bulk purchases please contact Macmillan Corporate and Premium
Sales Department at (800) 221-7945 x5442 or by email at specialmarkets@macmillan.com.

*For Krista:*
*Thank you for being my first* honest *reader, for always*
*loving Piper more than anyone else, and for showing me how*
*important sisters can be. Love you!*

CUT ME
FREE

# 1

The city embraces me. Shiny rectangles so tall I can barely make out where they end and the sky begins. They wrap me in shadow. Hiding me. Holding me. In this single moment, I feel safe here, and I don't remember the last time I felt safe anywhere. The sun sets against an unseen horizon, but I don't head back to the hotel. No one waits for me there.

The sounds and smells of this place are like a different world. It smells like people, so many people. I'm accustomed to the smell of emptiness, but it would be foreign in a place so full. No, it's more than full. It is bursting with life. The scent of Rittenhouse Square fills the air around me, green and lush. I'm encircled by millions of breaths taken at once—surrounded by life. The best thing the Parents ever did for me was to go down without giving me much trouble. At least I only had to escape once. I'm not positive that they're dead, but I certainly tried. And I really can't think about that now.

Instead, I need to live. Everything I've ever known is death and pain; being drenched in life feels good.

Closing my eyes, I extend my arms and the warmth of the city flows around me, flows through me. No more pain. No more claw-ing fingers dying to break another bone or raise another bruise on my pale skin. No more cruel eyes and words twisting my world. Now they are dying. Now they are dead.

And I don't regret what I've done.

I open my eyes and squint at the statue across from the bench I'm sitting on. It depicts a battle—fierce combat, lives at stake. A massive lion crushing a serpent beneath his claw in the final vic-tory of a fight to the death. In some ways, I relate more to these animals than to the people in the park around me. I struggle to move past my own battle, still remembering every moment of the fight for my life yet never able to celebrate the triumph.

Lifting my wrist, I check the time on my watch. It's a digital one I found in a kids' section of a department store. I haven't quite figured out the twirling hands of its more confusing counterpart. And the adult ones were all loose on my too thin wrists. There aren't many people in this section of Rittenhouse Square, and all of them were here when I arrived fifteen minutes ago. He's late. Only five minutes, but that's five minutes too many. There is no-where I need to be, but it doesn't matter. He's my fourth attempt. The first didn't show up. The second, I left the minute he let his eyes wander a little too freely. The third didn't seem intelligent enough to entrust my future in her hands. If I'm going to hire this Cameron Angelo person, I need to be sure he will do what I ask, when I ask. I need to be certain he knows his business.

If this doesn't work out, I'll move on to the next name that my money can buy me in a shady bar or dark alley. Illegal services are easy to obtain, especially in a big city like Philadelphia. If you can find the right places to search and are okay with paying for the information, you can get anything. The books Nana used to slip me in the dead of night were more educational than I ever imagined. The ones she'd let me keep taught me the most—*Flowers in the Attic*, *Oliver Twist*, and *Kidnapped*. She'd been planning my escape for a long time, but neither of us thought I'd be doing it alone.

We'd shared a favorite quote. The paper that held it had been as yellowed and wrinkled as Nana's hands, but I still wish I'd brought it with me. She'd ripped it from an old tattered book of English poets. Only two lines from a poem, but Nana said it should bring me hope.

"Though my soul may set in darkness, it will rise in perfect light; I have loved the stars too fondly to be fearful of the night."

I mutter the words three times under my breath, my heart holding tight to the quote with a grip stronger than my fear. There is nothing I need more right now than hope. I shove aside the aching pit that replaces my insides whenever I think of Nana or Sam and get to my feet. Switching my suitcase to my other hand, I squeeze it until my fingers stop trembling. I couldn't leave it in the hotel—it holds two hundred and thirteen thousand reasons not to. Only ten thousand less than it had when I packed it. Not bad for over a year on my own, but living under the radar doesn't exactly play well with extravagance anyway. Even now, it feels weird dragging my suitcase behind me when I know what it contains. I can feel everyone looking at it—at me.

A young girl walks past holding hands with a man and a cold rush spreads through me, like an arctic wind starting at my feet and blowing up through the winding tunnels of my veins. As plain as the city around me, I see her pain. She tugs down her pink sleeve, but it still isn't long enough to cover the bruises beneath. Her hand is wrapped in his, but it's limp, not holding on for support. It's trapped, ensnared.

Millions of memories of Sam pelt my brain, and my free hand digs around in my pocket for the black metal bolt I always carry with me. I rub my thumb across its worn ridges as I struggle to keep the images entombed. The past I wish I could bury forever crawls out of the darkness to haunt me again: Sam and me cowering in the dark corner of the attic, the Father's breath hot on my face as he pins me to the wall, the Mother ignoring my pleas to leave Sam and take me instead as she drags him down the stairs and slams the door, later followed by tears on his face and mine when he comes back with new bruises and cuts I couldn't prevent. I'd watched him sleep every night and dreaded the next week, the next day, the next hour, when it would begin all over again.

I force a choked breath in silent agony. The memories are too painful to touch. I skirt away from them and barricade myself in a corner of my mind, trying to pretend this little girl isn't suffering the same way my brother did.

The man with her reminds me of the Father, but the similarity isn't outward. It's like the same darkness radiates from him. I focus on the details, driving back the ache of confusing emotion with the unfaltering black-and-whiteness of logic. They look nothing alike. This man is younger, maybe forty, and his hair is dark. The Father had blond hair, like Sam and me, and his paranoia made him stay trim and in shape. This man is an overweight slob.

He stops to scratch his shoulder and she flinches when he raises his arm. Her dirty, dark hair falls across her face the way Sam's used to. She's hiding and no one else sees. She's dying and no one else notices. I battle through a wave of nausea and try to keep breathing.

I watch them walk away. Sam's small voice pleads in my head—tells me to save her.

*No one will save her but you.*

Like a magnet, I'm towed along in their wake and fighting the desperate need to do what I couldn't do for Sam. To stop this man before it's too late. I know I have to ignore it. I can't get involved. I must pretend I didn't see, but Sam won't let me.

*She needs you.*

I follow them to the edge of the park, keeping my distance. Just watching.

All I can do is watch—at least, for now.

"You give up too easy." A deep, warm voice speaks from behind me and I whirl to face him. My hands fly up in the defensive posture I know too well.

"Whoa, slow down." He takes two steps back and stares at me until I drop my arms to my sides. "Sorry. I just didn't want you to leave. You're"—he glances down at his phone—"Piper, right?"

"Yeah." I pivot to one side, keeping him in full view, but glance toward the back of the little girl disappearing from sight. The guilty feeling that I'm losing her is almost as strong as the surge of relief that she's gone. No longer my responsibility.

*No one else will save her.*

I suppress a shudder and ignore Sam's words. Focusing on

drawing a single deep breath, I release the bolt and draw my hand out of my pocket, fix my attention on the guy in front of me. It didn't take me more than a few days after I ran away to learn that noticing the details keeps me alive—both in and out of the attic. This situation is no different.

Cameron is tall with broad shoulders and chin-length brown hair. Olive skin, nose slightly broader than it should be. His jeans and red short-sleeved shirt fit him well but don't look new. He's confident, poised, and calm.

His stance tells me that he can more than hold his own in a fight, but that's not what I need help with. A genius is what I need, a criminal wizard. The hazel eyes returning my gaze are inspecting me as well. I can't deny the intelligence there. He might be smart, but he's too young. Not what I'm looking for.

"Thank you for coming, Cameron, but it's not going to work out." I turn and walk away, my suitcase wheels clicking rapidly on each crack in the sidewalk. *Click, click, click, click*—the rapid pulse of a city that seems as alive as the people that reside here. Each part of Philly is different. One section is a cozy tree-lined neighborhood, the next a bustling center of business. It makes me feel safe, like death can't follow me here. Even though deep inside I have no doubt death *can* follow me anywhere.

A second later he's walking beside me, his long legs easily matching my fastest pace. "Call me Cam."

"Fine, *Cam*." I don't miss a step even though the name is a little too close to my brother's for my comfort. "It's still not going to work out."

He glances at my luggage. "Looks like you gave up on me before we met. Either that or you're the youngest flight attendant I've ever seen. You have a flight to catch or something?"

"No. I just think we're done here." I shift my suitcase to my other side so I can be between him and it. Any future I might build depends on keeping it safe.

"And can I ask why?"

"You're too young."

He laughs, but it sputters like a dying car when he sees I'm serious. Then he lifts an eyebrow. "When you're the best, age doesn't matter. Besides, how old are you? Fifteen?"

"Seventeen." I don't admit that I'm not entirely certain. Time was so hard to track in the attic. And even before I'd been stuck in there when I was six, one of our neighbors—an old woman whose name I wish I could remember—was the only person who'd ever wished me a happy birthday. There is very little I can remember from the time before the Father. It wasn't good, but it was better. The pain was still there, it was just different. Exchanging hunger pains for bruises and scars wasn't my idea of an upgrade. Six years with the Mother and her addictions, then ten years with the Father and his.

"Then we're even. Not a good enough reason."

I stop and face Cam. A million instincts tell me to keep walking and ignore him. He'll give up eventually, but something about him makes me reluctant to leave. "Because you were late."

"I was here before you were."

"No." An image of every person who was in my section of the park when I arrived flashes through my head. "You weren't."

"May I?" He grins wide and then steps carefully behind me.

9

Raising an arm, he indicates a small break in one of the hedges on the other side of the statue. It would be nearly impossible to see from where I'd been waiting, but from that spot he could see this entire section of the park. I release my breath. Very smart.

"Fine." I turn around to face him and immediately take a step back. The smell of soap, mint, and something warm and woodsy overwhelms me—too close, way too close.

"So, am I rehired?" He leans forward and grins wide.

"To be that, you would've had to be hired to begin with."

"Then why are we meeting?"

Lifting the suitcase, I walk to a nearby tree and sit on the grass. When he sits down, he's again too close.

I squirm for a moment before scooting a little farther away from him. The guy has no sense of personal space. "This is the interview," I say.

He looks down at the now slightly larger gap between us and I'm surprised by how irritated I am when the corner of his mouth twitches. "Okay. An interview then. Shouldn't you ask me some questions?"

"What's your fee?" I toy with a single blade of grass by my knee that is longer than the others around it.

"Straight to money. You don't mess around, do you?"

"No, I don't." I meet his eyes. "And if you do—"

"I get it, I get it." He raises his hands and gives me an easy smile. "You're extremely strict and serious. I can handle it."

His sarcasm comes through loud and clear. Somehow he thinks he's in control of this situation, this conversation. I don't like it. He seems nice enough, but I don't know what to do with "nice." All

I *need* is someone who will get the job done and then leave me alone. I only met him two minutes ago and already Cam doesn't strike me as that kind of guy.

"This isn't a joke to me." Brushing the grass off my hands, I shift my weight to my feet and begin to stand when he grabs my forearm. Panic and adrenaline slam through my system and I can't breathe. I can't see him anymore. He's a shadow, a remnant of the Father. With one move, I twist my wrist, jerk it back, and break his grip. He shouldn't touch me. He has no idea what I'm capable of. Gasps of air escape my chest. I see Cam's eyes widen as fear and anger clash inside me, but his words cool them both immediately.

"Okay, slow down and breathe . . ." His voice brings clarity and eases my panic slightly. It's strong and firm like the Father's, a man's voice, but without threat or malice. "I understand. You want a new identity. That's what I can provide." Cam's tone is low and steady. He raises his hands in surrender and leans back a few inches. His gaze holds mine, and any trace of humor is gone. "I'll give you a different past and you can turn it into any future you want. I'll help you live under the radar—to live invisibly. I'm the best. My fee is seven thousand and I guarantee it's worth every cent."

His confidence sets me at ease. I relax back onto the grass and stare at the park around me. Like so many times since I escaped, I feel like someone is watching me. But it's not possible. Even if he survived, the Father couldn't have followed me—no, I have to ignore the feeling and instead focus on what I can control, on the decisions I have to make . . . on Cam.

Three different sources told me he was the clear choice and the only one to go to. That Cam was my best option. I'd only waited this long to contact him because I don't like taking the obvious path. It makes me feel predictable and vulnerable. But his connections and hacking skills are supposedly unmatched.

Plucking the extra-long grass blade from the ground, I run it across the back of my hand. He was here first, watching me and waiting. He seems to pick up on cues that I don't even realize I'm giving him. I'm beginning to see why he, even at his age, is the first name they gave me. Without looking his way, I give him my answer. "Fine. Meet me here tomorrow morning at ten. We start with a new identity, then an apartment. My hotel sucks."

It's getting dark. The nearby walkway lights up as the power to all the streetlamps comes on at once. The city prepares to fight off even the coming night. The light casts a strange glow in Cam's eyes as I get to my feet.

"Wait," he says.

"What?" I stare down at him, already impatient to leave. I don't like holding still for too long. Stillness reminds me of the attic. Unsurprisingly, I'm not a huge fan of small spaces either.

Cam sits forward and wraps one long arm around his knee. "I have questions for you."

"No."

"No? What do you mean?" His expression is incredulous, but I'm not going down this road. The sooner he understands that, the better.

"Did the meaning of the word 'no' change recently?" I keep my voice light as I rub my hands together, the chill of the evening coming faster than I expected.

"You aren't going to answer any questions? An interview goes both ways, you know." His eyes are piercing. "I haven't decided yet if I'm willing to help you."

The people who'd recommended him had suggested something like this was a possibility. Apparently, in the last year, he'd become very picky about the kind of clientele he was willing to take on.

"Two questions." I nod and try not to show how tightly wound this one concession makes me. "I'll answer if I can."

"Do you have a record?" His expression is grim.

"No. Last question." That was easy. Hard to have a record when no one knew we were in the attic in the first place. I wait for him to speak.

"Is anyone after you?"

"No." I shake my head and study the sidewalk around my black sneakers. Most of the time, I'm pretty sure no one is left. A shudder escapes, but I try to cover it with a shrug.

"What if I need to know more?"

I lower my chin. "If it's about anything that happened before I met you five minutes ago, then no. Call it the five-minute rule. It's unbreakable."

Cam hops to his feet so fast I take two steps back and tug my suitcase between us like a shield. Then he freezes, holding perfectly still until I relax my stance.

"Fine," he says. With his back to the streetlamp, his face is hidden in shadow. I can't see his expression, but there's a roughness in his voice that makes me uneasy. "We'll discuss it tomorrow."

He pivots on one foot and walks away. I know he can't hear me, but I respond as much to reassure myself as anything else.

"No. We won't."

# 2

Cam is sitting beside the fountain in Rittenhouse Square when I arrive the next morning. I'm only five minutes late, but I'd planned to be early. It had been harder than I expected to get moving this morning. Someone played music too loud in my hotel half the night, and I had nightmare after nightmare of the Father showing up and dragging me back to the attic. I can almost feel the circles under my eyes when I blink.

In the late-morning sunlight, the park smells like warm grass and chlorine from the fountain. It reminds me of the dirty swimming pool outside the motel on the outskirts of Cincinnati, where I'd stopped for a few days to sleep in a completely stationary room before boarding another bus. I watched families swim in it, but I don't understand the appeal of swimming pools. They're like giant chemical bathtubs that you have to share with other people. Besides, the idea of being immersed in water deeper than I am tall just sounds like another method of torture.

Cam leans forward and smiles when he sees me. His white shirt is unbuttoned with a gray T-shirt underneath, and for some reason it makes me nervous. Why must he appear so relaxed when my every nerve is being fried by the glare bouncing off his sunglasses?

"And I thought being punctual was important to you." He stands up and lowers his glasses until I can see the swirls in his hazel eyes. "You look terrible."

"Thanks," I mutter, and self-consciously shift my suitcase in front of me. Like that will help cover up my oversize T-shirt and faded jeans. "How kind of you to mention it."

"Come on." He pushes the glasses back up, and I wince when the glare blinds me again. He reaches down to the ground beside him and brings up two steaming cups that I hadn't noticed before. "Coffee will help."

I inspect his offering for a moment. I don't want to offend him, but avoiding risk is more important. "You first."

His brow lowers, and his eyes stay on mine as he takes a sip from the cup and then hands it to me. "Not afraid of germs, I see."

"They're less scary than other things you could've put in there." This isn't about Cam, and it bothers me that he's making it sound like it is. Trust is something I've learned to live without. It's better this way—safer—for both of us. I watch the steam rising from the cup. I've never had coffee, but I have to get used to trying new things. The scalding, bitter liquid coats my insides with warmth and I do my best not to sputter. "Thanks."

Cam laughs. "That bad, huh?"

"Horrible." I take another sip and can't resist making a face. "I guess it's an acquired taste."

A beautiful girl with long black hair and eyelashes to match walks around the fountain and stands next to Cam. She's close to him in age. A girlfriend maybe? If this is a girlfriend, I'm gone. I don't have time for silly distractions. She waves and I raise an eyebrow, waiting for him to explain.

"This is my associate, Lily."

"An associate was *not* part of our deal."

"You will want me to be." Lily winks at me.

Cam takes a sip of his coffee and grins. "She's going to help us find the new you."

It's been an hour since we got here and Lily hasn't stopped squinting at me the entire time. We're in a back alley in an abandoned barbershop that somehow still has running water—hot water, however, appears to be too big of a request. Everything in the room is covered in a layer of dust. The air smells like it's been drenched in hair dye and left out to mold. The only thing keeping it breathable is the fact that Lily put on too much perfume. Every other breath is filled with a hefty dose of vanilla and spice. My nose tingles in a chemical daze and I rub the tip of it with my hand. Five baskets of scissors, brushes, and combs are spread out on the table near us like a bizarre assortment of medieval torture devices.

Lily raises her scissors, snips another section of damp hair, and I try unsuccessfully not to flinch. If there is any hair left at all when she's finished, I'll be amazed. The floor around the lumpy old barber chair I'm sitting on is covered with long dark strands. They look so foreign even though I know they used to be my own golden hair. I'd convinced Lily to let me wash my hair myself, after she dyed it. It's still difficult to sit motionless when she's touching parts of me, even if I can't exactly feel it.

I hear Cam's voice softly from another room. Whoever he's talking to, he doesn't sound happy with them. The only word I've been able to make out clearly is "no." After a few more minutes, I hear "ciao" and an electronic beep before Cam walks through the door holding a white sheet and a large paper bag. When his eyes meet mine, he whistles.

"Brunette suits you." He nods. "Now I might actually believe you're seventeen."

My hand flies up to where my long blond hair used to rest across my shoulders, but there's nothing there. Lily shakes her head and spins my chair to face the mirror.

For the first time in months I'm too shocked to be reminded of Sam's lifeless eyes by looking in my own. Only the reflection is not me—or, at least, it doesn't feel like me. My hair, which has never been dyed and has only been cut a handful of times in my life, is gone. In my place is a girl I'd never recognize as myself in a million years. She blinks her wide blue eyes at me and they're the only thing I recognize about her.

My new hair is so dark it's nearly black, and it's cut in a jagged line above my shoulders. It's confident, daring, and I love it. This is what I want: for the old me to disappear. I will no longer see the blond hair like the Father's that made it seem like he'll never truly be in the past. I can't look at everything I've already done wrong, only the things I can choose to do right from here on out.

"It's perfect," I say.

Lily dips into a little curtsy. "What can I say? I have mad skills."

She reaches into a white bag and pulls out a long silver tube. I don't know what it is, but the way she squints and walks straight up to my face makes me squirm. When she bends down close, I can count the flecks of gold in her brown eyes. I hold my breath. I know she's trying to help me, but I don't remember the last time I felt this uncomfortable.

By the time Lily separates the tube, reveals a mascara wand, and brings it toward my eye, I can't sit still anymore.

"Wait! No, no, stop." I make my body go limp and slide down out of the chair, scrambling around her on my hands and knees. My heart pounds in my chest as I try to get to my feet.

Lily jumps back to avoid falling on me. "Hey! What are you doing?" She stares at me like I'm the weirdest thing she's ever seen.

I've seen mascara in makeup commercials. It's fine if other people want to wear it. I just don't appreciate it zooming toward my eye like some sort of weapon.

Cam's voice comes from behind Lily and startles me. I've almost forgotten he is here. "Don't worry, Lily. She doesn't need it."

"Fine by me," Lily mutters with a frown as she closes the tube and sticks it in her white bag. By the time she drops the bag into one of the baskets, she has a neutral expression back on her face, but there is something hesitant behind her eyes now.

I'm used to that. It's happened on buses across the country. As hard as I try, sooner or later people recognize I'm not as normal as I pretend to be.

Usually, I try to be gone by the time they figure that out.

Retaking my seat, I stare in the mirror to avoid seeing the look Cam and Lily are sharing behind me. Although my hair was blond before Lily got her hands on it, my eyelashes and eyebrows have always been dark. And if I can get by without poking devices near my eyes, I want to.

I can't hold back a tiny smile when I reach up to touch one of the little spikes of hair on my neck. Both the smile and the hair are foreign and wonderful. I watch through the dirty mirror as Cam drapes a sheet over a partition in the back of the room and faces me.

"I have two options for you." He drags a chair out. Throwing one long leg over it, he sits down. "Do you feel more like a Suzanna or a Charlotte?"

I frown. "Neither. Are those my only options?"

"Yes."

"I think she could pull off a Charlotte." Lily dunks some scissors in a jar of blue solution and squints at me over her shoulder. "Yeah, definitely more than a Suzanna. I knew a Suzanna once. She was horrible."

"Charlotte it is." Cam stands, reaches into the bag, and withdraws some papers and a camera.

"Fine. Do I have a last name?" I stretch one toe down to the floor and push against the ground until my chair spins toward him.

"Yes, it's, uh . . ." He flips past the first page and examines the second. "Thompson. And good news, Miss Charlotte. You're now eighteen and have your GED."

"Charlotte Thompson." My new name feels like the lie it is when I say it out loud, but I'll get over it. After all, Piper isn't an official name either. When they had put me up in the attic I didn't mind at first. At least I got to eat there. The Mother never cared

19

much whether I ate or not, she was always too focused on her next fix. But once we were with the Father, he wanted me to be stronger to withstand what he had in store for me. The Father insisted on calling me Girl. I was punished for saying my real name and eventually I forced myself to forget it, but I think it might have started with an A. When Sam was born, they just called him Boy. I'd picked the name Sam for my brother because it felt warm and we didn't have enough warmth. We'd used our secret names at night and in whispers, only when no one else could hear.

I'd started calling myself Piper after I read a page torn out of a fairy-tale book we had in the attic. We didn't have the whole story, so I'd made up part of it on my own. The page said the Pied Piper got mad at some parents and played his music to lead their children away. I pretended the parents in the story were bad, too—that the Piper was saving the children. I wished I could do that for Sam. I wanted to take him away. But I hadn't, and now it was too late.

The bad parents won in my story, but that wasn't the end. They aren't winning anymore.

One perk of them being paranoid hermits is that their house was in the middle of nowhere. No friends, no neighbors, no one to come looking for them for a very long time. No one else ever knew that Sam and I even existed except for Nana, and she'd only found out about us when her cancer set in and she came to live with the Parents before she died. I've wondered how life would have been if we'd lived with Nana before the attic. She never would have let the Mother take me away. She'd said so a hundred times and I choose to believe it was true.

One day when both the Parents were outside, I'd made enough

noise that Nana had discovered us. I still remember the fury in the Parents' faces as she told them she'd called the police to report what the Parents had done. It was the first time I ever tasted hope. The first time anyone ever made me wonder if we could be worth fighting for. Before the officers showed up, Sam and I were gagged, bound, and secured to the attic floor. For added emphasis, the Father hit Sam hard enough to knock him out and made it clear that Nana and Sam would pay even more if I made a sound. I was too scared to do anything but cry in silence as I listened to the Father tell them Nana was dying of cancer. He produced a paper stating that her medication could bring on vivid hallucinations. The police chuckled with the Parents about how crazy the story sounded and told them to keep a better eye on Nana.

They did.

All the phones in the house were gone within an hour, outside locks were installed on every door and window within a day, and Sam and I didn't see Nana again for two weeks. Each night I'd gone to sleep worrying about what the Parents had done to her, and the laughter of the officers wouldn't stop echoing in my head.

But now, the Parents are gone, Nana is gone, Sam is gone. And even I am being wiped away, replaced by someone named Charlotte.

*You will always be Piper.*

Stacking the papers on the countertop, Cam twists to face me and tosses me a phone. I only catch it out of instinct.

"What's this?"

"It's a burner phone." At my blank expression, he sticks his hands in his pockets and continues. "Prepaid disposable cell phone.

So I can get in touch with you if I need to. You don't want a phone with a plan, and you don't want to keep the same phone for too long, at least not for a while, they're too easy to track. But don't change phones without letting me know."

"What if I need to find you?" I flip open the small black phone and then close it again. I tilt my head to one side. "Do I need to keep leaving messages with that bartender? Lenny's Bar was kind of a dump. I'd rather not go back there if I don't have to."

Cam laughs. "No. You're a client now. My phone number is already saved in your contact list."

"Oh." For some reason this makes me nervous. I lower my gaze just in case he can see it in my face. "Okay."

"If you have any kind of trouble, contact me first, not the police," Cam continues, and Lily yawns like she's heard this speech before and isn't interested in hearing it again. "Even if you think you're being careful and report something anonymously, they will still have your number and you'll have to ditch the phone. Otherwise the cops can usually find you if they want to. And I doubt you want them poking around in your life or your past. Keep your head down, don't cause any problems, and you should be fine."

I nod, my eyes still on Lily's feet. My experiences with the police haven't exactly been pleasant. Contacting them isn't something I can picture myself doing.

Cam waits until I raise my eyes to him before speaking again. "So, do you think you can get used to it? You'll be Charlotte forever if you do this right."

I reach up and touch the ends of my almost-dry hair. My voice is small in my ears when it comes out and I wish I sounded more confident. "Yeah, I can be Charlotte."

"Good. I have to ask you a question."

"Sorry. Five-minute rule, remember?" I hold my hands up like I'm helpless to break it and his jaw flexes. Lily is leaning against the counter across from me, watching us like it's some kind of sporting event. When I glance at her, she shrugs, but there's a tightness to her expression that wasn't there before. Reaching into my pocket, I grip my bolt tightly. I started prying it from the bars over the attic window on the day Sam was born. It had taken me nearly a month of pushing, pulling, and hitting to loosen it even a bit. A year, and more than a few scars on my hands later, I finally got this first bolt out. It is one of only two things I brought with me when I escaped. I'd never actually gotten out through the window, but it didn't matter. The bolt was the first time I started trying. It helps me remember things I can't afford to forget.

It reminds me I'm not weak. If I can escape the Parents, I can handle anything.

Cam's voice snaps me back to the present and I raise my gaze to focus on him.

"Relax, it isn't about the past." Cam walks closer, his expression serious. "It's about the future. The five-minute rule doesn't apply."

"Still might not answer it, but go ahead." I scoot back in my seat, my fingers loosening their grip automatically.

"What do you plan to do with Charlotte?"

I stare at him. Not exactly what I was expecting. "Huh?"

"Your new identity." He takes another step closer. "If you're careful and you take care of it—you know, stay out of trouble, pay your debts, lie low—then she'll last a lot longer."

I meet his eye. "I'll be nice to Charlotte."

Lily must've decided our conversation isn't interesting anymore, because she turns to her supplies and starts packing them in organized bundles and baskets.

"Good. If you trash this identity, I won't give you a new one." Cam is frowning now. I'm beginning to wonder what kind of person he thinks I am. The skin on my arms crawls as I admit to myself that I couldn't answer that question if I tried. "I only deal with people who treat my work with respect."

"Sounds fair."

Cam extends a hand to me. As I look at it, he waits patiently for me to take it. Dread makes my gut clench, both at the idea of him touching me and the knowledge that I don't deserve to be touched. My breath quickens and my fingers squeeze the black bit of metal in my pocket. It takes all my control not to sprint past him and out the door. Running can't be the answer, not anymore.

Instead, I draw a slow deep breath, get to my feet, and step around him with a shake of my head. "I . . . I really don't want anyone to touch me. It isn't personal."

Lily freezes in the middle of packing a group of combs. I notice her roll her eyes at my words, but Cam doesn't seem bothered.

"Not a problem, I kind of gathered you felt that way yesterday." With a shrug he gestures for me to walk toward the curtain. "But it's time to smile for the camera."

# 3

We climb the stairs to the fourth apartment on Cam's list. Unlike the first two, this one is on a well-lit street in a safer section of town. Unlike the third one, there isn't a dead cat on the fire escape.

When I'd objected to the awful smell from the poor cat, Cam rolled his eyes and said I was too picky. Lily decided she was done apartment hunting and went home. She kissed him on the cheek before she left and then waved at me when she saw I was watching. I'm relieved she's gone. I know that kind of affection is supposed to be normal, natural even, but I still haven't gotten used to seeing it.

The building's manager, Janice, unlocks the apartment and steps aside. She's fifty-something with a fuzzy jacket and fuzzier hair. The apartment is on the third and top floor on Lombard Street. It comes furnished, which is good since everything I own would fit in the cabinet under the sink. The space is smaller than the first two apartments, but clean—and all the apartments are bigger than the attic. Through the large window I can see a playground across the way and several nearby rooftop terraces. There is a slightly worn, brown leather couch facing the window, and a tan armchair tucked into the corner. Two walls are exposed red brick, and for some reason they make me feel warm inside.

So open—not like the attic. I can breathe here. I can *live* here.

Cam sits at the oak dining table, waiting and watching as I walk through. Janice sighs a few times, and after she starts tapping her foot Cam shifts forward.

"Do you think you could give us a minute to discuss?"

"Sure." Her smile for him could melt butter. "I'll be in my place. Let me know when you're done." She gives me an appraising and wary glance as she walks out, and I put on the sweetest expression I can manage. Cam chuckles after the door closes.

"What?" I glance at him as I run my hand over a brick that is a slightly darker red than the rest.

"Just your face. You look like you're in pain." He inclines his head toward the door.

I drop my hand back to my side and turn to face him. "I was trying for trustworthy."

"Yeah, maybe you should work on that."

"Being trustworthy?" Raising an eyebrow, I wait for him to show signs of discomfort, but he doesn't. He knows what I'm doing. Maybe I didn't need to hire someone quite *this* smart.

"*Looking* trustworthy."

I move to the bedroom. There's a queen-size bed with a gray blanket and matching curtains on the window. I stare at the gloomy expanse, imagining the empty floor beneath the bed. It is so big. Such a waste of space when sleeping on the floor is more comfortable. Beds are too soft.

I open the closet and peek inside. It isn't huge, but it's well organized. One half is set up for shoes and has several shelves; the other has a bar for hangers and open space below for storage. Everything about this place is right. It feels like home already, or maybe what I think a home should feel like. I'm realizing how lucky I am to work with Cam. Getting an apartment like this without having to do a background check would be impossible without his connections. Even if it does come with a bump in the rent for what he calls the "anonymity bonus." I step back and brush off my jeans before I close the closet door.

"This will work."

"Okay, then sit down."

I walk back to the table but don't pull out a chair. "Why?"

"Because I have more questions for you."

"No. Those two at the park are the only ones you're getting. Do the words 'five-minute rule' mean nothing to you?" I groan with a quick shake of my head and turn away. I have the door open and I'm halfway into the hall before he stands and speaks.

"Janice trusts me, not you."

I lower my chin and stare hard into his eyes. "And I don't really trust either of you, so what's your point?"

"You can trust me."

I just watch him, waiting for him to continue. There is no reason to discuss this.

"Janice . . ." He looks like he's searching for the right words. "Well, let's start with the fact that she has more in common with you than you think. Her name's origin for example."

I'm not all that surprised. For her to let me stay here based solely on Cam's recommendation, I figured it had to be something like that. Still, the confirmation makes me suddenly wary. "And what is *she* hiding from? Did you ask her as many questions as you're trying to ask me?"

"Yes." His gaze hardens and he continues. "And she was a lot more forthcoming than you've been. She is a very good woman who was in a bad situation."

I nod, not pushing to know more. They can keep their secrets if they let me keep mine.

"The point is, without my okay, she'll never let you rent this place. Especially without filling out an application or running a background check, which I don't think you want her to do, *Charlotte*." Cam steps in front of me. He waits, knowing I don't like it when he stands so close. I can see it in his eyes.

Lowering my gaze, I inch back into the apartment, my spine prickling with frustration even as I do what he wants.

"Good, now sit down and answer a few simple questions for me."

My feet echo oddly in the mostly empty space as I reluctantly drag them back to the table. "What do you want to know?"

Cam takes the seat across from me. "What are you running from?"

"Who says I'm running?" I knock my knuckles against the wood table. "I'm getting an apartment—*if* I can get your permission. Looks to me like I'm staying."

"You ran from somewhere to stay here," Cam says. His eyes stare through me as I study the wood grain on the table. The swirls and loops help me focus. I have no problem lying to him if it means he'll drop this and leave me alone. God knows I've done worse.

"Why do you care? I thought I was hiring you so I wouldn't have to answer these kinds of questions."

"You are." Cam takes a deep breath and lets it out slowly. "I just like to know that I'm not helping dangerous criminals. Asking a couple of questions helps me sleep at night."

I fake a laugh and am happy to hear that it sounds less awkward than it feels being forced out of my chest. "Do I look like a dangerous criminal to you?"

He doesn't answer, but he waits until I meet his eyes. They intimidate me, but I refuse to even blink. After a few seconds, I realize the best way to end this conversation. I'm not the only one with secrets.

"What happened to the real Charlotte Thompson?" I ask.

Cam blinks, and I see something new in his expression, but it isn't the guilt I was expecting—more like resignation.

"Her mom died. She went to live with her dad in France. I don't think she'll be coming back—at least not for a long time."

I stand, but Cam grabs my hand before I can get away. I jerk it out of his hold and resist a thousand impulses that tell me to grab the chair or the vase and hit him with it for touching me when he knows I don't welcome it. When he drops his hand and looks up at me, all the violent urges fizzle like lit matches in water. I expect to see hunger, a thirst for power and dominance. But instead his eyes are sad, pleading. And they steal my breath away.

"Tell me you're running from the bad things others did." His voice is barely above a whisper. "And not the bad things you did."

I swallow and take a step back. "Yeah, others." Then the apartment feels much smaller, and I need to get away. Turning, I walk into the hallway, down the stairs, and out into the night air. My brain fills with the images I've been fighting off for more than a year. The monster I'd become, the knife in my hand, the violence I'd never have believed could come from me, the blood . . . so much blood. I press my palms against my eyes and try to shove it all away. They were the monsters, not me.

*You are good, Piper.*

Sam's voice calms me down, like always. Four deep gulps of the chilly evening air later, I watch the way the sky fades from the light pink at the horizon up to navy overhead, the perfect shift of one color into a completely different one. My old life could fade away and become something new. If only I am brave enough to make it happen.

Cam walks down to where I wait. I'm the picture of patience and calm, pushing aside wave upon wave of panic at everything I'm doing—everything I've done. I'm an expert at this. If I repeat that a few more times, it's sure to be true.

He stuffs his hands in his pockets. "So, I know you don't seem to have to worry much about money, but have you thought about—what now?"

My mind stops its whirling. "What do you mean?"

"Are you getting a job? Going to school?" He kicks the back of one shoe lightly against the step behind him, and for the first time since I met him he seems uncertain.

"Oh, I can go to school?" I haven't attended school a single day in my life. I was supposed to start, but the Father took us back and it never happened. I've spent the last year trying to learn what I can where I can—devouring newspapers, magazines, books, anything

I can get my hands on. The first month, when I couldn't stop shaking long enough to be seen outside without drawing attention to myself, I'd spent long days and sleepless nights trying to absorb culture, customs—life—all through television sets in my hotel rooms. I tried so hard to add on to everything Nana managed to teach me in only a few short months. Still, the idea of going to school seems as foreign as going to Mars.

When I realize Cam is squinting at me I go on. "Can I go to college as Charlotte? Can Charlotte go?"

"You might need more documentation from me, but that shouldn't be a problem."

I nod and try not to reveal how overwhelmed I feel. It's a heavy freedom, like someone gave me wings so large I can barely stand beneath their weight. I've never had so many options in my life. "I think I'll wait. Get a job first and maybe go to school next year."

"Okay." He peers at me hard for a few seconds before continuing. "If you decide you need help on the job front, let me know."

A small laugh escapes my lips, and from the way his face hardens I wish I could suck it back in. "Why? Are you hiring?"

"No." Cam shifts his weight onto the balls of his feet and leans toward me. "But if I'm sure I can trust you, I might know someone who is."

He's so close I see the light reflecting in his eyes. I smell his mint gum.

"Don't." My voice is barely above a whisper.

"Don't what?" His eyes are holding mine, and I struggle against the urge to run.

"Don't trust me."

31

# 4

Three days later, I watch a little boy sitting on the edge of the Rittenhouse Square fountain and smile as he kicks his feet in the cold water and squeals. My heart aches that Sam never made a noise like that in his entire life. The most we ever had were quiet giggles when I read him stories in the attic. Only at night when we were sure no one could hear us—that was our time.

I shift my position on the bench across from the fountain and check the clock again. There's still an hour before I'm supposed to meet Cam with the other half of my payment. Until then, I will stay in the sun. My pale skin is already pink, and I love it. I probably shouldn't because I've already had a sunburn once and it was anything but fun, but it feels like proof that I can go outside. Now I never have to go back in if I don't want to. The freedom is exhilarating and terrifying at the same time. Sometimes it is too much.

A shiver chills me from the inside out and I glance around the park again to make sure no one is looking at me too closely, no stranger staring too hard, but they barely seem to notice other people are here. Everyone is too absorbed in their own lives to pay attention to anything else, and that's just fine with me.

I spent half of my first week in the city locked in my hotel room hiding in the bathtub. I'd adjusted partly to life outside the attic by then, but the city is so much more. I came here because it is the opposite of a small attic in a cabin in the wilderness. But it is the opposite to the point where nothing is small. So much of everything I've never known—holding me, binding me, drowning me in vastness. I needed a moment of smallness and security to reorient myself in this new world. But I'm doing better now. The most important thing is to remember to keep breathing. Nana said as long as I keep breathing everything will work itself out.

I stretch, trying to absorb even more of the sunlight, but this time the warmth reminds me I'm alive. I'm alive and Sam is dead. He was six. No six-year-old should die. It's wrong. The whole damn world is wrong. He will never get to be seven.

The rough bark of the tree scratches against my back, so I sit forward, and all at once I forget about sunlight and warmth. She's here. It's the same girl from before, and I hear Sam pleading again. Her clothes are as dirty as the first time. This time I can clearly make out a new cigarette burn on the back of her hand.

My eyes search the park. Someone else has to see; it's so obvious. The mother of the boy on the edge of the fountain sits beside him, reading her magazine. Other people are on phones or deep in conversation. Even a policeman glances at her and then looks away with no sign of really seeing her. My frustration burns like a branding iron. I want to make them all see what they're blind to.

*It's like X-ray vision, Piper. You're the superhero who has it. They aren't heroes. You have to be her hero.*

Ever since the night Nana told us stories and explained to Sam and me what a superhero was, he'd been convinced I was one. I wish I'd had something super inside of me. If I had, I could've saved him.

The girl stumbles, and I grip the grass with my hands as I see the man shift his thumb and push on the circle of red, raw skin in the center of her burn. She doesn't even gasp, but I see her back stiffen from the pain as she hurries to catch up.

I'm on my feet and following them out of Rittenhouse Square before I realize it. Keeping half a city block between us, I almost miss it when they duck down an alley behind a sleazy bar and disappear into a back entrance. An old comic book store is on the other side of the street. I cross, go inside, and wait. I flip through comic after comic without really paying any attention. I can't drop my gaze from the bar entrance.

*Don't lose her again, Piper. She needs you.*

Standing and watching, I wait at the window display until I see them come out an hour later. Even from across the street it is clear he's spent the entire time drinking. Instead of holding her hand, he drags her along by the hair. For the first time, I see her whole face and realize that her features are distinctly Asian. His are not.

*He probably kidnapped her. See? I told you.*

It doesn't matter though. Sam and I know better than anyone that a kid doesn't have to be stolen from their family to be in danger. I wait until they get a little farther down the street before sneaking out of the shop and following again. Sam and I feel everything the little girl does: the fear of how he'll hurt her next, the dread of how much worse it could turn when she gets home, the need to do everything perfectly right even though she knows it won't be enough to save her from more pain.

At the next corner they turn right, and I follow them to a building in South Philly seven blocks away. He pulls her into a dingy basement apartment and I walk past, trying not to be too obvious as I check the place out.

An alley leads to an area at the rear of the building that probably was grass at one point but now is just overgrown weeds and a single large tree. The stench of garbage is so strong I cover my nose as I sneak around and peek through the only window I can find.

One pane is very dirty but I can still see through it, and the other is broken and half covered by a piece of cardboard. A television is the only noise I hear coming from inside.

I crouch in the shadows of the tree. It's dark now, and the branches hang so low I can barely make out my hand in front of my face. If I hold very still, he shouldn't be able to see me here, but I can see in the apartment as he drags the little girl through the kitchen.

At first, I think he's heading to the fridge, but he walks past it and opens a miniature door to a space under the stairs. Inside, I see a blanket and a box of crackers with a small, bloody handprint on the label. With a shove, he pushes her inside, and I flinch at the impact as she lands hard on her knees. Then he closes the door behind her, slides a lock into place, and grabs a beer from the fridge.

Trembling, I wrap my arms across my knees as he turns off the light and leaves the kitchen. I can still hear the TV, but there is no noise from the girl. No sign of life. If she ever fought him, she gave up long ago. No one else would understand that, but I do. It's easy to underestimate how terrifying it is to fight back when you've never had to do it. It takes almost an hour and every ounce of my self-control to ignore Sam pleading in my head and get to my feet.

*Help her! Save her, please.*

I walk home in the darkness to my new life in my new apartment.

And nothing feels new at all.

Even through the pillow over my head, I can hear the pounding no matter how much I wish I couldn't. When images of the girl in her cold cupboard aren't keeping me awake, nightmares of burying Sam under the old pine tree torment me. I don't allow myself to think about what happened after I threw on the last shovelful of dirt.

My brain feels ready to explode through my forehead, and when the pounding stops it's the sweetest relief I've felt in a long time—until it starts again. I feel the warmth on the floor beside me and it takes a moment to remember that it isn't coming from Sam. Sitting up, I drag the pillow off my head and blink in the brilliantly bright light pouring through my window. My fingers run across the small electric blanket. I've had it for nearly a year, but it still looks new. I guess when you don't use it the normal way, it shows. I didn't need it for the cold—I'm used to being cold. What I couldn't ever get used to was sleeping without the heat of my little brother curled up by my side. I never lie under it, but lying next to it is the only way I can get comfortable enough to sleep.

The pounding starts again and it takes almost a full minute for my brain to realize the noise is someone knocking on the door. My heart thuds hard against the wall of my chest in time with the knocking and I can't quite breathe. He's found me. He's finally found me.

I should've known he couldn't be killed. Something as evil as the Father wouldn't surrender to a simple end like death.

It doesn't matter. I will not give up now. Stumbling to the kitchen, I pull a knife from the drawer as silently as possible. I grip the cold handle with trembling fingers and inch toward the door. One step—two steps—three, and then I hear Cam muttering on the other side before I even get my eye to the peephole.

"You better be okay."

Every bit of air in my body pushes out like a gale, and I place the knife back in the drawer.

"Hold on." My voice is lost somewhere in my throat and what comes out is unintelligible. I hear a *thump* and when I look through the peephole I see Cam pressing his ear against the other side of the door.

"Charlotte?" His voice is soft now and he waits. When I unlock the first of my seven locks—one of my favorite things about this apartment—I hear him release his breath. I look at the door to the fire escape and remind myself again to buy more locks for it. With only two, the fire escape is vulnerable. I refuse to be vulnerable, not anymore. Whoever lived here last obviously didn't consider it a risk.

They weren't me.

By the time I get the door open, his angry glare could melt glass and he doesn't wait for me to invite him in.

"Where were you last night?"

The other half of the payment—I'd forgotten about it when I saw the girl.

"I'm sorry." My voice feels scratchy, like a cat has been set loose in my throat.

Cam frowns and walks into my kitchen. When he returns a moment later with a glass of water I'm so stunned I don't know what to say. He pulls out a chair and waits for me to sit before handing me the drink. I take a sip while I try to find an appropriate response to his kindness. A simple thank-you doesn't seem like enough.

"Are you sick? Is something wrong?" At the shake of my head he says, "You don't look well."

I rub my eyes and sigh. "You keep telling me that."

"What happened?"

"It was a rough night." I stand up, wanting to avoid more questions. "Wait here. I'll get your money."

"No. That's not . . ." When I pause and wait for him to finish, he only shrugs. "Fine."

My first day in the apartment, I put a safe behind a panel in my closet. Under the mattress or in my suitcase didn't seem like good places to store the money—my money now. It was Nana's before she got sick, and she told me where the Parents kept it, under a loose board beneath their bed. My safe feels like a wiser choice.

Digging through my closet, I push aside the only thing besides my bolt that I brought with me from my old home, Sam's favorite puppet. Just seeing it sends a wave of sadness and regret crashing down on me. It's tangled in its own strings, and it takes me a moment to gently move it completely out of the way. There'd been a few puppets stuffed up in the attic with us. Sam was afraid of all of them except this one, a tiny girl with giant blue eyes and blond hair. He called it his Piper-Puppet. When the Parents would drag me out of the attic, he'd always be hiding in a corner, clutching it in his thin arms when they brought me back.

I smooth the puppet's blond hair and set her gently aside before entering my combination. I used Sam's favorite number (because it was the age he'd been when we met Nana), followed by Nana's (because of Christmas), and then mine (because if luck exists, it's screwed me over time and again): 5-25-13. Opening the door, I take out thirty-five hundred dollars and then close it again.

When I come back into the room, I see Cam standing over the stack of mirrors I hid behind the chair. The only mirror that remains on the wall is the one in the bathroom, and that's because I think I need a crowbar to get it down. His expression hovers somewhere between surprise and amusement.

"I've never met a girl who didn't like mirrors."

I shrug and hold out the money. "Appearances are overrated."

It's fast, but I can't miss his eyes sweeping from my bare feet up to my crazy bed-head hair. There's an unmistakable twitch at the corner of his mouth, and I'm suddenly very aware of my blue polka-dot pajama pants and bright orange tank top.

I sigh and mutter under my breath, "An opinion demonstrated by my choice of clothing."

Cam grins wide and I'm totally unprepared for the way it makes my stomach wobble inside me.

"Uh"—I step backward and run into my table—"that's all you needed, right?"

His eyes take in my quick movement, but he doesn't mention it. "Any luck finding a job?"

"No, but my luck should improve once I start trying." Pulling out a chair, I sit in it and wait for him to leave. The pounding in my head has eased, but not much.

"Six blocks southeast of here in the Italian Market, there is a restaurant named Angelo's." Cam tucks the money inside his pocket without counting it. "Meet me there at five."

"Why?" His constant amused expression is starting to bother me. "I have the rest of Charlotte's papers. Now I've paid you the rest of the money. I thought we were done."

"We aren't." He shrugs and walks to the door. "Not quite yet. Five—don't be late." Cam closes the door behind him without waiting for me to agree. The echo of it shutting mingles with my groan. Each of the seven pins and bolts slides into place under my fingertips, reassuring me as I close off the outside world and lock myself away. Something about that separation makes me feel like everything will be better when I wake up.

It doesn't matter that I know it's a lie.

# 5

By afternoon my headache has dulled, but Sam won't shut up.

*Go back. We need to know she is still okay.*

She's living in a cupboard, of course she isn't okay.

*Help her, Piper.*

I know his voice isn't real. That he's dead and I'm essentially arguing with myself. But it helps me feel like he's still with me. And if that means I'm walking a bit on the crazy side of the sanity line, I'm okay with that. I've lived through reality—didn't care much for it.

Slow, deep breaths keep me calm while I shower and get ready, but I can't say the same for Sam. He's like a spring in my brain. Every motion I make that doesn't take us closer to saving the girl winds him tighter. The pressure begins to feel like an unstable land mine waiting for the slightest trigger to set it off.

Locking up my apartment, I turn and nearly step on a blond girl sitting at the top of the stairs. At my gasp, she glances around and beams up at me.

"Hi." She lifts up a stuffed bear from her lap and waves at me with one of its arms.

"Hi." I say a quick prayer in my head that she's real because a hallucination like this would put me about a mile over the sanity line, and that's too far—even for me. "Are you lost?"

Her blond hair bounces when she shakes her head, and then she hops toward me. "No. I'm playing hide-and-seek," she whispers.

I glance down the stairs but see no one. Cam told me the guy who lives below me is a businessman who's gone traveling most of the time, and Janice seems a little old to have a daughter this young. "With the bear?" I whisper back.

She giggles and I can't help but smile. "No, but you're funny."

This girl with the long blond hair and happy grin is me from another life—the sister that Sam should've had. It takes all my strength to stay upright as a pounding wave of loss and sorrow threatens to drown me. Sam would've loved this version of me. He would've been happier with her.

He would've lived.

A door opens below us and I hear Janice's voice muttering, "Rachel, so help me." When she looks up at both of us, she freezes.

"You found me! You're good at this game, Grams." Rachel tucks her bear under her arm and hops down the stairs. When she reaches the bottom, she takes Janice's hand and points up at me. "But she's better. She found me first."

Janice crouches down by Rachel. "You have to stay in Grams's apartment or we can't play this game anymore. It's not safe out here."

"It's okay though. I was with . . ." Rachel turns to me and tilts her head to the side. "What's your name?"

I take a breath and a couple of steps before answering. "Charlotte."

The name is foreign on my tongue, but I need to get used to it. "But your grandma is right. You have to stay inside with her."

Rachel shrugs. "Okay. Bye, Charlotte." She skips past Janice and into her apartment. Her grandma follows her in and casts me a half smile before closing the door behind her, and I hear the lock slide into place.

"Bye, Rachel." I sigh to myself, trying to ignore the giant hole in my heart the girl has stretched wide just by existing. Then I head out the door into the afternoon sunlight.

At Rittenhouse Square, I wait on the bench with a magazine I picked up on the way. Which celebrity might be pregnant and whether she cheated on her husband doesn't hold my interest, and I glance up at every girl that walks by. The city feels different today, more hostile somehow. Even in full daylight, the shadows seem deeper; the contrast between the light and dark more ominous. The people seem less busy and more calculating, almost sinister. Instead of hiding me, Philly feels like it's trapping me. The towering buildings bordering the square no longer make me safe. I am closed in, claustrophobic, and I don't like it.

When the man finally comes through, I nearly miss him because he's alone. My stomach clenches. Sam won't even speak to me anymore because we both know it's probably too late.

Following this stranger will do me no good; there is only one place he might trust to leave her alone. I try not to break into a panicked run as I make my way back to the disgusting hole of an apartment I'd seen them in the night before. In the daylight, I can see all the garbage, cigarette butts, and discarded needles lining the alley that I hadn't noticed in the dark. Under the warm sun, the stench of rotten food is so strong I hold my breath for the length of the side street. I'm still not used to the smell of decay. The Parents were always so neat. So clean about everything—everything except what they did to us.

Once I get behind the building, panic takes over and I throw myself into the filthy kitchen window well. Nature has taken over and the wood around the well is mostly gone, barely leaving room for me to fit. Most of the window is above ground level and my crouching back is warmed by sunlight, but I shiver from a sudden cold sweat when I peek inside and find the room dark and empty. I can hear and see no one, and the door to her dungeon under the stairs hangs open.

No longer caring about caution, I knock hard on the window, clinging to the remnant of hope I have left in spite of Sam's whimpering in my head.

"Please be in there," I whisper as I knock louder. "Please don't be dead alrea—"

I freeze as I see the tiniest bit of movement in a corner of the room. The dingy curtain below the sink rippled—at least, I think it did. My pulse thumps loud in my ears as I push my face hard against the glass trying to make out any motion. Then I see them.

Ten small toes poking out from under the curtain.

My heart explodes in my chest with the need to see her move again. Please let her be alive.

I knock louder and speak into the glass. "Girl? Can you hear me? Move if you're okay."

After what feels like an eternity, the curtain ripples as it slides a few inches to the side and I can see her eyes shining in the darkness. Her ankles are bound together with a chain that is secured to the wall, but her hands are free. I see a battered half-empty water bottle beside her and the box of crackers from yesterday. We gape at each other, and even with the sounds of the city around me, all I hear is my own breathing.

She inches forward just slightly, and even though I can't hear her, I see the words her mouth forms.

"Please. Help me."

Sam is humming in my head, the same song he used to hum when he was in pain but wasn't allowed to cry. My heart shatters into a million pieces of shrapnel, and each one rips through me, drawing blood. I nod and search for a rock—anything that can break through the cardboard and any remaining glass left behind it and let me save her. My hand lands on a small stone. It isn't much, but it should do the job.

When I look up though, she frantically shakes her head, waves at me to go away, and tugs the curtain closed in front of her. A new light shines from the front of the apartment and I scramble away from the window well and back into the shade of the tree. Even here the sun is too bright today. He will see me. I know his type. If he knows there is anyone who might help her, she'll be dead before I get the chance.

There is no choice. If I want her to live, I have to leave and come back later.

Dragging myself to the opposite side of the tree trunk and out of sight, I concentrate on slowing my shallow breathing. In and out, in and out—the rhythm matches Sam's song in my head and he hums even louder. Only every few seconds, I hear his voice catch as he chokes back a sob.

I get to my feet. Trying to shake off the icy coldness that has settled within me, I walk home in the sunlight.

The apartment with the girl is only eight blocks from Angelo's. It was hard to convince Sam that I needed to come to this restaurant instead of going back for her. It's startling that only a few city blocks separate places so drastically different—like the dark and light within each person. They're so close together, occupying the same space, but still worlds apart.

Angelo's is warm and inviting, even from across the street. Vivid red-and-white-checked curtains frame the windows and every table has a glowing candle. It's the kind of place I want to feel at home in, even if I don't.

My hair is still slightly damp from my second shower of the day. I'd been covered in filth when I'd gotten home, both mind and body. The water only seemed to help with the body. The image of the girl's dirty face, her mouth pleading for me to help her, won't leave me alone.

And Sam is only making it worse.

*Go back, Piper. Please go back.*

"I will, but I can't until he leaves her alone again," I mutter, knowing that talking to myself in public is never a good plan.

Drawing my shoulders back, I cross the street and walk through the front door. The aroma of fresh-baked bread and spaghetti sauce nearly knocks me off my feet and my stomach rumbles for the first time today. A low murmur of people talking and laughing fills the room with cozy warmth. It's so new to me that I want to sit down and soak it in until my skin gets pruney. The girl at the host station is helping a couple to their table, but I don't see Cam, so I wait.

The wall by the door is dominated by pictures. Old and new, big groups and small, most are families with adults and children, but a few have people in chef uniforms—and I recognize the black jacket the hostess has on. I walk closer to a photo with a younger version of Cam, Lily, and a smaller girl with Lily's hair. Lily has one arm around each and they're grinning so wide I can count their teeth. A few adults stand behind them, and for the first time I wonder if they're related.

"Sorry." Cam's voice comes from directly behind me, and I spin to face him. He has me pinned between him and the wall of photos. Before I can decide the best way to escape, he sees my panic and steps back. "Thanks for coming."

The way he seems to read me makes me uncomfortable. I shift on my feet before turning back to the pictures. I reach my finger up and touch an engraving on the wooden frame. "Is she your sister?"

"Lily?" He turns to look at the frame, but I'm surprised to see him wince and close his eyes for a moment.

"Yes." I study my fingers, rubbing my knuckles together, wondering why I'm anxious about his answer.

"No."

"Oh." I want to kick myself when it comes out sounding disappointed.

Cam laughs under his breath, but not low enough that I can't hear. "Do you want her to be?"

"No." I keep my voice even and don't answer too fast. "I was just wondering."

"That's too bad." He gives the hostess a friendly wave as she hurries past, seeming frazzled.

I watch him in confusion. "What do you mean?"

Gesturing for me to follow, he leads the way toward a waiting area off to one side that has a few empty benches. He acts like he didn't hear me. "Have you ever worked at a restaurant?"

"W-what?" I blink hard and try to figure out how the conversation ended up here.

"A restaurant?" He raises one eyebrow, and that damn smile is back. When I stare at him like an idiot instead of answering, he continues. "People come here to eat? They pay you?"

"Oh, no. I haven't." When realization finally dawns, I frown. "I told you I didn't need help finding a job."

"I know." He steps closer and inclines his head toward the girl busily leading customers to tables. "But Mary is leaving and Angelo's really needs a hostess we can count on. Lily can show you how to do it. It's pretty simple."

I run a hand along the back of a bench and raise one eyebrow at him. "Are you the manager here? Lawbreaker by day, Italian chef by night?"

"No, but Lily is one of the assistant managers. She can't cook to save her life." He takes another step and I resist the urge to move away. "Our grandparents own it."

I can see so many emotions in his eyes—laughter, hope, concern. I've never met someone who can let their guard down this way. It scares me.

With my small motion, he freezes, but his eyes don't change. "Lily is my cousin."

"Oh, right." My heart warms and it spreads up my neck to my cheeks. It's uncomfortable so I turn and take a seat on the bench. When he pivots to face me, his eyes are impossible to read. The sudden barrier I see there hurts more than I expect, and I don't know what changed.

"So, will you do it?"

I should say no. I know it, but I can't make the word come out. "You don't work here?"

"No, I help my aunt Jessie at her studio."

"Studio?" I pride myself on how quickly I learn. I'd taught myself to read when I was little by watching the Parents' TV through a crack in the boards of the attic floor. The commercials were my favorite part. They always said words while printing them on the screen. There were words printed on the bars over the attic window. I'd hoped if I could know what they said it would tell me how to get them open and escape. But it was only the name of the company that made them. Even now, I devour books to keep learning, but "studio" is one of those hard words that have multiple meanings.

He shrugs. "What can I say? My side business isn't exactly legit. I like to know I can protect myself."

"Okay." So some kind of fighting place? I squint and tilt my head to one side. My mind tries to put Cam into a box that includes violence, but he doesn't fit there easily. "But Lily wants me to work here?"

49

"She will."

"You don't know that."

"I do." He grins. The slightest quirk at the corner of his mouth tells me he's lying, but I don't call him on it as he continues. "Come on. I already know how you feel about being punctual. Who doesn't want that in an employee?" He winks, and in spite of his teasing, I find myself nodding without any further thought. When his grin widens and I see a flash of a dimple, I can't even bring myself to regret it.

"I do care about being punctual."

"Yes, just apparently not when it comes to meeting me."

He kind of has a point. I was late once, and when I was supposed to meet him with the money I hadn't even shown up. I move my lips to speak, but when I can't decide how to respond I just close them and wait.

"Great. I'll ask Lily to check the schedule and let you know when you can start training. Do you want to have dinner or should I walk you out?" He extends a hand to me, and this time he waits as I hesitate. His eyes are a challenge, daring me to take it. A fiery burst of anger flares inside me and I glare back as I slide to one side and slip off the bench without touching him.

"Don't." My one word is a low growl, a warning to back off, to keep his distance.

People only cause pain, and I'm no different, even now. Hurt shines in his eyes as he drops his arm, and part of me wishes I could take it back. He turns away with a shake of his head and walks out of the waiting room. I'm left alone and I stretch my hand out before me, wondering what the heat from his touch would feel like. Longing for that tiny connection with humanity aches, and only fear helps me resist the urge to call for him to return.

Less than a minute passes before he leans back in the room and the guarded smile has returned. He lifts a hand to show me a bag with a to-go box tucked inside. "You can take this with you. The marinara will blow your mind."

# 6

I'm beginning to seriously consider the merits of sleeping pills. It's pretty difficult to sleep with a little boy's voice talking nonstop in your head. The only way I got any rest last night was to give in to Sam. I promised I'd go back for the girl today. That I would not leave without her again.

No clue how I'm going to keep that promise.

The shade of the tree behind the man's apartment is quickly becoming my regular hangout. He is home, the girl probably locked beneath the stairs. I wait. The leaves above me rustle and I tingle with their restlessness. I stretch my fingers and rub them along my jeans over my knees and down to grip my ankles. The need to move, to be free to act, is overwhelming. She is so small and so helpless in her miniature prison.

I know exactly how she feels, how easy it is to be trapped in this world filled with monsters. But now I am free. Now I can move, and still I must wait.

I hate waiting.

The man moves through the apartment with no fear. I want to

make him tremble with her fear the way I do. To feel the pain and terror he so enjoys causing. But I won't let myself give in to those urges—this is what separates me from him. Instead, I watch him from the shadows as he drinks another beer and makes a phone call.

He disappears from the kitchen for fifteen minutes. I keep checking my watch, wishing he would go away. When he comes back, his hair is wet and he's wearing black pants and a clean shirt. Now he doesn't look like someone capable of keeping a girl locked in a cupboard. He appears so normal I almost doubt myself, but I know better. The Parents seemed extremely normal—it meant nothing. They were monsters, too.

Tugging on a jacket, he sticks his phone in his pocket and heads for the front door. On the way out, he slams the palm of his hand against the door the girl is trapped behind. He mutters a few words and then leaves. I tug on the weeds and let them fall through my fingers, counting one hundred of them before allowing myself to hope. He's gone. This is my chance.

My heartbeat almost deafens me. For once, Sam is silent. I glance at the buildings around me. They're tall, dark, and still. They keep watch. The city sees what I'm doing. It knows everything, but the people don't. A few men sit on a porch at the end of the alley, but they're occupied with their own business. Several motels I'd stayed at across the country were in neighborhoods like this one. I'd learned quickly that no one would ask questions. When someone is hurt in these types of places, people close their curtains and turn their heads instead of running to help.

Darting across to the window, I decide to risk a cut from the remaining glass and kick the cardboard inside. Careful to avoid the jagged shards, I reach my hand in, unhook the latch, and slide the frame aside. In less than ten seconds, I'm standing in the apartment.

It isn't cold, but I shiver anyway. The weight of the bolt in my pocket lends me strength as I look around. Stacks of mail are scattered on the table. The same name printed on each: Steve Brothers. A sick laugh rises in my throat. A *brother* to whom exactly?

I keep my footsteps quiet as I cross the kitchen. My throat tightens and I think of the million different ways I could terrify this child. Crouching before the door, I brush the wood with the knuckles of one hand. The words don't want to come. "Hi, I'm here to rescue you." It feels inadequate.

*Just tell her you want to help her, silly.*

Hearing Sam's voice gives me strength. I know—knew—him better than anyone. Is this girl really so different? I run my palm down the door, but before I can utter a word, I hear her.

"Hello?" she calls. Her voice isn't nearly as small or weak as I expect and it takes me by surprise.

"Hi," I reply. Mine isn't as strong and I clear my throat. "Please don't be afraid. I want to help you."

"Are you the girl by the window?" she asks, and I catch the first hint of suspicion in her tone.

"Yes."

"You came back?"

"Yes."

"Why?" Now I hear them, the small quick breaths that show the fear even when her voice doesn't. "Who are you?"

I take a deep breath and let my body crumple to the floor. Pressing my fingers against my temples, I struggle for an answer to her impossible question. What do I say? That I'm a killer? A fake teenager with a stolen name? A girl who let my brother die and couldn't do anything to stop it?

"I'm you." It's the only answer that makes sense at the moment. "Only older."

It's quiet for so long that I wonder if she's decided not to talk to me anymore, and then I hear her slide away from the door.

"Please hurry." All the strength in her voice is gone, drained. "I don't know how long he'll be gone."

"Do you know where he keeps the key?"

"With him." She sounds devastated. "Always with him."

"Don't give up yet," I mutter as I search the room. "I don't need a key."

I find nothing in the kitchen or living room that is of any use. In the bedroom, I open the closet and lose the ability to breathe. Memories pinch, prod, and slice at me with visions of my past. So many ways to inflict pain, the closet is filled with different kinds of chains, gags, whips, nooses, spikes, and countless other things I wish I didn't recognize. The Father had a closet like this for his tools, too. This one is messier, a reflection of the man who made it. I hold tight to the bedpost and say a quick prayer to anyone listening, hoping Brothers hasn't used everything in his collection on that poor girl.

My foot bumps against something metal as I back up. I look down and there it is, exactly what I need to set her free—a baseball bat.

"Are you there?" I hear her calling from the kitchen, the soft words barely audible through her sobs. "Please don't leave me here."

Swallowing back the disgust that sits in my throat like a ball of glue, I close the closet doors and hurry back to her.

"Don't worry. I'm not leaving without you." I study the hinges and lock on the door, trying to decide the best place to hit. My hands squeeze the cold metal of the bat on impulse, itching to destroy something. "I made a promise."

The crying stops. "To who?"

"That doesn't matter." The latch the lock goes through is attached to old wood, the paint chipped and fading. If I hit that part just right, it should work. As I draw back to swing, a small squeak comes from the girl.

"Go! You have to hide!" Then I hear it, keys jangling at the front door. He's back.

"Okay, shh." Images of every part of the apartment flash through my head. Taking the bat with me, I slide into one of the two hiding spots I'd seen—the small gap between the fridge and the wall. There is no way I'm going in the torture closet. I try not to think of what squishes against the bottom of my shoe as I get in place just before the door screeches open.

I focus on trying to keep each breath level and quiet. He can't find me here. If he does, I'll fight, but the girl and I are probably both dead. I'm endlessly grateful no one else can hear Sam freaking out in my head.

*No, no—not again, Piper. No more being stuck with bad people. No more. We have to get out of here.*

I tighten my grip on the bat as he moves through the apartment—breathe in, breathe out. My fingers are so damp I'm afraid it may slip from my grasp. He's in the kitchen now, so close I can hear him breathe. Can he hear me?

He fumbles with his keys as he unlocks her cupboard door. From my position I can't see them, but I hear a whimper from the girl and a low growl from Steve Brothers.

A shuffling noise moves away from me, out of the kitchen, and I risk taking a peek. His arm is wrapped tight against her throat, her feet barely touching the ground. I see terror in her eyes as they meet mine. My hand flies to my mouth just in time to stifle my gasp.

Brothers is taking her to the closet.

*Stop him, Piper. Do something.*

Chains rattle in the bedroom, then a sharp metallic scrape echoes down the hall. My eardrums vibrate with the noise even after it stops. Sam pleads in my head as I inch out from behind the fridge and grip the bat with two hands. A small scream comes before it's quickly muffled, and I know he's using one of his gags.

Sliding along the wall, I move to a spot where I can see into the room. The girl's hands are chained above her head with her back to me. A strap from one of the gags stretches across her face and around her head.

Brothers stands behind her. He grips a small but vicious-looking knife in one hand and a lit cigarette in the other. The knife has four blades coming from a single handle, and I see in my head what it will do to her skin. The image makes me light-headed. His stance is calm and powerful. This is where he's in control, and he enjoys every second of her pain. I see his face in a mirror on the opposite wall; a cruel smirk curves his lips as he watches her. There's a hunger in his eyes that makes me want to throw up—I've seen it before in the eyes of the Parents.

But I stopped them and I must stop Steve Brothers.

Sam is humming in my head. I fight not to react as flashes of pain and blood from the past haunt us both. A powerful need washes over me. I've felt it before. It scares me. I'm trapped, ensnared like the girl. The fear of what I know I can do battles against the understanding of exactly what he will do to her if I don't.

Familiar fury pumps through my veins and I resist the urge to pounce. I don't need my bolt anymore. I feel my strength pulsing with every heartbeat, and that's what scares me. My goal is to save her, not to destroy him, no matter how much he deserves it. I don't let myself move an inch until I can draw in one slow breath after another. Brothers has an entire closet full of weapons within his reach, I have a bat. If I'm going to get the girl or myself out of here alive, I can't lose control—not this time, not again.

But I *will* hurt him if it means saving her.

Taking two steps into the room, I move in silence. I'd perfected moving without sound back in the attic. It is instinct now. Brothers walks closer to the girl and I freeze. He lifts her shirt and my eyes close tight when I get a glimpse of her back. So many healed slices, burns, and cuts, there is no skin without scars. Sam hums louder and I can't hear anything else. I focus on breathing until I can calm down.

*He is bad, Piper. Stop him.*

When I open my eyes again, he's still watching her, and I know

I must make my move soon. He's dropped the knife back to his side and takes a long drag on his cigarette. Two steps closer, I lift the bat over my shoulder. I try to convince myself I can save her. I can stop him. Still, in my head, I see the blood. The Parents and all the blood—I didn't care about killing the Parents, but I hated the blood.

My hands shake. The bat wobbles. I glance in the mirror and every piece of me turns to ice. His eyes, dark and hungry, are staring straight at me.

And he smiles.

I yelp and try to swing the bat, but he's ready. He moves his arm to block it and turns with his knife, catching me across the side and slicing my skin with the blades. It burns like a red-hot poker, but I don't cry out.

"You're a pretty one." He breathes as he grabs my hair with one hand and brings the knife toward my neck, but he doesn't cut me. He wants me to be afraid. Fury boils in my veins, and I know he's made a big mistake.

Because I am *done* letting people feed off my fear.

I jerk back the bat and slam him in the gut with it. When he doubles over, his head is right there and I don't hesitate.

The bat hits his skull with an audible *thunk*. I whack it again to be certain he will stay down, and part of me wants to keep hitting him, keep hurting him. He collapses to the floor. Taking a deep, shaking breath, I instead say the words that help me be strong, the words that keep me sane.

"I am *nothing* like you."

There is no movement and no blood. I force myself to release the bat, tugging back one finger at a time until it falls to the floor. His cigarette rolls from his hand and lands on the dingy brown rug in front of the dresser. It catches fire almost immediately but takes its time—like it wants me to decide its fate. The smell of smoke fills my nose and I move to stamp it out.

*No, don't. Leave it.*

The cold hatred in Sam's voice is foreign, and I remember, again, that it isn't really my little brother. He's a piece of me. A piece that thinks Steve Brothers deserves to burn.

I withdraw my foot and watch the baby flames. Something about fire fascinates me. It lives alone and dances with no partner. Fire is beauty and destruction, life and death wrapped up in one glowing ball of light. The girl whimpers again and I snap back into the moment. The fire has started to spread. We need to get out of here.

The torture closet surrounds me as I step toward her and into her world of pain. I wince from the throbbing in my side as I reach up to release the cuffs on the girl's wrists. All the devices scare me in a way that I didn't believe possible after everything I've seen. Once her hands are free, I work on the strap tying her gag in place. We've turned sideways now, and she is like a statue. When I follow her gaze I see her staring at Brothers. She's only a child. I move to block her view as I finish releasing the strap and drop the gag to the floor.

With a shake of her head, she steps around me and stands over him. Tears roll down her cheeks, but I hear nothing—no sobs or whimpers, just silence. I can't help her, not here and now, because the fire is creeping down the rug between Brothers's sprawled left leg and the brittle wood of the dresser. We have to leave. Hesitating for only an instant, I reach out my hand to her. She is like Sam, she needs me—touching her isn't like touching others, it's different. When she stares at my outstretched fingers, I know how she feels and what she thinks. It isn't safe to touch people or trust them. It hurts.

But I want her to feel safe. So I wait.

Turning back to Brothers, she whispers something I can't make out and stomps on his hand as the fire spreads to the leg of his pants. I blink as she turns to me, places her hand in mine, and pulls me toward the door.

I falter and look back at the man lying still on the floor. The edge of one pant leg is on fire now, too. If we leave him here like this . . . the girl tugs on my hand again. She looks desperate to leave, to escape while she has the chance. Part of me thinks this is wrong and recognizes that we're killing him. Another part delights in it. I'm torn in two and neither side is winning. Am I the murderer or the savior?

Sam doesn't answer in my head this time. I'm not sure I want him to. I walk out with the girl and close the door tight behind us.

# 7

My navy shirt hides my bloody side as we walk down the street. It was a good choice. A white one would've stained. Not to mention people would've noticed. Red bloodstains on a white shirt are pretty much impossible to hide. I want to touch my ribs, to lift my shirt and assess the damage, but the girl has a death grip on my hand. It reminds me of Sam in a way that makes me smile and want to scream at the same time. Still, I feel like there are eyes on me, on the blood, on us. I want to be faster than we can walk.

At the next corner, I step out and wave down a cab with my free hand, hoping no one notices how it shakes. My stomach flops as the car pulls over and I try to breathe around the sudden knot in my gut. The idea of climbing into a car alone with a stranger has always kept me on crowded buses and trains. Taxis leave me exposed and defenseless. They're a risk I've avoided, until now. I look down at the girl and know we need to get out of this neighborhood as fast as possible. For her sake, I'll do it.

Giving the driver an address on Pine, a block away from my apartment, seems like a smart decision. He nods without even a glance in my direction and speaks into the headset he has on his ear. Perfect, he can talk to whoever is on his phone all he wants. Distraction is my friend right now.

"I don't know your name." I keep my voice low when I turn to the girl, even though she isn't as jumpy as I expect her to be. My chaotic mind whirls over everything that just happened. I was strong enough to stop myself from hitting him again, but not strong enough to stop the fire. Pushing the thought aside, I lock it away for now and focus on the girl. She is safe. That's what matters.

"Yeah." She peers at me, her face as blank as a fresh sheet of paper beneath the tear tracks on her dirty cheeks. Her dark eyes guard her secrets well. "I don't know yours either."

I can't hide a small smile. I like this girl. Which name should I tell her? Can I trust her with my past? The answer comes quickly, but it isn't about trust. She has enough baggage without having to carry mine.

"Charlotte."

She watches me for a second, and I almost wonder if she can tell I'm lying. I wait and she shrugs, her shoulder-length black hair falling across her face.

"I'm Sanda."

"Okay." I take a deep breath. Now what? "I don't live too far from here. We're going there first."

"First? Then where?" Her nose crinkles up in confusion.

"Then I guess we should talk about where to take you." I check to make sure the driver is still focused on his phone call. When he coughs and responds loudly into his headset, I continue. "A shelter or the police station maybe?"

Sanda's haunted eyes remain on the back of the seat in front of us. She doesn't answer, but her grip on my hand tightens even more.

"You aren't related to that man—"

"No." Her answer is quick and sharp enough to draw blood.

Breathing a sigh of relief, I squeeze her hand lightly. "Do you know where your parents are?"

"Where are yours?"

I flinch. "Well, okay then." But in my head, I'm already defending her. After what she's just been through, would I behave any differently? I'd been the same way. I need to let her catch her breath for a moment before grilling her. We ride in silence for a few blocks before she looks over at me. I can see the remorse in her eyes as she speaks.

"I'm sorry. My parents are dead. My brother and I lived in an orphanage in Myanmar. I was taken when I was small."

"You're still small."

"Small-*er*." She levels her chin at me and I nod. "I cleaned for a rich family until almost a year ago. Then they sold me to *him*." Her voice drips hatred and I don't ask her more.

"Is English your first language?"

"I only know a few words that aren't English. I've been here for as long as I can remember. Before that I only know what people have told me happened." She hunches over, studying her dirty fingernails.

"How old are you?"

"I'm pretty sure that I'm nine." She straightens her back and nods, clearly proud to have an answer.

Unfortunately, I understand perfectly. Without a birth certificate or anyone who cares enough to celebrate, it's hard to keep track. At least Sam and I had each other and Nana. I don't remember the years before Sam very well except being hungry with the Mother, but there wasn't much worth remembering. This girl has been alone for a long time. She doesn't look much bigger than Sam, but we'd mostly been fed regularly up until the last year before Sam died . . . one of the only kindnesses the Father did for us, and then he took that away, too. The Father always said being healthy made us bleed better.

Perhaps "kindness" isn't the right word.

"Do you know when you were born?"

"No. But I think maybe in the fall?"

"Why?"

"Well." She stares at her feet now and seems embarrassed. "Because I like to pretend all the kids that dress up for Halloween are celebrating with me even though I never get to dress up."

Shoving aside the emotion welling up inside me, I smile. Sam had been born when the leaves started changing color outside. His next birthday isn't too far away. My stomach tightens at just the thought. It will be the second one since he died. The first was a couple of months after I'd run. When I'd walked out of the motel room in Nebraska and a leaf fell at my feet, I fled back in and spent a week straight sobbing in a dark corner. I'd wished a thousand times since then that I knew the exact day. Something I could mark on a calendar and celebrate for him. He would've been eight this year. The week he died, the attic was hot, but not yet so hot that we had no choice but to lie on the slightly cooler wood floor instead of our tattered blankets to keep from getting dehydrated.

I blink again and again, forcing my eyes to see this girl instead of my brother, but it's so hard not to see Sam when I look at her. My words come out wavering at first before gaining strength. "Th-that sounds like a perfect time of year for a birthday."

Her answering grin is so wide it lights up her entire face.

The taxi pulls over. My hand trembles when I try to count out the fare. The bills are pretty simple. It's the coins that cause me problems. That's why I never carry any. So many small metal things, and I'm supposed to remember what each is worth and which ones add up to what. It's too hard and complicated. There are coins all over the streets of Philly that I've dropped, hoping someone who knows how to use them will pick them up. I hand the driver the cash as we climb out.

A woman sitting on her nearby porch gapes at me. I look down and realize the blood is seeping onto my tan pants. I sigh. Why didn't I wear dark jeans?

Because I didn't pick my outfit based on hiding blood, that's why.

I tug on Sanda's hand until she is walking a bit in front of me and blocks the woman's view. The girl sees my side, grimaces, but doesn't ask any questions.

"Let's hurry. We're only a block away." I quicken my step. "We can figure everything out there."

"Okay."

* * *

My first-aid kit is one of the few things I had before I got to the city. I'd picked up pieces of it on my way here—Band-Aids in Nebraska, Steri-Strips in Iowa, Neosporin in Illinois, bandages and hydrogen peroxide in Ohio. It's a road map of where I've been. A guide to how I got here.

And if there's one thing I'm an expert at, it's bandaging myself up.

Lifting the corner of my shirt, I survey the damage. There is quite a bit of blood. I close my eyes tight and take a deep breath—I hate blood. The cuts are mostly thin and shallow, only one deep gash that needs to be closed.

I grab a clean cloth, run it under cold water, and press it against my side. Pain burns across the right half of my abdomen. Sanda seems worried, and I smile through my gritted teeth to reassure her. I'm just glad I stopped him before she had fresh cuts, too.

"So, you don't want me to drop you off with the police?" The water runs pink as I squeeze some of the blood out of my cloth and rewet it. I look away.

"No." Sanda's dirty hair falls into her eyes as she shakes her head. "The family who owned me before called me ill-illegal. They said the police will send me back if they find me." She bites her lip and closes her eyes tight. "It's not much better there."

Forcing myself not to cringe, I press the cloth against my side again. It's a little better now, but the deepest cut refuses to stop bleeding. I push harder against it and a small groan escapes my lips. "Then where should I take you?"

Sanda shuffles her feet, opens her eyes, and stares at the white tile floor between her dirty shoes.

I know what I *should* do—the *normal* thing to do—but how can I do it? I don't trust the police. If I could help her it could be my chance to make up for failing Sam so completely.

I'd do everything I could to keep Sanda safe, but how am I supposed to take care of her? I'm only just figuring out how to take care of myself.

She shifts her weight and I can see her discomfort. Her entire life has been wrong. Everything she knows is pain. How do I know that anywhere I take her won't lead back to the past? I can't protect her if she's gone. Even if she ends up with a healthy, normal family—assuming they actually exist—how could they understand? No one else will be able to begin to comprehend what she's been through the way I can.

*Saving her is more than simply setting her free.*

Just what I need, Sam is starting to sound like one of the "healers" I'd seen on late-night TV.

This time he doesn't laugh.

*She needs you, Piper. Like I needed you.*

The voice in my head is giving me a guilt trip. Perfect.

I sigh and open a package of Steri-Strips. The bleeding has finally slowed. Spraying my whole side with Bactine, I wait for it to dry before holding the sides of the cut closed with two fingers. With my other hand, I secure it with Steri-Strips until I don't need my fingers to hold it shut anymore. Then I grab the Neosporin, gauze, and paper tape to cover the area and keep it clean. As I'm wrapping my waist with a bandage to keep everything in place, I survey my work. It isn't my best, but it will do.

"Where did you learn to do all that?" Her eyes are wide.

"I had to take care of myself." I walk past her to my room and change into some clean clothes. The navy shirt has a couple of gashes in it and the pants are beyond stained. I toss them both in the garbage when I walk back to the kitchen.

When I come in wearing fresh clean clothes, Sanda takes a step back and her cheeks flush red. She turns away, but I can see her fingering the edge of her dirty shirt with one hand. The girl needs a shower—or fifteen. To start, I gesture for her to follow me and give her a soapy cloth in the bathroom to clean her face, arms, and hands. Up next we'll get her some new clothes and food.

I sit on the edge of my couch and wait for her to join me. The last thing she needs is someone new pushing her around, telling her what to do. After a few minutes, she returns from the bathroom with all her exposed skin scrubbed clean.

"What now?" She lifts one eyebrow and spreads her hands out before her. I can see one of them shaking before she tucks it behind her back.

I grab my Avengers wallet off the counter and stick it in my pocket. Purses are too big, too bulky—even the smallest ones. They slow me down. I'd picked this wallet from the little boys' section of a Kansas department store a week after I left the attic. Besides, if I want to carry more than just money, a backpack is more practical than some pretty, frilly bag that bounces against my hip or slides off my shoulder when I run. "I was thinking we could grab some food. Then maybe get you some new clothes. If you want?"

Her eyes light up like miniature suns and I can hear Sam giggle in my head. I take a quick breath against the raw pain it brings. I can count on one hand the times I heard him make a happy noise like that. Sanda walks to me, grips my hand in hers, and nods.

"Yes, please."

# 8

Sanda had devoured the sandwich in seconds, but now she sits quietly with a strained expression on her face and both arms wrapped around her stomach. The chips and apple sit untouched on the table before her, but I don't say anything. I remember how hard it was at first. Wanting to eat everything you see, but the pain from introducing new foods, or more food than you're used to, can be horrible.

"It's okay to take it easy." I watch people walk past the window. "You'll have food tomorrow. I promise."

She lets out her breath in a gush and pushes the tray in front of her to one side. "Thank you. It hurts."

"I know."

Her eyes remain on me for a while before she says anything else. "You know everything."

A short chuckle bursts free before I see the tears in her eyes. I lean forward and place one hand open on the table before her. When she places her fingers in mine, I respond. "I don't actually, but I'm trying."

"You understand, though, and you're strong and brave. You're not afraid." She frowns and tightens her grip. "You can fight."

I lower my face until I can see her eyes. "I'm terrified . . . always."

One tear slips free from her lashes and slides down her cheek. "You don't seem—"

"I am. And it took me a very long time to fight, too long." Swallowing hard, I bring my other hand up and hold it out before her. Her eyes widen as she sees my fingers tremble, and I finish. "But if we don't fight, they win."

Sanda nods, her small face determined. "I want to learn to fight. Can you teach me?"

"No, I'm barely learning myself." Her face falls and I hurry on. "But I think I might know someone who could teach us both."


When we return home with two bags of new clothes, I follow Sanda up the stairs to my apartment building. I nearly run her over when she freezes in place just inside the door. I glance past her and see Janice's granddaughter Rachel, smiling sweetly from her spot on the steps up to our apartment.

"Hi, Rachel."

"Hi, Charlotte! I didn't know you had kids!"

I sputter. "I don't. This is my cousin."

Sanda's wide eyes turn up to me, and I see the fear she's trying to hide. "Rachel is my neighbor and she's very nice." My heart breaks for her. Being afraid of everything new and different is hard enough, but when you've spent so little time around "normal," *everything* feels so new and different.

Sanda nods and takes a tentative step toward Rachel but doesn't speak.

The door opens and Janice peeks out at the hallway. The worry erases from her face when she sees Rachel, but then she sees me and it returns full force. Her eyes drop to Sanda and the worry is replaced with confusion. I watch her eyes take in the dirty hair and clothes and wish again that we could've cleaned her up more before going out anywhere.

"This is my cousin. She'll be staying with me for a little while."

"Your cousin?" Janice looks at Sanda, who tries to smile but then takes a step back toward me.

I try to cover for the fact that Sanda and I don't exactly look related. "Yeah, a distant cousin."

Janice nods without a word and waves at Sanda, visibly relaxing. It's strange. Am I more trustworthy if I take care of a kid?

"How old are you, sweetie?" Janice's voice is kind.

"Nine."

I'm proud of Sanda for not following it with her customary "I think." We picked a Halloween birthday for her when I explained that she needs to pretend to know how old she is, even if she's not sure.

"How fun!" Janice takes on the overly excited tone that many "normal" adults use with kids. When I notice Sanda's mouth drop open a little I barely suppress a laugh. "That's how old my Rachel is! Maybe you can come over to hang out sometime?"

Sanda gives Rachel a shy smile and turns to me.

"Sure, maybe we can find a good time for that later." I slide along behind Sanda, trying to casually nudge her toward the stairs with one of the shopping bags. "Good night."

"Okay, take care." Her expression is appraising, but her lips are drawn into a tight line and she hurries Rachel inside and closes the door harder than necessary.

I sigh as I walk up the stairs with Sanda close behind me.

"I'm not sure she likes you very much," Sanda says, looking puzzled. "That's too bad."

I nod. "Yep, it sure is."

My phone rings as I open the door and let Sanda inside. The ringtone is terrible, jangling in an absurdly loud and annoying way. The screen says "Cam" and I flip it open. I try to remember how I've seen people talk on the phone on TV shows. It's not like I grew up doing it.

"Hello?"

"Charlotte?"

It takes me a few seconds before I remember that's me. "Oh, right. This is her."

Cam snorts. "You're going to have to do better than that."

"Yeah, I'm working on it." I run my hand across the railing and hesitate on the landing outside my apartment door. "Everything okay?"

"Yep, Lily just worked out the schedule. Sorry for the late notice, but can you come to training tomorrow night at five?"

I hear Lily mumble something in the background and she

doesn't exactly sound pleased. I'm not sure what I'll do with Sanda, but I have a day to figure it out. Besides, now is not the time to get on Cam's bad side. With Sanda, I'll need his help longer than I expected. "Yeah, I think so."

"Great, thanks again."

I groan. "Don't thank me yet."

"Yeah, yeah, you'll do great. I'll see if I can stop by the restaurant."

"I didn't think you worked there."

"I don't, but I help the family out in the storage room whenever my grandpa isn't well enough to come in."

"Oh, I see." I'm not sure how to respond, and I'm still confused about why he would be coming in tomorrow.

"See you then." And he hangs up without another word.


"I'm just supposed to ask her to hang out with me?" Sanda takes two steps down from our door before turning to face me again. After two showers, a night of sleep, and some clean clothes, she's like a new kid—on the outside at least. "And then wait for her to answer?"

"I think so." I haven't had much experience with this either, but my reply actually appears to make Sanda more nervous. Reaching out, I squeeze her shoulder. "It will be fine. I promise."

"But what if she says no? Or what if . . ." Her dark eyes study the pink straps on her new shoes, and I see a familiar pain. A shame that burns your heart until you know everyone can see it. Her right hand crosses over and she rubs a thin scar peeking out below the edge of her sleeve. "Are you sure she's safe? And what if Rachel sees, or Janice?"

I kneel down and wait until her eyes meet mine. "Rachel is healthy and happy. Janice is a good person. And if they ask, you should tell them that someone used to hurt you and that's why you're with me now. So I can keep you safe. You don't have to, and you shouldn't really, tell them anything more than that."

Her expression relaxes a little. She squeezes my hand and her eyes fill with warmth that steals the breath from my chest. Sam used to look at me the same way. It is devotion I didn't deserve—don't deserve—but I'm working toward it. Her voice is only a whisper when she speaks again.

"Thank you for keeping me safe."

I nod, unable to come up with any response. Sanda throws her arms around me in a tight hug and I feel better than I have all day.

We walk the rest of the way down the stairs, and Sanda's hand is shaking when she knocks. In less than five seconds, Rachel flings the door wide open and grins.

"Hi! I was thinking about you all day, but Grams said I had to wait until you got settled. You seem settled. Want to see my room?" She gives Sanda no time to answer, grabs her hand and drags her into the apartment. Sanda follows in stunned silence, but then a grin spreads across her face.

Janice wipes her hands on a towel and walks out of the kitchen. She waves for me to come in and I close the door behind me. Her apartment makes mine look like a barren wasteland. It's warm, cozy, and clean, with the exception of a few dolls and toys scattered about. It is lived in—like a home.

As I stand in the doorway, I count the locks on it. There are only four. One of the windows is open to allow in a breeze, like an invitation. This apartment is at street level. It's so easy to break in. Can I really leave her here when it's this vulnerable?

"Well, that didn't take long." Janice gestures toward the next room where Rachel is showing Sanda a dollhouse. The blond girl keeps handing Sanda dolls and is talking a million words a minute. I smile as Sanda struggles to hold about fifteen dolls without dropping any before Rachel giggles and takes some back.

I have my answer. If Rachel is safe here, Sanda can be, too. Besides, having a friend will be so good for her. "They'll have fun together," I say.

"She looks better." Janice's gaze is piercing and I turn away. "Than last night, I mean."

"New clothes will do that for a girl, I guess." I hurry on before she can ask questions. "We were planning on inviting Rachel up to our apartment."

Janice shakes her head. "They're fine here, if that's okay with you. I'm sure we have more toys, anyway."

"Well, I was hoping I could take Rachel off your hands for an hour and give you a break, because then I kind of need a favor tonight." This is even more uncomfortable than I expected. I'm not used to asking for help. And I don't like needing it.

She doesn't say anything, waiting for me to finish.

"I got a job working at a restaurant and I need to go in for training in an hour." I look back toward Sanda again and she grins and waves. "I was hoping she could stay here with Rachel while I'm gone. I'd be happy to pay you."

Janice watches me for a moment before nodding. "No need to pay or to watch Rachel first. It's actually nice for me, too. I get more done when someone else can entertain Rachel for a little while. Your cousin is always welcome."

I start to let out a breath of relief, but she holds up a hand and the air stops in my throat, choking me.

"One problem though." She leans forward and whispers, "I don't think you ever told me her name."

"Oh, right." I remember to keep breathing. "It's Sanda."

"Great. Sanda will be fine here until you get home." Janice pats my shoulder and I hold perfectly still. "What time does your shift end?"

I give her an apologetic wince. "It'll be a little late, between ten and eleven. Are you sure you don't want me to pay you for baby-sitting?"

She shakes her head. "I'm sure. I'll send them to bed at nine anyway, so any time after that really doesn't count. Rachel has an extra bed in her room for when her dad is home on leave. If you bring down some pajamas for Sanda, you can just carry her up when you get home."

I'm speechless. I expected Janice would watch Sanda if I paid enough, but not this kind of generosity. There is nothing I can say, but I'll make this up to her somehow.

"Thank you." I can see it in her eyes as she nods. Janice knows how much this means to me. "I'll be right back with her things."

As I turn toward the door, there's a light tug on my hand. Sanda is standing behind me, biting her lip. She wraps her fingers around mine and I squat down to her level.

"What is it?"

"You will come back?" She's squeezing my hand so hard it almost hurts, and she stares at the carpet between us like it might split into a mighty chasm and separate us at any moment. "You promise?"

"I promise." I wrap her in my arms and give her a quick hug like I used to give Sam, then pull away and lean my forehead against hers. "I'm not leaving you."

# 9

Mary stands at the host station with a happy grin when I walk in, and I wonder why Cam *ever* believed I'd be good at this job.

"Are you waiting for someone or would you like a table for one?"

"Neither. I'm here for training."

Her grin widens and she laughs. "Oh, you're the new me!"

Her unending exuberance leaves me wanting to escape—either that or find her brightness and volume options and turn them down a few notches. "Uh, I suppose so. Where can I find Lily?"

She points toward the back of the restaurant. "Take the left hall past the men's room."

The narrow hallway has a large IF YOU DON'T WORK HERE, YOU'RE PROBABLY LOST—EMPLOYEES ONLY sign across the top. I check around to make sure no one is watching me before I walk under it. It's hard to think of myself as qualified to be called an "employee."

Lily is scribbling furiously on a stack of papers at a desk in a room on the right. I'm amazed at how fast her hand flies through the motions. I must go slow and push hard just to get the words to be readable. Of course, I haven't been writing that long.

"Hello, Charlotte." Her expression is guarded when she stands up.

"Hi." I have a sudden urge to apologize for the way I'd been thrust upon her, but my gut tells me that apologies won't get me anywhere with Lily. "So, where do I start?"

She gathers the stack of papers from the desk and walks toward a large black safe on one side of the room. "Tell me what you've done before."

I shrink in on myself a little. I'd assumed Cam would tell her I had no experience. "Nothing, really."

She doesn't look surprised, and I realize he did tell her. She's toying with me, and doing it well.

When I instinctively reach in my pocket I'm shocked to find it empty. I'd forgotten my bolt? I never forget it. But I'd been so focused on making sure Sanda had everything she needed. Can I make it through an entire night without it? My hands sweat and I force my feet to stay in place long enough to let me think. No running, not yet.

"If you don't want me here, you can just tell me." My voice comes out smaller than I expect so I pull my shoulders back and stand straighter.

I'd been worried about leaving Sanda anyway. Maybe Lily will send me away. I could go home to Sanda and still wouldn't get on Cam's bad side. It's the best-case scenario, really.

"I didn't say that." Lily pauses, her fingers hovering over the keypad on the safe. She looks up at me. I study my hands as she enters the code, but when I hear the door creak open I can't resist taking a peek. The safe contains some metal drawers with cash in them, but not much. A stack of paper sits on the top shelf and on the bottom I see the black metal butt of a gun. My heart skips a beat and I'm hot and cold at the same time. I *really* don't like guns. I know exactly how it feels when all you can see is the barrel pointed at you and everything else falls away.

Of course, even the Father's gun couldn't stop me after they killed Sam.

Shaking off the sudden rush of fear, I watch as Lily closes the safe.

"Let's get started."

I follow Lily down the hallway. She stops near the storage room and peers inside. "Gino, can you show the new girl around? Give her a tour and everything?"

No one responds, but Lily nods and speaks over her shoulder as she walks to the office. "He'll be right out. Just wait here."

I stand in the hallway alone, feeling inadequate and trying to remember every TV show I ever watched that had a restaurant. It isn't helpful. Mostly they were comedies with the staff's bad service being the punch line. I doubt Lily would want me learning from them.

The door before me swings open and a guy a couple of years older than me steps out and wipes his hands on his apron. He's not much taller than me, but his shoulders are wide. His dark eyes land on me but he doesn't say a word.

"Are you Gino?" I grab a notepad and pencil out of my back pocket and pray he doesn't want to shake my hand.

He nods and his eyes go from my feet all the way up to my

head. It makes me intensely uncomfortable and I wish I could have the tour from Mary or even Lily.

"This is the storage room." He points to the room behind him and his soft voice surprises me. "For food supplies. We have another one for cleaning and office stuff. Follow me."

He gives me the full tour and explains the sections of the dining room.

"What is your name?"

"Huh?" I'm barely listening as I stare hard at the dining room tables and try to memorize where each section begins and ends. My notepad is back in my pocket. I've learned from experience that my brain works much faster than my fingers. "Oh, it's Charlotte. I'm Charlotte."

When I turn and raise my eyes, he's studying me again. "I am quiet, so people don't think I'm smart, but I pay attention. I don't know why Cam wanted you working here, but don't upset Lily. She's not as tough as she seems."

I wonder for the first time if he knows more about me than he should.

"I don't intend to."

I spend the second part of my shift watching Mary and Lily at the host station. I already know I need to spend more time practicing my writing. Whenever we're busy, they want me to write down people's last names on a list. Just the thought makes my hands sweat. How am I supposed to guess how to spell people's last names? I didn't even have a last name myself until I became Charlotte.

I rub the back of my neck, feeling the tension build up there with every passing minute. I've been away too long. My mind keeps drifting back to Sanda. The last time Sam had been out of my sight—but no, this is different. My hand presses gently against the still-healing gash on my side. No one else wants to hurt her. She's safe.

Sanda is safe.

"Are you listening, Charlotte?" Lily's voice breaks through my trance.

Mary whistles under her breath and walks toward the bathroom. "Potty break."

"I'm sorry, Lily. I got distracted for a minute." I try to focus.

"By what?" She levels her gaze at me and is obviously expecting an answer. My eyes fall on the frame on the wall behind her and I decide it's a better option than the truth.

"That picture." I point to the wall behind her. "Is that your sister?"

Lily's body freezes mid-turn, and I can actually see a physical struggle to breathe beneath the abrupt tension in her shoulders. When she finally speaks it is low and furious. "Was—she *was* my sister."

The sudden pain in her face makes me wish I'd thought of anything else to say. "Lily, I'm so—"

"Look." Her pain is quickly hidden behind a glare that burns my skin like the city's asphalt on a hot day. "I know you're only here because Cam wants you to be, and I'm not going to do you the favor of firing you. Do your job and stay away from me."

Mary walks up as Lily storms back toward her office. All she says is "Wow" before another couple comes in and she turns her happy smile back on to greet them.

When Mary comes back after escorting them to their table, she raises one eyebrow at me like a challenge. "So you and Lily aren't going to be besties. Big whoop. Angelo's still needs a new me, and since you haven't left yet, I'm assuming you still need this job for one reason or another. You try this time."

"Okay." Forcing my hands not to shake, I step up to the booth and try to smile at the next couple that walks through the door. From their reluctant approach, I'm guessing my attempt isn't coming off the way I hope. I drop it and give up on friendly. I try for nonthreatening instead. "Welcome to Angelo's. Table for two?"

They nod and I lead them to a nearby booth.

When I come back, Mary isn't even trying not to laugh. A flush rises to my cheeks.

"Maybe we should find a place for you in the kitchen. Don't want you scaring off the customers." She grins.

"At least I'm trying," I mutter under my breath.

She pats my arm. "Go take a break and we'll try again when you come back."

"Okay."

As I head toward the break room, I sense it. The feeling that someone is watching me. I turn, expecting to find Lily's eyes on me once again, but I can see her back through the door to the kitchen. Still, the hairs on my arms stand on end and my fingers are cold with fear.

My senses have never steered me wrong before. I don't intend to ignore them now.

I keep walking but do a quick sweep of the restaurant. There are three sections of tables, and I get the distinct impression someone in one of the far side booths has his eyes on me. It's darker in that half of the room. Once I'm safely tucked into the nearest hallway, I peek around the corner, but it's no use. No matter how I squint, I still can't make out the features of a guy in the back corner. It's hard to tell with his hat so low and the collar of his coat up so high, but it's like he's staring right at me . . . right through me. I can't remember Mary seating anyone at that table.

"Hey," Cam whispers from behind me, his lips so close, they almost touch my ear. I spin and hit him in the stomach with my fist. He grunts and doubles over.

"I'm sorry." I grimace and head farther down the corridor to the break room. "Why did you sneak up on me like that?"

"I didn't." He's still trying to get his breath back. "I called 'Charlotte' three times, but you didn't respond. I didn't want to shout your real name across the restaurant."

"Oh, I didn't hear you." I have to step closer to Cam to let Gino pass with a tray of food. I notice a slight shake of his head before he walks out into the dining room and I turn my attention to Cam.

"What's going on?" His eyes watch close, taking in my every movement. It's unsettling.

"I'm considering a change of careers already." My shoulders slump forward. "I told you I wouldn't be any good at this."

"Not that." Cam reaches up to put one hand on my upper arm, but when my eyes widen he drops it again. "What happened just now? You seem spooked."

"Nothing." I shrug. "I felt like someone was watching me."

His eyebrows drop lower. "Where?"

"I'm sure it's nothing." The goose bumps on my arm tell me, and probably Cam, that it isn't nothing. I rub my hand across my skin, planning to check it out myself when I'm done talking to Cam. My other hand keeps diving into my pocket and searching around for the bolt, even though I know it won't be there. I silently curse myself again for forgetting it.

"We both know you're running from something. You hired me to help you." His face is just above my ear and with two quick steps he switches our positions so I'm the one against the wall. "Tell me where he is."

I stare in his eyes, trying to show him I don't need his help, but he doesn't flinch.

"Where?"

"Fine. Far corner booth, left side."

He gives me a dark smile before stepping out into the dining room and leaving me alone in the hall. After a few deep breaths, I try to convince myself that this one time my senses were wrong. They were off somehow. Nothing and no one was watching me.

Cam returns, leads me down the hall past the break room and into an empty office currently being used for storage. I can't tell anything from his expression.

"Well?"

"Stay here. I'll be right back." He shuts the door behind him.

I'm starting to panic. Maybe my instinct was right. Had someone found the Parents' bodies and connected them to me? Did they find me? That seems like a stretch. Or worse, was it possible they weren't really dead?

It couldn't be. Images of blood-soaked clothing and carpets fill my vision as I drop onto the couch. Everything was over after they made me bury Sam. It was too late for any of us.

Flashes of emotion, the pure wild fury, the way my vision slanted to one side, they all pound against my brain like captives against a locked door. Everything is vivid, the colors skewed until all I see is red. The Mother comes to get my chains after I throw the last shovelful of dirt over my brother's body. When she clicks open the locks, she puts the knife to my back and tells me to go inside. I've seen her scars. I know what I am to her. She used to be the Father's victim. He used to hurt her like he does me. That's why she agreed to stay with him. They made a deal. I'm her substitute, her shield. Sam was an accident. They hadn't wanted her to get pregnant. I'd heard them talking about it. I guess two shields were better than one. And now she's grown to like the power of causing pain to others the same way the Father does.

The Mother nudges me, causing the dull blade of her knife to cut into the skin of my back. It hurts, but I can't feel the pain like I could before. She wants me back in my dark attic where Sam won't be waiting for me. He won't ever be with me again.

"The Boy is gone. Go upstairs."

When I turn to face her instead, her stance is relaxed. She knows I won't fight, I never have before. I was too afraid. Of what? That they'll kill me? That would be a relief now. I deserve it after what I let them do to Sam.

"His name is Sam." My words are ice and fire, frigid and furious.

She stumbles and then takes another step forward. "What did you say?"

"I said, his name is Sam. And my name is Piper."

"You little . . ." She walks toward me. Her head is an easy target, so within reach. There is no logic, only wrath, only bitter hatred as I swing the shovel and she's down. The formidable opponent so easily stomped beneath my feet. I let the shovel fall to the earth beside her.

I stand over the Mother, panting, my thoughts trapped in a hazy fog where everyone I've ever known is dead or dying. Everyone but the man who deserves it most. The Father curses when he walks onto the porch and his eyes meet mine. It is the first time—the only time—I've seen fear in their blue depths. It lingers there for only an instant, until they harden and he steps backward. He doesn't even blink as he moves slowly, steadily, toward the rack just inside the door where he keeps his gun. I can see it in his eyes. The game is over. It's time to sweep away the toys.

He's going to kill me, but not before I do everything in my power to make him pay for what he did to my little brother.

My heart pounds blood through my veins so fast that everything else slows in comparison. I reach down and tug the knife free from beneath the Mother's hand. My muscles coil beneath me and explode up as I launch forward. My fury won't let me stop. His fingers scratch across the wood, flipping the latch, but I'm faster than either of us expects. My knife slices through his arm. Damaging his muscle, so when he reaches for the gun it dangles limply from his fingers.

Losing Nana and Sam in a few weeks was more than even

I could take. The Father said they were punished for my mistakes. Both of their deaths were my fault. Now he had been punished, too.

I shake my head hard and push my palms against my temples, trying to shove away the images of what I'd done. I don't want to see this, don't want to think about the loss of control and sanity. About the blood pumping in my ears so loud, so hard I couldn't think. Couldn't do anything but stab him. Even with the gun in his grasp, the Father couldn't protect himself from the monster I'd become.

They were barely alive when I walked to their bedroom, took the money they'd stolen from Nana, and ran.

I push my fingertips hard over my eyelids. No more thinking about them. They couldn't have survived. Impossible.

*Not them. No, not them again. Never again.*

Who else could've been watching me from the booth? I'd walked past Brothers's apartment today on my way to work. It is little more than rubble. He couldn't have survived that. Every instinct urges me to run home to Sanda, just in case, to be certain he hasn't taken her again.

*He deserved to die. He had to. He was a bad man.*

My chest hurts, quick gasps burn my lungs. I focus my energy and draw in a deep breath, trying to keep it as steady as I can. Whatever is happening, now is not the time to panic.

Cam walks in, smiling, and I'm across the room in an instant.

"What happened?" My fingers are gripping onto his shirt before I realize what I'm doing, but I don't care. "Who is it?"

"Whoa, calm down." He curses under his breath and wraps

both arms around me. Everything inside me withdraws from the world, the fear, his touch. I crumple to the floor and scoot into the corner to escape.

He keeps talking, his voice low enough I can barely hear him with my face buried against my knees. "I'm so sorry I scared you." The remorse in his tone is pure and his concern reaches out to me through it, offering acceptance that I don't know how to receive. "There isn't anyone in that booth. Mary doesn't remember seating anyone there. Your eyes must've been playing tricks on you."

My fingers are balled into fists that refuse to release, and my emotion leaves me in a huge gush. I lean my head against the wall behind me, unable to hold it up under the mountain of everything that has happened in the last year. Flashes of Sam's body, his fresh grave, the blood, the Parents, the burning house, Brothers's closet, Sanda's eyes. They pelt me from every direction, unexpected, like hail in a summer storm. I don't cry—I can't. But I'm humming, and Sam's humming, and I feel I might break under the weight of everything I've done, everything I've lost.

I don't know how many minutes pass, but when I become aware again Cam is sitting beside me, as close as possible without touching me. I hear a slight scratching sound and look down to see he's rubbing his hand against the ground beside my fist, like somehow the comfort will pass through the ground and into me. I steal choking gasps of air. I don't know when I stopped humming, but Sam continues in my head. It's slower, quieter. Like Sam is trying to make me feel better.

I've calmed enough to be embarrassed now, but I'm not. The wall that keeps my past carefully caged has crumbled and I can't do anything to rebuild it. It's good not to be alone, that Cam didn't leave me, didn't run away. He raises his hand off the ground, holding it still in the air, and waits. Without his saying a word, I know he wants to help. Sucking in a deep breath, I realize I want it, too—a small piece of protection, of human comfort. My hand shudders as I slide it beneath his and he lowers his hand to rest over my still-closed fist. It's better than I hoped. He shouldn't feel good, not this good. But his warmth penetrates my skin and sinks deep into me. His smell fills me with peace and knowledge that everything will be okay. I want to stay here. I want him to help me through it. More than that, I think I need someone if I'm going to make it through this at all. I can't do it alone.

And that scares me more than the disappearing man from the corner booth.

The door opens and Lily walks in. Her jaw drops, then her lips curve into a sneer. I move to twist my fist free, but Cam's hand tightens and won't let me go.

"If you two are done making out, maybe she can go help Mary. She doesn't get any privileges because of you, Cam. Specifically, taking an extra-long break just so you can 'make sure she's all right,'" she mutters, as she walks toward the door, but her next words are crystal clear. "She looks just fine to me."

As soon as she walks out, Cam releases his grip. I slide my hand out and get up from the floor. Yeah, *now* I'm embarrassed. It's important he understand that this doesn't . . . can't mean anything—even if I am still overwhelmed by his kindness and the warmth lingering from his hand on mine. "Thank you, and I'm sorry. I've had a hard time lately and you were there. It won't happen again."

He gets to his feet and moves toward the door. His eyes are guarded, but I can see a lingering sadness beneath. "It's fine. I'm only doing what you paid me for."

A very tall, very loud man blocks the door before it's even all the way open. "Hey, Marco!" He slaps Cam across the shoulder. I move a few steps back. The name Marco sends a chill through my veins and suddenly makes Cam look less trustworthy in my eyes.

"Me and the boys need to talk to you about a few things."

Cam shakes his head before the other man even finishes. "Not now, Oscar."

"Oh, now's not convenient for you, is it? What if we decide not to make it optional?" His voice lowers a bit and he turns and his eyes find mine, looking me over before he leers back at Cam. "Well now, who is this?"

Cam's expression flashes anger as he glances back at me, but just as quickly it's gone. "Her name is Charlotte."

Oscar winks and nudges Cam with his elbow. "Yeah, sure it is."

Cam ignores him and continues. "She's new. She'll be replacing Mary."

"I'd better get back to work. Thanks for your help, Marco." I slide past them into the hallway. The way Oscar's eyes move over me is making my skin crawl to get away.

"No." Cam's voice is sharp, but his eyes beg me not to argue, not this time, so I stay silent. He turns back to Oscar. "Wait in Lily's office. I'll be right there."

Oscar inclines his head and grins at me before walking away.

I follow Cam back into the room, staying close to the door. Everything he's ever told me suddenly feels colored with shadows of doubt.

"Marco is my first name. Marco Cameron Angelo." He stares me straight in the eye as he continues. "My mom wanted Cameron, my dad wanted a family name, and I prefer my mom's choice."

I tilt my chin down but don't say anything. He steps closer, and with my back against the door already, I can't retreat. "I swear to you. You clearly have your reasons not to trust people, but I want you to trust me. Everything I've told you is true."

His warmth seems to jump across the inches between us, and I have to fight the pull I feel toward him.

"Trust doesn't matter. Neither does your name, honestly, and I'd better get to work before Lily comes for me." I give him a half smile and continue. "I really don't want to face her wrath any more than I have to."

Cam sighs, resigned, then reaches out and inches even closer, grabbing the handle to the door behind me. Every move he makes, every word he utters fills me with a confused sort of longing. It makes me feel like I'm losing control, and I know I shouldn't like that, but somehow it isn't bad with him. "I'd hate to get you in any more trouble with Lily on your first day." His breath is warm through the fabric covering my shoulder.

I slide a step to my right so he can open the door, then I walk through it without a word or a glance back in his direction.

* * *

Before I leave for the night, I'm certain I've proven I'm the worst employee ever. I used the wrong cleanser and stained the bathroom counter, broke three glasses, and offended their most loyal customer when I couldn't make myself shake his hand.

"I'm sorry. Maybe next time will be better?" I shouldn't have agreed to take this job to begin with.

"It wasn't *that* bad," Lily lies, then shrugs and groans as she rolls her shoulders back. "I'm exhausted."

"Right, thanks. I'll see you later." I walk to the door, but when I open it I see a man standing across the street in the shadows. He doesn't move, he watches, he waits. My body goes cold and I step back, slamming the heavy door. It's the only thing I can put between us besides the city street and the night air. When I hear a crash I scramble behind a table and everything is silent.

Through the window on the door, I see the man across the street step out of the shadow. His short gray hair shines in the light of the approaching bus. It stops and he climbs on board. I take a deep breath and stand up, relaxing my tense muscles. Then I hear a soft sob and the scraping of glass against the wood floor.

"Lily?"

When I step forward, I see her crouched on the ground behind the host station. Broken bits of glass cover the ground before her. Cradled in her hands is the picture frame with her sister that I'd asked about earlier. Tears slide down her face, and I don't know what to say. It must've fallen off the wall when I slammed the door.

All I can think is how it would crush me if someone had broken a picture of Sam.

"Get out." Her voice sounds haunted. Gino walks over from the back room, and without a word moves to help clean up the glass. His eyes are cold and accusing when he glares up at me.

I struggle to find the right words, any words to express how sorry I am, but it doesn't matter. I know, were I in her place, there is nothing anyone could say or do to ease the pain. I whisper, "I'm sorry," as I slip out the door into the night.

# 10

Jessie's Studio is a martial arts school on the corner a few blocks from my apartment. They specialize in a form of self-defense called Krav Maga. The studio is actually a bit closer than Angelo's. I hadn't warned Cam about Sanda when I asked him to teach me. I figure if I spring her on him, he might be less likely to argue and ask questions in front of her. At least that's what I hope.

Sanda and I are a few minutes early so we sit beside the wall while another class is finishing up. Eight adults move in sync with the instructor. Sway to one side, duck, sway to the other, kick, punch, punch—it's a violent dance. I'm glad I'm not on the receiving end of the instructor's kicks. She's petite, not much taller than me, and probably in her late forties. Her feet could do serious damage though. I wonder if this is Cam's aunt. Her dark eyes remind me of Lily's, but more friendly, which says a lot considering she just pinned a guy twice her size to the mat in two moves.

Sanda's watching every motion like she's trying to burn them into her memory. Her shining hair feels like evidence that I'm still a good person. I don't know how I'm going to make this work, but the only thing I'm sure of is that any life I build for her could dis-appear in an instant.

And if that happens, I want Sanda to be able to get in a few good kicks the next time she meets someone like Steve Brothers.

His name sends a chill down my spine and the dream from last night flashes through my mind. She's been with me five days now, but the memory of what I did to save her is still fresh. Nightmares of Brothers's skin melting in the flames as he screams and writhes on the dirty brown rug are far too regular. I'd been relieved more than once when Sanda woke me up—until I'd realized she was screaming, too.

Nightmares are just part of the territory. No matter how far we run, we can't escape the memories of where we've been.

I tried letting her borrow the electric blanket, but then we were both restless. She didn't understand why it helped me and I didn't feel ready to tell her about Sam. She sleeps better now that I started lying on the bed next to her. She doesn't let go of my hand most of the time. This morning, I'd thought it was Sam's hand for a few sweet moments. When I saw her dark hair instead of his spiky blond mess, it destroyed me all over again. I'm glad Sanda was sound asleep so she didn't see me fall apart.

The instructor and her class bow to each other and their les-son ends. The people gather their belongings to leave, and I get to my feet with Sanda only a moment behind me. The teacher walks over.

"Hello! What can I help you with?" she asks as she takes a long swig from her water bottle.

"Hi, I'm Charlotte. We have an appointment with Cam."

"I'm Jessie." She smiles and points across the room to where a guy just came in. I have to blink twice to recognize him. "He's right over there."

Cam looks like an entirely different person in loose sweatpants and a sleeveless white shirt. His biceps are far more intimidating than I expected, but the rest of him is so casual, he could've walked in off the beach. The way his brown hair falls across his face as he sets down his bag doesn't help.

"Um, wow," I say. I'm not sure what I expected, but it wasn't this.

I don't realize I'd said it aloud, let alone how it sounded, until Jessie sputters the water she's drinking and coughs. My cheeks burn and I turn my attention toward smoothing Sanda's hair. "I'm sorry."

Jessie glances behind her and Cam tilts his head toward us. "He may not look that experienced, but he's my nephew. He really is the best. He teaches all the private lessons." She grins and her skin wrinkles around her eyes. "Give him an hour, and I promise you won't be disappointed."

I nod with an exaggerated sigh, knowing Cam is listening.

When I turn his way, he's leaning against the wall watching us with his arms crossed over his chest. He walks forward, his voice echoing in the large room. "Is this a friend of yours?"

"Yes, this is Sanda."

He extends a hand to her and waits. She pivots to face him and stares at his fingers a moment before I see her swallow and place her hand in his. My heart aches; I know how hard that was for her. In so many ways, I wish I were more like her.

"Very nice to meet you." He raises his face to watch me, leaving a list of implied questions in the air between us.

I clap my hands together. "Okay, so where do we begin?"

Cam laughs. "You want to dive in?"

"I think that might be best." My voice sounds a little shaky. I know I'll have to let him touch me. I've been preparing myself. The idea alone turns me into a boiling pit of emotions, but I know I have to try.

"Are you ready?" His voice is soft and smooth, like silk across a hard floor. Taking a few steps closer, his hazel eyes bore into mine. Judging from how shocked he'd seemed when I asked for lessons, he *must* have an idea how hard this will be for me. Somehow, knowing he understands doesn't make it any easier.

"I am." Sanda speaks from beside me. She is scared, but I can tell she's trying hard to be brave. I'm filled with sympathy. The first few weeks are the most difficult . . . especially around boys.

I step forward, but Cam motions for me to stay and beckons Sanda until she stands in front of him. "I'm going to take a minute to figure out what you two already know." He kneels down by her and smiles, but I know him better. I see recognition in his eyes as they take in her fear. This is Cam after all. The first thing I learned about him was he always sees more than you want him to. "You look strong. How old are you?"

Sanda glances back at me and waits for my nod before answering. "I'm nine."

His grin widens and he hops back up on his feet, moving fluidly into a defensive position. "Okay, Sanda. I want you to put your arms up like this. I'm going to come after you, like I'm going to grab you, and you try to stop me."

Sanda doesn't move and her face seems like it's turned to stone.

My instincts flare and I have a strong urge to grab Sanda and run. "Wait, can we have a minute first?"

Cam stands and walks back to his water bottle. He shrugs like he couldn't care less, but his eyes never leave us.

Sanda walks over to me and I kneel down before her. "This isn't going to be easy. He's going to try to touch you. He will touch you."

Her eyes are filled with panic and determination. "But it's okay?"

"No, it's never okay unless you feel okay, but I think we both need what he can teach us. You know?" With Cam listening, I don't want to say anything more specific. He might not be super-excited about teaching a killer like me how to defend herself. "For safety, in the future."

Her lip trembles but she nods and turns back to face him. I can't stand seeing her fear and not taking it away, not trying to erase it when I know I can. Maybe we don't have to do this, maybe not yet, not today. I don't want to let Cam touch me any more than she does.

"Maybe we should start with something else." I take two steps forward, but he raises his hand again for me to stay put. I stop, but watch Sanda closely. She takes another step toward the middle of the mat.

"I promise, I won't hurt you." His voice is soft now and he bends low enough to meet her gaze. I see his eyes take in her shaking frame, and he waits as Sanda starts breathing again. "Do anything you want to me. Punch, hit, bite, pull my hair—anything to try to stop me. Okay?"

She nods slowly and raises her hands in front of her.

Cam drops low and comes closer. She kicks one foot and misses; it's feeble and tentative, but it's a start. She glances at me, and when I smile something in her expression changes. Her eyes turn back to Cam, and as they narrow I see a fierce fire in them I've never seen before.

He inches near and reaches one hand for her foot. She lifts it and stomps down hard, barely missing his fingers as he jerks away. A low chuckle escapes him and he stands up. With a move so quick I almost miss it, he grabs her arm. Sanda collapses to the floor so unexpectedly that he loses his grip and she's free again. He nods in approval as she gets to her feet, then he steps in a tight circle before diving in and wrapping both arms around her. She struggles with her arms pinned to her sides, but the way he's holding her, she can't get enough momentum to make her legs useful.

He keeps her in place for long enough to prove she's stuck before returning her gently to the floor. She whips around and throws her fists up in front of her again, but he waves his hands and takes a step back.

"Great job, Sanda. You're a real fighter. I like that."

She doesn't drop her arms. I can read the uncertainty in her expression; she doesn't trust him to stop. I walk over and slowly push her arms down with my hands. Kneeling, I hold out a water bottle from the bag we brought with us.

"Good. It's over now." I keep my voice low until I see her eyes focus and she grabs the water. This girl is so strong, so much more than I expected. My hand shakes by my side, knowing I'm next. I *will* find that same strength inside myself somehow. "Go sit down while I take a turn."

I stand and Cam raises an eyebrow at me while Sanda walks to a bench by the wall. When I get to the mat, he winks and then crouches a little. "Ready?"

"Am I allowed to pull hair and bite, too?" I roll my shoulders back and draw in a slightly uneven breath.

"Sure." A grin spreads across his face. "If you get the chance."

I bend my knees and bring my hands up in front of me. It feels comfortable and like a mistake at the same time. The Parents never came at me with their bare fists. And I learned quickly that defending myself against wooden boards, knives, or leather belts with only my hands never worked out very well. I have the scars to prove it.

He ducks in and tries to grab my elbow. My heart races and adrenaline pumps through my veins. I whip my arm out straight and catch his cheek with the back of my hand. He dodges away at the last second, so it doesn't hit hard, but we both stand there, stunned.

"You're fast." His eyes are wide; the smile comes back even bigger. "Nice."

"Thanks?" I bring my arms back up as he returns to his stance. After a few feints for my arms again, he dives for my leg, but I lightly step out of the way. Huh, I *am* fast. How about that? The fear of him touching me dissolves a bit and I'm filled with an odd sense of pride. I grin, and Cam does, too.

He moves to one side, then dives in quick and wraps both arms around my waist. The panic floods back, slamming me hard and leaving me breathless. At the same moment, pain explodes at my side and I cry out. He immediately loosens his grip and lowers me to the floor. He's so close I can smell his deodorant, but all I can think about is the wet metallic scent of blood.

"What the hell?" Cam jerks his arm away. We both look down as spots of red appear on my clothes. His eyes scan the room, but he doesn't seem to find whatever he's looking for. He swears and tugs off his shirt, pressing it against my side. He doesn't pull back when he sees me flinch, but his voice drops into a low growl that sounds more like a chain saw than silk. "Why didn't you tell me you were hurt?"

"I forgot." It'd been healing so nicely, too. I roll away, trying to escape the weird sensations his exposed chest sends through me, when he leans in close and it fills my vision. And I'd thought his biceps were intimidating . . . I keep trying to get up on my feet, but Cam pushes me back down. I'm used to having bumps and bruises. I'm not used to being around people that care whether or not they make me bleed.

Cam tugs at the corner of my shirt and I try to push his hands away.

"You forgot?" he says, as he glares at me, presses my hands down by my sides, and lifts the corner of my shirt. I hear him mutter under his breath when he sees blood already soaking through my bandage and examines the smaller, healing gashes encircling it.

"Okay, we're done for the day." Cam stands up and moves behind me. Hooking one hand below my left arm, he lifts me to my feet with surprisingly little effort. As soon as I'm up, I twist to escape his grip. "I live next door. Let me grab my first-aid kit and I'll help clean you up," he says.

*No, no, no. Bad idea.*

"No."

"Yes."

"No."

"P-Charlotte." He groans and shakes his head. "I hurt you. The least I can do is clean up the mess I made."

"Not your fault. I was already hurt. It was stupid not to tell you." I grab my backpack and hand it to Sanda, who is standing between us with huge eyes. Before she has a chance to heft it over her shoulder, Cam takes it and wraps the strap around his fist.

"Fine, then. You *were* stupid not to tell me. You got blood all over my arm and my shirt. The least you can do is let me help so I won't lose my job for letting a *new client* leave with blood streaming down her side."

I wait for him to back down, but from his expression I know he won't. The silence between us hangs thick until Sanda stifles a giggle, and Cam winks at her before glaring at me again.

"We aren't going home with you." I raise my hand to stop him when he opens his mouth to argue again. "But if you're really concerned, I'll let you walk us to our apartment."

His expression is defeated in such an overdramatic way that Sanda laughs again and I can't help but smile. He yanks on the backpack. "Fine, but I'm carrying the bag."

"Okay. I don't want to carry it anyway," Sanda says over her shoulder as she walks out the door in front of us.

Cam bows his head and extends his hand toward the door. "Ladies first."

Maybe taking lessons here is a bad idea. Fifteen minutes into our first lesson and I'm already bleeding. No one has even hit me yet.

# 11

Sanda walks ten feet in front of us on the way home. I think she wants to prove she can walk alone, but about once every minute I see her check to make sure we're still there. I pretend not to notice.

"So what's the story with you two?" Cam asks. Despite the sweatpants and the hoodie he threw on over his exposed chest, Cam still somehow manages to walk with purpose *and* appear so relaxed it borders on lazy. It's impressive.

"No story," I reply. My voice is a little colder than I intend, and I bite my tongue softly between my teeth.

"Everyone has a story." Cam lowers his chin and turns my way. "You don't want to tell me yours . . . yet."

We walk in silence, and I'm surprised at how comfortable it is. I half believed letting him touch me would ruin any ability for me to relax around him ever again—instead, the opposite seems true. The whole city is tranquil when I'm next to him, the people friendlier, the streets peaceful. It's like even the buildings around us are cozier, more at ease when he's by my side. Every few seconds he glances at my shirt to check the bleeding but never says anything about it.

"I can guess what made you decide to take Krav Maga. You clearly need it." Cam keeps his eyes on Sanda and his voice low. "Her, too?"

My instinct is to not tell him anything, but I've already tried that and because of it I'm ruining another perfectly good outfit with my blood. I press his shirt harder against my side and wince. "She might need it even more than I do."

His jaw tightens, and we walk in silence for a moment before he responds. "Then I'll have to make sure not to let you two down."

Unfamiliar warmth spreads through me, but I keep my eyes on the back of Sanda's feet.

We make our way up the steps to our apartment building. When I unlock the door and let Sanda in, Cam is right behind me.

"Thanks. We'll be fine from here." I hand him back his shirt and try to pretend it isn't covered in my blood. The apartment needs to be for Sanda and me alone, especially tonight. I lowered some walls between Cam and me when I let him touch me. If replacing them with ones made of brick and stone is my only option for now, it will do. Not any closer, not yet.

"Look, I'll wait here if you want. You don't have to let me in." Cam's eyes darken as he stares at the amount of blood on the ruined shirt. "But you're pale and I'm not leaving until I'm sure you don't need to go to the hospital."

I shake my head, but he crosses his arms over his chest and sits down on the steps to our building. His smile irritates me as he leans back, like he has all the time in the world.

"You know"—he tilts his head toward me like he's sharing a secret—"I'm pretty good at first aid."

"You know"—I lean down toward him a bit but pain shoots through my side so I bolt up straight—"so am I."

He sits and waits, but his playful expression is gone.

"Fine," I say, stomping my feet harder than normal as I head inside. "Wait here."

When I follow Sanda through the door and up the stairs, I hear Janice's door open.

"Hel—" She gasps. Closing my eyes for a moment, I groan as I pivot to face her. She stands frozen in her doorway, staring at the blood that's begun to spread across my side to the back of my shirt.

"I had an accident. Excuse me for rushing, but as you can see, I need my first-aid kit." I try to spread my hands out in front of me, but the motion hurts too much and I return them to my side.

Janice glances from me to Sanda, backs away, and closes the door to her apartment quietly.

By the time we've made it up the stairs and into our apartment, my head is pounding and my side has gone numb. Sanda runs into the bathroom and is back in our room with my first-aid kit before I can even ask.

"Thanks."

I lift my shirt and once again survey the damage. I've really got to stop bleeding like this. My vision tilts. Yep, I still hate blood. The Steri-Strips dangle uselessly from each side of the newly opened gash. I gently remove them and resist the urge to cry out as I re-clean the wound. The injury isn't quite as bad, but now I'll definitely have a nasty scar.

I bite my lip as I finish applying new strips and put on a fresh bandage. Sanda is sitting out on the couch flipping through an old

*Sports Illustrated* that was here when I moved in. Gingerly, I tug a new shirt over my head as I hear a knock on the door. My heart flies into my throat, but my reaction is nothing compared to Sanda's. In an instant, she's in our room again, has flung the door closed and is cowering behind me.

A memory of Sam rises unbidden to the surface of my mind and I see him running to his hiding spot every time the attic door opens. The Parents didn't even make it to the top of the stairs before his skin paled to the shade of a ghost. I'd tried my best to protect him. To focus their anger on me so they'd leave him alone, but with two of them I couldn't always keep him safe.

*You didn't hurt me, Piper. It was them. Never you.*

So many times I'd wanted to make them stop, to hurt them back, but I'd always been too afraid. I'd been a coward. I was too scared until it was too late . . . and then I was the only one left to save.

My breath is so shaky when I draw it in I wonder if any oxygen comes with it. Crouching down beside Sanda, I lift her chin and look in her eyes.

"It's okay. It's probably Cam. You can stay here," I whisper, silently cursing him in my head for scaring her like this. "Crawl onto the bed. Hide under the blankets. I'll let you know when it's safe."

Her dark eyes are filled with terrors that only the two of us know. She turns and climbs under the covers. Even when I can't see her anymore, I see the blankets tremble with fear.

I walk to the door and check through the peephole. Janice stands uncertainly in the hall outside. She wrings her fingers together and then raises her hand to knock again, but hesitates. She returns it to her side and pivots to leave before I turn back the locks and open the door.

"Hi," I say.

"Oh, yes. Good." Her eyes go immediately to my side and she smiles weakly. "I'm glad to see you're okay."

"Yeah." Was this why she'd come? "I'm fine. Thanks."

"How long is Sanda staying with you?" she asks.

"I'm not sure. It will probably be quite a while." I frown. "Is it going to be a problem?"

"No, not at all." Her eyes widen. "But I was wondering . . . if she's going to stay, school starts in a few weeks and I could help you get her registered if you'd like. Rachel will be new, too. She'd love to have a friend at school."

"School?" The word is foreign in my mouth. I hadn't even considered it. Of course Sanda should go to school. Besides the TV that I was able to see through the crack in the attic floor, I'd learned what little I know from a used kindergarten workbook, a stack of old novels, and a radio that Nana snuck up to me when no one was looking. Does Sanda even know how to read? If not, I'll do my best to teach her. "Yes. I'd really like your help with that."

"Really? Great! That's great." Janice seems so surprised I wonder why she even asked. "Get her paperwork together." At my blank expression she goes on. "Birth certificate and social security card, and I'll let you know when I get the registration information. Cam can help you—"

"Right, perfect," I interrupt.

"And I assume that you are done with school then?"

"Yes. I'm done for now at least, maybe college someday." I start to close my door before either of us can reveal any more than we should. "Thank you, Janice."

"Charlotte?" She puts her hand up to stop me. And her cheeks flush as she continues. "Cam is downstairs. He isn't the one who caused your accident . . . is he?"

"Cam?" My voice does this weird squeaky thing when I say his name. "No, he's just making sure I'm okay."

"And are you?" She looks down at my side again even though there is no longer any evidence of my injury.

"Yes." I give her a firm nod and smile. "I'm fine."

"Good," Janice says, studying the floor between us for a moment without speaking. I wonder for the hundredth time what she thinks about me. I have no idea what the terms of Cam's arrangement with her are. Although, since she's also a client, she's probably realized that Charlotte isn't my real name. "Do you want me to send him up?"

"No," I say too quickly, and her eyebrows shoot up. "No, that's okay. I'll come down in a second. Thanks."

She purses her lips and turns as I close the door tight. I head straight for the bedroom. Sanda's lump is still under the blankets, but it has stopped shaking. Kneeling beside the bed, I let her hear my voice before touching the covers.

"It's okay, Sanda." I lift them high enough to see her. Twin dark pools shine back at me and she blinks twice before responding.

"Who . . . who was it?"

"Janice. She wants to know if you'd like to go to school with Rachel."

Sanda scoots closer and pulls the blanket off her head. "School?" She's almost reverent as she speaks the word.

"You've never been to school?"

"No. Never."

"Would you like to go?"

Her eyes are enormous as she gapes at me. "Could I? Really?"

"Yes."

"Oh, Charlotte." Her hand reaches for mine and she pulls me down until my head is right in front of hers. Her eyes shine as she whispers, "That would be the best thing I could ever imagine in my whole entire life."

And then both of her tiny arms are wrapped so tight around my neck I can barely breathe, especially since I'm laughing and she's laughing, and it feels so good to laugh. I hug her back and let myself be happy for a moment, knowing this would make Sam proud.

I will protect her. I will keep her safe. I will give her what Sam should've had.

"Thank you, Charlotte."

"You're welcome." Grinning, I sit her back on the bed and extract myself from her arms. "We need to talk about the school arrangements more, but first I need to go and send Cam home."

Sanda is bouncing on the bed as I walk out and down the stairs. Cam gets to his feet as soon as I open the apartment building door. I'm taken aback by the relief that washes over his face when he sees me.

"You're okay," he says.

"I told you I was fine."

"I was starting to think I'd have to bust in and call an ambulance."

"Sorry, Janice distracted me."

"Oh yeah, I saw her." Cam's eyes almost glow when he grins. Bubbles of warmth burst inside me. "She's never acted suspicious of me before, but I worried she might call and report me if I sat out here any longer. What did you tell her?"

"She asked me if you caused my 'accident,'" I tell him with a shrug.

His eyes are pained as he takes a step closer. "Did you say yes?" With me standing on a step, I'm almost as tall as him. I try to back away, but my heels bump against the next step up.

"No." My voice sounds weak, so I clear my throat and try again. "No. It wasn't your fault."

"Does that mean you're going to keep taking lessons?"

I laugh. "Yes."

"On one condition." He leans back when he notices my heels ram into the step behind me for the second time. "You have to warn me about any injuries before each class."

Finally, I can take a full breath. "I'll try."

"Tuesday night, then."

"Wait." My hand reaches forward to stop him without thought and I stick it back in my pocket. His brow furrows as he waits for me to continue. "Could you come by tomorrow morning, around ten? I need help with something."

His eyes search mine for the answers he never finds. "I'll be here." He turns back toward the studio, but I catch the slightest whisper across the darkness between us. "Good night."

# 12

The family Sanda used to clean for gave her a few early reader and chapter books their kids had grown out of. She told me they wanted her to be able to read the labels on the groceries when she put them away. Math is a different matter, but she does know how to count from the times they made her scrub the bathtub with one thousand strokes using an old toothbrush. The woman she'd worked for had listened to her count out loud, and if she missed a number she had to start over.

Sanda had become an excellent counter.

"Are you sure they'll let me go to school?" she asks as we wait on the steps in front of our apartment. Her hair is so glossy black in the sunlight it's like the midnight sky, but not the one here in the city. The heartbeat of Philadelphia pushes that kind of inky darkness away. It is like a country sky without the stars.

"They will if you have the right papers."

"And that's what we're doing today?" She seems uncertain. I know she's afraid to get her hopes up. That's why I have to be sure not to disappoint her.

"Yep. Cam doesn't know it yet, but he'll help with that."

When I see him coming down the street, heat spreads across my cheeks at the memory of his bare chest last night. I focus on the ground, trying to force my body to stop all the weird reactions it has to his presence. Lately, he creates a war inside me every time we're together. I don't like being a battleground.

His brown hair curls a little around his ears. It's so cute that it's unfair. His lips curve into a smile, and I wonder how long he'll keep that up after I tell him what I want. This is quite a favor, but I'm planning to pay him the same rate as before, so I don't know why he would have a problem with it. Even as I think about it, I know that isn't the real problem. The real problem is that he wants answers. So far, I haven't given him any.

And Sanda brings with her a whole new set of questions.

"Hi." His eyes flick to Sanda before he continues. "Charlotte. Hi, Sanda."

Sanda gives a little wave but hides behind me when I get to my feet and speak.

"Hi. Thanks for coming. Let's go inside."

"Oh, wow. Such an honor to know I'm welcome in the building this morning." He grins as he holds open the door for us and we head up the stairs to the apartment.

"I think it's smart to keep strange boys out of my house at night." I raise one eyebrow. "You disagree?"

"At least you're honest about thinking I'm strange." He winks as I turn toward the stairs.

Sanda rushes forward to walk up ahead of us, and I know she is trying to keep me between her and Cam. Sadness settles in my chest, but at the same time I understand her. These kinds of instincts will keep her alive.

"I need you to do what you do," I say as we enter the apartment.

"What I do?" Now he's all business.

"I was hoping you could help her start over." I extend one hand toward where Sanda has taken a seat on the arm of the couch. "The way you helped me?"

His eyes flash and he glances at her and back to me. "Piper . . ."

I flinch when he slips and uses my real name. His face tightens when he realizes his mistake, but he doesn't back down. Ignoring the confusion on Sanda's upturned face, I push harder. "She needs it for the same reasons I did."

"And what are those reasons again?" Cam's frustration is so clear on his face. It demands the answers I keep refusing him.

I groan. "I'll be happy to pay the same amount as before."

"That doesn't matter." He's angry now, but after Sanda flinches, his voice becomes low and controlled. "I want to help you. God knows I do, but you keep too many secrets. Where did she come from? Why is she here?"

"She's my cousin." I cross my arms over my chest.

"Lies are not going to work. You're asking a lot here." He steps closer and turns so his back is to Sanda. He's hesitant as he slowly places his hands on my shoulders, and I fight not to jerk away as a jolt of fire runs through my body. "Why don't you know by now that you can trust me?"

"She was in trouble." I stare into his eyes and beg him not to push for more. I can't risk telling him everything now. If he knew about the Parents or that I'd left Brothers to burn, he'd never understand. I can't risk Sanda's future by telling him, not until I have her papers. "I'm trying to help her get out of a bad situation. Please, for now, can't that be enough?"

"You're killing me. You know that?" he mutters, and removes his hands, sticking them in his back pockets. Tingles still run down my arms, amazing and terrifying. I freeze, not moving, barely breathing until I can get him to say yes.

"Please, Cam."

"Fine." He closes his eyes and gives a reluctant nod. I finally feel like I can relax again. "If you promise to answer any ten questions I want after we're done."

Well, the relaxing didn't last long. My back stiffens. Why can't he leave my secrets alone? "Please, don't—"

"Sorry, it's a deal breaker. I think you're familiar with that concept." He leans forward and his hazel eyes suck me in. Cam has the power here, pretending otherwise is pointless. He extends his hand and waits. I'd never have imagined myself agreeing to a demand like this, but this is for Sanda and her future.

"Okay, fine. *After* we're done." But I can't stop my hand from trembling as I place it in his and agree to reveal every secret that keeps me safe.


Sanda's new name is Sandra, which is pretty much perfect. There's much less risk of her forgetting it and it's easy to explain the nickname. It's actually Sandra Roberts, which Sanda loves because one of Rachel's dolls is named Robert. Rachel told her he was named after her dad. He's in the military; so was her mom until she died in Afghanistan. Rachel said her parents' job was to be heroes to keep us safe. It works for me. Sanda needs more heroes in her life.

From the bits and pieces I'd picked up from Rachel, Janice has run into some obstacles in her life also. She used to be involved with some guy who was less than willing to let her go. That explains Janice's need for Cam's services.

Maybe we're all hiding more scars under the surface than it seems.

Cam had more options with identities for someone Sanda's age, so he picked the closest thing to her real name. When all a person has is a birth certificate and a Social Security number, it's easier to become them since there's very little legal photo identification stored anywhere. The real Sandra was a good fit because even though she lived in Missouri before she died of leukemia, her mother was Japanese, which made Sandra half Asian in all her records.

Sandra had only been eight years old when she died. I can't decide if it makes me feel better or worse that even a happy childhood can end in such tragedy. Terrible things happen all the time. Does this make my failure to save Sam any better? It doesn't feel that way.

We didn't tell Sanda about Sandra's death. I'm sure it would make her sad. According to the obituary, the girl had a loving family. At least someone buried her in a real grave with a real tombstone. At least her family mourns her. Cam said he hacked in and deleted the death certificate entries, so Sanda can have this identity as long as she wants.

"Well, what do you think?" Lily spins Sanda around in her chair to face the mirror. She's only cut off a couple of inches and made her hair all one length, but the change on Sanda's face is dramatic as she stares at herself in the mirror. Her dark eyes are wide as she reaches up and touches the ends. I can't help but smile, remembering how I felt after Lily worked her magic on me.

"I look pretty," Sanda whispers, and lets out a shaky breath, but she doesn't take her eyes off the mirror. "Thank you."

"No problem, kid." Lily's face softens more than I've seen in days, until she raises her eyes to meet mine.

"Thanks, Lily." I try to give her a smile, but her expression only tightens in response.

"Yeah, yeah . . . making hopes and dreams come true," she mutters, but I think I see confusion in her face as she stuffs her scissors and combs in the bag. "Just a regular Wednesday for me."

"I guess I'm up." Cam walks in and tugs a stool over in front of us. "Ready to see my art?"

Sanda blinks at him and then up at me. "Sure?"

"I've gotta go." Lily walks out the door without waiting for any of us to respond.

Cam frowns, shakes his head, and leads the way into a room behind the barbershop area. I prefer it back here with no windows. The attic had only the one covered with bars and it was so dirty on the outside it was hard to see through. I don't want anyone to be able to look at me when I can't see them.

The front door opens and closes again and Sanda gives a squeak before Cam reassures her.

"Lily must've forgotten something." He walks back to the main barber room and it's immediately obvious that it isn't Lily.

"Now isn't a good time." Cam's voice sounds cold and foreign.

"You can't walk away. That's not how it works with blood." The man's voice sounds familiar, but I can't place it.

I move to stand between Sanda and the door without a second thought, and I feel her small hands grip the back of my shirt as she looks around me.

"I've made no promises to you. Besides, why can't you go to him?" I hear something foreign in Cam's tone that I've never heard there before, and it shakes me to the core. I hear fear.

"It's a lot of work for one guy, Marco." The name brings Oscar, the thug from Angelo's, back to the forefront of my mind and I realize that's where I know the voice from. "And you know that he's busy with other odd jobs, too. We need you both."

Cam's voice lowers so I have to strain to make it out. "If I promise to think about it, will you leave now? We aren't alone."

A few seconds of silence pass before I hear Oscar reply. "You got that pretty chick from the other night hidden away, don't you?" He chuckles low then finishes. "See? Told you we was blood. You're just like your pops."

I hear the front door swing open again, then Cam's voice. "I'll call you tonight and I'll think it over."

"Okay. Have a fun afternoon," Oscar's voice singsongs before I hear the door shut again, and this time the reassuring click of a lock slides into place.

Cam comes back looking flushed and angry.

"Everything okay?" I ask, as he starts moving boxes and tools around a little more forcefully than necessary. Sanda still hides behind me, and I know he isn't intending to scare her, but she jumps every time he slams something new down on the table.

"Yes." He stops and forces out a puff of air before pivoting to face me. His eyes go immediately to Sanda and he winces.

"Who is that guy?" I ask, putting my arm around Sanda and nudging her forward to stand beside me.

"Oh, are we asking questions now?" His voice is soft, but the edge to it still stings. "How about you go first."

Sanda stiffens under my hand, and I look down before I take a step toward the door. "Maybe we should finish this later."

"No." Cam closes his eyes tight and slumps down on the edge of the table before opening them again. His gaze is full of apology before he says the words. "I'm really sorry—to both of you."

I nod without speaking. I have even less right to his secrets than he has to mine. We take seats on the empty table opposite Cam. He looks at us for a moment then stands, and we watch him fly around the room, moving from one fancy piece of equipment to the next. Some of the detailing he does by machine, some by hand. He has a briefcase of folders with different kinds of paper carefully separated into files.

I'm surprised that all this is tucked away in a room behind the abandoned barbershop. I'd seen some of the equipment when I'd been turned into Charlotte by Cam and Lily, but I hadn't been in this room before. There's a couch and a few tables. It's very clean and there's electricity and cold water, but I wonder how comfortable he is having all of this here. The equipment alone must be worth a lot of money, not to mention how much trouble it would cause if the wrong people found it. He sails through the motions effortlessly, his hands moving so fast I can barely keep up with what he's doing. After he gets going, he's intent and focused. I'm not sure he even remembers we're here.

I'm amazed again by the precision that goes into this work. The people who recommended Cam were right. He is the best. His hand glides deftly across a paper, adding a few details to a seal. If forging documents is what Oscar wants help with, I can see why he won't leave Cam alone.

"Where did you learn to do this?" My voice comes out breathy and heat pulses through my face. "I mean, did someone teach you?"

He laughs with his back to me but doesn't answer. After a moment, he turns and puts down the long slender tool he's been using.

"Aren't you the curious one today?" He grins at Sanda. She giggles and her hands fly up to cover her mouth. Cam glances at me and his brow furrows. When Sanda lowers her hands, her smile remains and my heart warms at the sight.

That is the response of a normal girl. One who hasn't grown up in a nightmare. It's a hint at something, a new beginning, a clue that I am doing something right.

He picks up a new tool with a tiny silver hook on the end and turns toward the passport. "My dad taught me. I started helping him when I was ten."

"So this is some kind of *family* business you're taking over?" I hear the sneer in my voice when I speak the word "family," but

I can't stop it. Then I think of the word Oscar used: "blood." Is this what he meant? Cam stiffens but doesn't even look in my direction before answering.

"No. I lived with him then. No idea where he is now." He tilts his head to one side and moves the passport under what I think might be a microscope. "But I don't need his help anymore. I'm better than he ever was."

"Oh." I stop asking questions. I'm not sure if Cam is uncomfortable, but I know I would be. Sanda, however, doesn't seem to have the same concerns.

"Who do you live with now?" She's leaning forward and watching his every move. Nudging her, I get her attention and shake my head. She nods.

"My aunt." He blows across the paper he's working on and smiles. "Oh, and Lily."

"How do you know Lily?" Her words come out and then she lowers her head and swings her legs, sheepish. I can't help but laugh because she looks so much like a girl I'd seen in a cartoon on TV.

Cam's eyes fly up to mine. "You should really do that more often." He doesn't turn away, and the warmth from his grin spreads across the room between us and soaks through my skin until I turn my attention to the desk beside me.

He puts down what he's working on and steps closer. "Lily's my cousin."

"Oh." Sanda still has red in her cheeks. "I have to go to the bathroom."

She jumps down and runs into the hall. I hear a door click shut and then it's silent. The quiet charges the room in an instant as

I watch Cam move closer. This time I don't want him to move away. Everything I've ever known tells me it's not safe, but I'm beginning to trust him. For whatever reason, he's always here when I need him, and I like that.

"You see how easy that was?" He takes another step until his hips are an inch away from my knees at the edge of the table. Not touching, but almost.

"What?" My mouth is dry. I'd kill for some water . . . well, not literally. I'm slightly nauseated that I have to clarify. I lick my lips and now Cam is looking at them. I shift my position on the table and slide back a little. He raises his gaze to my eyes.

"It was easy to answer your questions. I trust you." He places his hands on the table beside my own. Again, so close, but not touching.

It's harder to breathe and I really hope he can't tell. I swear if we turned off the lights we'd be able to see the sparks jumping from his hand to mine. It's tangible. I search his eyes and resist the urge to blink. "Easy, but maybe not smart. How do you know you can trust me? Maybe you shouldn't."

"Are you telling me not to?" He dips his head forward until his eyes are so close I'm drowning in the eddies of green and brown.

"No." Wrong answer, idiot.

"Good." He slides his hands closer until they're almost touching mine. His smile widens when I swallow hard but don't move away. Then the *click* of a door shutting from the other room snaps me out of it.

I jerk my hands away, and I notice the flash of amusement in his expression as he turns back to the papers. Sanda walks in and hops up on the table as Cam puts the documents in a stack and places them on my lap.

I'm suddenly very glad that Sam has kept his mouth shut this whole time. I don't need to hear what he has to say. I don't need Sam to tell me to stay away from Cam. I'm too . . . Cam is too . . . I run one hand over the side of the other. It still tingles. We're just not a good idea. I'm not a good idea with anyone.

"You were born in Missouri." He turns to Sanda and everything returns to normal but my heart rate. "I'm going to get you into the system for a school down there, and then we'll print some transcripts so Charlotte can get you registered."

"Registered?" She bounces so hard on the table I nearly fall off. "So I really can go to school?"

Cam nods and his eyes land on me for a second before he smiles at Sanda. "You really can."

Her eyes tear up and she jumps off the table, but then hesitates and turns back to me. Reaching up, she pulls me down so she can whisper in my ear. "Is he safe?"

From the surprise I see in Cam's eyes, I know he heard her. I don't look away when I whisper back. "Yes, he's a good guy."

Before I realize what she's doing, she turns and throws both arms around Cam's neck. I can hear her quiet whisper against his shoulder. "Thank you."

He barely had a chance to move his arm out of the way before she attacked him. Now he sits with his mouth wide open and his eyes on me. When he gently wraps both hands across her back, his expression shows me that he understands more than I believed he could. He pats her back with one hand, and I see a familiar pain in

126

his eyes. I know very little about him, but maybe his life hasn't been as easy as I thought.

I move my lips to echo her words, but no sound comes out. "Thank you."

Cam gives Sanda a small squeeze but keeps his eyes on me as he answers us both. "You're very welcome."

# 13

By our second week of Krav Maga, I can see Sanda's confidence growing after every session. My wound is better. It's beginning to scar over. I suppose we're both scarring over. And I'm starting to worry about how normal it seems when Cam touches me.

He's made a habit of walking us home afterward. I don't mind. Something has me feeling a little shaky lately. Probably simple paranoia, but it makes me more comfortable to have him nearby, just the same.

Sanda skips along in front of us. She learned it from Rachel. It's her new favorite thing to do. She calls it "happy walking," and Rachel giggles when she says that but doesn't correct her. If not for the scars curling down Sanda's arms, I'd probably think she looks like any other kid. Playing with Rachel has been so good for her. It makes me happy. Lately, I'm only a little sad when I think of Sam and wish he could've had a friend like that.

"What's on your mind?" Cam doesn't take his eyes off Sanda, but his focus shifts to me.

"Nothing. The past." A shiver runs through me. Even now, the strange prickling of someone watching, someone following us, nags at the edges of my awareness. I glance around, but there are many people on the street and no one seems to pay particular attention to us. Shrugging it off, I kick a pebble along the sidewalk and try to answer as truthfully as possible while still not telling him anything. "Things I shouldn't think about."

"Why not?"

"Because they're over. Why should I?"

Cam doesn't answer for half a block, and I focus my attention on Sanda, thinking the conversation is over. When he finally speaks it seems like his mind is on something so far away he can't touch it—or he doesn't want to. "My aunt Jessie always tells me if I can't deal with things enough to move forward, they'll never truly be in the past."

I try to laugh it off but stop when I hear how cold and biting it sounds. "Your aunt sounds like she should write for one of the self-help shows I've seen on late-night TV."

He turns his eyes to me and his focus is right back on the here and now. "I've been in enough fights to pay attention to scars." His voice lowers to a whisper. "What happened to Sanda?"

I know he's really asking about both of us. I've seen the look in his eyes when he notices the burn marks above my right elbow, or the way my left arm won't straighten all the way anymore thanks to a particularly bad break. Drawing in a slow breath and counting to ten, I choose my words carefully.

"Drop it. Whatever it is, I'm sure she doesn't want to explain it to someone who is practically a stranger." My words are as hard and icy as an avalanche as they spill out of my mouth. I'd meant a stranger *to Sanda*, but I can't find the words to clarify. Cam's spine stiffens.

"Consider it dropped, but you still owe me—"

"I know." I want to apologize, but I don't know how.

We're half a block from our apartment, but he stops walking. "I better get back. Wouldn't want to get in trouble by walking a *stranger* home. See you guys on Thursday."

Neither Sanda nor I get a chance to respond before he turns and jogs toward the studio. A jagged stab of regret strikes me straight in the heart, and I wonder how I should've responded. We stand staring at his retreating back until he's out of sight, and then Sanda grabs my hand and begins walking again.

"He's not bad." Sanda's voice is soft and thoughtful.

"What do you mean?" I struggle to shift from under the sudden weight of anxiety that threatens to bury me. I feel safer with him, but when he's gone I feel more vulnerable and I hate that. Lately, my fears shout at me whenever I'm alone and I don't understand why.

*Hurry. Something isn't right.*

Sam's words make every hair on my body stand on end. The sensation of being watched only grows stronger now that Cam is out of sight. I squint at people across the street. Their movements seem anxious, frantic. The buildings of Philly tower over us like the gods of tragedy I've read about in a dusty old book Nana had snuck into the attic. Never intervening, only observing as we crumble beneath the weight of our own mistakes. Shaking off the ominous air, I pick up the pace.

"Cam is one of the good guys and he's nice to you." Sanda

widens her eyes at me as she hurries to keep up. They seem to see through me in a way most people can't. "Why aren't you nice back?"

I sigh and it burns a little in my throat. "Because I'm not a nice person."

She shakes her head and stares at the bottom step. "No, that's not it."

Smiling, I guide her up the stairs to our apartment building. "Well, let me know if you figure it out."

Sanda makes cute snoring noises when she's asleep, but not when she's having one of her nightmares. Bad dreams make her whimper, cry, and even scream.

I stand in the doorway to our bedroom and listen. Her snoring reassures me. She's alive, breathing and happy. No one will come to steal her away while I sleep. I won't wake up and have to bury her cold body under a tree.

I walk into the bathroom and glance again at the only mirror left up in my apartment. I've never dyed my hair before, but I may have to learn how. My blond roots will show at some point and asking Lily for help doesn't seem like a good plan. I feel bad about mentioning her sister, and even more terrible about breaking the picture, but I don't know how to fix it. I'm not sure it can be fixed.

After taking a shower, I wrap up in my robe and towel off my hair as I walk into the living room. Pacing helps me think, and I love that I can move anywhere in my apartment and never have to duck. There were only a few places in the attic where I could stand upright. Nana made me stand in them as often as I could so my back wouldn't start to curve from hunching too much. Sam never got tall enough to need to duck.

I move to the window and watch the street below. It's late now and there are very few people outside. A couple walks near the corner, holding hands and smiling. I wonder what it's like to be them, to trust someone with your heart that way. Are they foolish?

A tiny red glow in the park across the street catches my attention. It's dim and then moves a little and glows brighter. A cigarette, I think. It's a man standing under the tree and smoking a cigarette. My heart pounds loud in my ears as I back away from the window. It's probably a coincidence. It's just a man having a smoke in the park, nothing to be afraid of.

Ducking down, I sneak along the wall to the light switches. I turn off every light in the apartment and then creep back to the window. Careful to stay far enough away so that he can't see me, I peer into the darkness where he smokes and waits. He never turns away from my building. It's hard to tell from here, but the angle of his face seems to be aimed up toward the top floor, my floor, *my window.*

He throws the butt of his cigarette at the ground, turns and walks away. Once he leaves the shade of the tree, I see the same low hat and high collar I saw in the booth at the restaurant. An icy hand clamps down on my chest and makes it hard to breathe.

I don't know who he is, but he's real. He's here . . . and he's watching me.

# 14

I blink a few more times, trying to make my tear ducts start working to soothe my sandpaper eyes. I'm perched in the same position I've been in for hours. I'm not sure how many, but the sky outside has turned from black to navy and is rapidly progressing to violet. I don't know why I'm still here. I watched him walk away, but I know I can't sleep now. The idea of going to bed while the man could still come back haunts me.

The ghosts of my past and present keep me stuck in one place. In some ways, they always have.

Instinct and logic are too busy creating a battlefield in my head to allow sleep anyway. Logic tells me I'm taking this too far. The man might not have been here for me. Maybe he was just a man out for a smoke in the park. Maybe he was just staring at my window because he saw me before the lights went out and was watching to see if I . . . if I what? If I'd left? If I'd gone to sleep?

I let out a shaky breath. Even the good and logical scenarios still make the man sound like a thief—or something worse.

My gut tells me something else. He was standing there for me, but why? Who is he? For the millionth time in the last hour, I run through my short list of possibilities: the Father, Brothers, the police. The figure was too broad-shouldered to be the Mother, plus she didn't smoke like my other two main suspects. The Father should be dead, the Parents should both be dead—and Brothers, too. I've left a trail of dead bodies in my wake, which makes the police the most logical answer, but there was something about the figure that seemed far too menacing for that.

*They are dead. They are dead. They are dead.*

Sam's mantra isn't helping things. It sets my nerves on edge even more than they already are. I almost wish he'd go back to the humming he'd been doing for the last few hours.

I shiver and grab a throw from the back of the couch. Pulling the scratchy material across my shoulders, I lean my head against the window frame and wait for the sun. Wait for the light to bring sense back into my life, to drive the fear away once again.


He's here. The Father squeezes my arm too tight. He wakes me from a dreamless sleep to a world of pain. He stands over me, stares at me, but doesn't see me. His hair is perfect, every strand in place. His clothes are spotless as always. He wears a raincoat when he cuts us. Wouldn't want to let any of our blood stain his shirt. Everything about him and his life is orderly and well kept. Everything except for Sam and me. We are the dirty things. His secrets.

I reach out for Sam's small fingers beside me, but he isn't there. My heart pounds in my head and I bolt upright, my gaze searching his hiding places. The corner where he hides with his Piper-Puppet.

The scrap of blanket he puts over his head when we play together. Everything is in its place—everything except for Sam.

They took him while I slept and he isn't back yet. If the Father has come for me . . . why didn't he bring back Sam?

"Get up." The Father's voice spills contempt and disgust. "You have to bury the Boy."

Getting to my feet, I blink and try to process his words. He walks out and comes back carrying Sam. He hands over my brother's small, lifeless frame. His skin is so pale, so cold, and I can see what killed him. One cut on his arm is too much, too deep, and he is too frail. His body gave up fighting to repair itself time after time.

"You should've made him stronger. When the fight ends, so does the fun." The Father yawns, stretches, and walks down the attic stairs. "But you know that. You understand me. You always have."

I barely hear his words because in my head my voice is screaming. Again and again, never halting, never even breathing.

*IT SHOULD HAVE BEEN ME.*


My heart explodes with pain and I reach out for the figure in front of me. Everything I feel and see drowns in wave upon wave of maddening rage. I will kill the Father again if he's back. I'll kill him over and over for what he did.

"Charlotte?" The small whimpering voice freezes me, and I blink my eyes against the bright light streaming in through the window. "Please don't."

*Stop, Piper! No more hurting.*

Sam's voice chills me and my heart skips a beat. He's dead. The Father said . . . but wait . . .

Sanda swims through my vision for a moment before settling into place before me. She clutches the sides of her pajamas with her hands and her whole body is trembling. My hands are raised toward her, the ends of my fingers curved into claws. I can see it in her eyes, the fear I've seen in Sam's so many times. Someone is coming after her, someone is going to hurt her—and this time it's me.

I drop my arms to my sides as horror rolls through my body like a tsunami, leaving me bruised and devastated.

"I'm so sorry, Sanda." Every part of me aches to hug her. I need to show her, and myself, that I'm not one of them. Not one of the people that cause pain.

But I do cause pain. I just hope it's only to the people that deserve it and that hurting them doesn't turn me into them. I clench my hands by my thighs. I can't touch her, not now, not yet. She needs time.

"I was having a nightmare."

Her shaking subsides some, but her lower lip trembles when she speaks again. It pains me to know I've caused it. "Why did you sleep out here?"

"Good question," I say, stretching. My body aches all over as I ease myself up onto the couch. I steal one last peek out the window. Even in the bright sunlight I need to see that he isn't back before I can let myself relax. "I was looking out the window, making sure we were safe, and I fell asleep."

Sanda sits on the couch, too, but on the opposite end.

"I'm very sorry," I say again, and wait for her dark eyes to meet mine.

She doesn't turn away like I expect. "Why did Cam call you Piper?"

I should've seen this question coming, but somehow it still surprises me. I want to protect Sanda from my past, but right now she needs to remember we're both the same. The truth will help her see that.

"Because Piper is my old name." I scoot closer to her on the couch. She doesn't back away. "Like you have Sanda and your new name, Sandra. I have Piper and Charlotte."

She nods like this is what she was expecting to hear. Her lip has stopped trembling and I feel a bit better. After a moment of silence, she crawls across the couch and sits beside me. Her head rests against my chest and her breathing slows. "I'm glad you escaped. I'm glad you're Charlotte now."

"Me, too." I rest my chin against her head and wrap an arm around her, trying hard to ignore the chill in my stomach that makes me wonder if I escaped at all.

I stand surrounded by charred wooden beams. They rise from the ash at my feet like a fossilized dragon claw straight out of fiction, waiting for the perfect moment to crush me. Every time the wind blows I can't keep from coughing. Somehow what happened in Brothers's apartment is poisoning my new world. It's a dead wasteland in the beating heart of the city. It is venom snaking through the veins of my new life and killing it cell by cell.

The rooms are barely recognizable and I only have a few minutes. I'm dreading what comes next. Meeting with Cam is the last thing I want to do right now, especially because it's time to make good on my promise. I finally have to answer his questions.

Sam didn't want to come back here. He seems to think if we pretend the man we saw outside last night was a dream, then it will all go away.

I've tried that before. It never works. Nightmares never just stay in my head.

I shove aside a beam with the toe of my shoe, and a shudder runs through me at what is exposed beneath it. Blinking at the sunlight glinting off the blade of a knife, I wrap my arms tighter around myself. I'm standing where his closet used to be, the torture closet. Using the side of my foot, I push a pile of ash over the blade, burying it along with everything else from this apartment that should remain hidden.

No one put this fire out before it was too late. No fireman rushed in to save him as others worked to dash out the flames. If there was any justice in this world, I'd be certain he died an excruciating death.

But there's never been any justice for me. Only what I've created for myself.

I pick my steps carefully in the shifting debris as I make my way back to the street. My chest loosens. It's easier to breathe now that I'm standing on the other side of the road. Could Brothers have somehow survived this? I walk down the street backward until the cancerous building is out of sight. Something won't let me turn my back on where the monster lived.

# 15

Cam asked me to meet him at Angelo's, and I shift uncomfortably in the lobby as I wait. I avoid coming in on my days off because the restaurant is always busy and I feel guilty I'm not helping. That and I spend most of my time with Sanda. I'm not sure I want everyone there to know about Sanda yet. The fewer people that know that I suddenly have a young girl living with me, the safer she'll be.

Cam walks out of the storage room and hangs the inventory count sheet up on its usual hook outside the door. I groan, but as much as I try to resist, he brings out a smile in me. Grinning back, he loosens the collar on his black shirt as he walks over. Nothing ever looks bad on him. He could wear overalls and somehow still be hot.

"Hi." His dimples seem to pop out at me like miniature black holes when he grins, irresistibly drawing me in.

"Are we staying here?" I glance toward the host station, where Lily is watching us and whispering something to Gino. A movement in the corner catches my eye and I see Oscar wave at me with a smirk.

"No." Cam frowns and opens the door for me to exit.

As we walk into the sunlight I feel lighter already—until I remember why we're here. I've canceled the last two times he tried to get me to live up to my end of the deal. He's losing patience. Still, I can't help but try to stall a little longer.

"Will she ever stop hating me so much?"

"Lily?"

"Yeah."

Cam's eyes turn me into thin tissue paper—weak, transparent, and, from what I can tell, totally useless. Part of me likes everything about being around him, the other part screams in frustration that I can't put up walls near him the way I wish I could.

"She doesn't hate you, but I think she's worried about me."

I nod and my jaw tightens. Lily is more perceptive than I thought. She sees through the mask I'm trying so hard to keep on. "She thinks I'm dangerous."

Cam's laugh surprises me. "Yeah, but not in the way you're thinking."

"How do you know what I'm thinking?" I stop and face him, my walls up as high as I can get them.

"Easy." Cam reaches toward my shoulder but then sticks his hand back in his pocket instead. He catches my eye and continues. "I just mean that she knows how I feel about you. And she's untrusting and overprotective."

I blink and breathe. And breathe again. My mind refuses to process what he's saying. My walls crumble and I'm left standing, exposed. I can't think of a single thing to say.

After watching me for what seems like an eternity, he turns and offers his elbow to me. "Is this better? More comfortable for you?"

Words still elude me, but I link my arm through his and am surprised to find it is more comfortable with my skin against his shirt than touching his skin directly.

"Thank you," I murmur.

He doesn't seem to mind that I don't say anything else. Of the books Nana brought me, only a couple had romance. I know I'm supposed to say something back when a guy talks about his feelings for me, but I don't have any idea what. The warmth spreading through my chest and down my arms really isn't helping me figure it out either. My cheeks are hot, and now that I've turned away, I can't meet Cam's eyes.

*Eww.*

Perfect. With Sam's comments in my head, I'll never find the right words.

"Are you hungry?" Cam's voice is so warm I wish I could wrap myself up in it.

"Hungry?" I repeat, still unable to return his gaze.

"Ruth's Deli is around the corner. It's a great sandwich place where they put comic strips on the tables. It's fun."

This time he stops and slowly lifts my chin up with one finger until I meet his eyes. They are so different, so exposed. I can see him the way he sees me, even when I don't want him to. I can see that he means what he said about his feelings for me.

And I realize for the first time that something inside me wants him to mean it, wishes I deserved it.

"I . . . I don't want . . ." Now that I know what I want to say, my voice isn't cooperating.

"Oh, we can go someplace else." Cam starts to turn until I squeeze his elbow and drag him over next to the building. This is a much busier street than the last one. I don't want to say this with dozens of people pushing to get past me.

"What is it?" Cam bends down, his expression intense. "Is something wrong?"

"No." I swallow hard and release his arm, rubbing my hands together. The words finally come, but it's even harder than I expected to be this vulnerable—to trust him with the feelings I barely understand myself. "I don't want Lily to be right."

His eyes hold mine, but he doesn't respond. I wonder for a moment if he heard me, then he inches closer until his arms, his chest, his hands and every other piece of him are only a breath away. I don't step back. His smell envelops me in a way his arms can't yet. He smells like warmth. Like life and happiness. I can't pull away.

"She isn't right." His breath is hot against my hair. Being so close to him drives away my ghosts. It's like everything can be what I've always wanted. The nightmares can finally end if I will simply lean forward and let him hold me.

My reason wiggles its way to the surface and argues with my desire to be happy. Even Cam can't work miracles. And as I've proven again and again, I *am* dangerous.

I push aside the doubts and close my eyes, drawing in another breath of him. Frozen an inch away from my possible refuge, I cling to the hope that he could be right.

# 16

Ruth's Deli is every bit as great as Cam said. There are so many sandwich toppings it's overwhelming. Some of them even sound made up. When Cam asks if I want banana peppers, I smile, expecting it to be some kind of joke. I'd heard of bananas and peppers, but a banana pepper? Who thought those should be put together? Once I realize he is serious, I shake my head and stick with the ones I know.

"Just tomatoes and lettuce, please," I say, glancing down and trying not to appear as awkward as I feel. Cam winks at me when he catches my eye.

"Good choice."

My sandwich is incredible, but the tables are my favorite part. I'd spent an hour in a comic book store while following Brothers, but never actually looked at comics. These are newspaper comics and they seem more focused on humor, so I devour them. Cam smiles at me as I read every one under the glass surface of our table. Some of them I don't fully understand, but it's still amazing how they fit so much information and humor into the tiny boxes.

Every time a new table empties, I move over with my drink and read the comics there. After an hour, Cam holds up a hand as I stand to move again.

"Not yet." He waits as I retake my seat, his expression serious for the first time since we walked in the door. "It's time to answer my questions."

I nod and rub my knuckles against my jeans, moving over the lump of the bolt in my pocket for reassurance. I'd hoped he would drop it, but I understand why he won't. If I were him, I wouldn't.

I study the spot in the middle of the table where our hands would meet if I were a different girl. The way his eyes meet mine sends tingles through my entire body. I love it and at the same time I'm scared to death by how it makes me feel. This is risky, maybe even stupid.

Probably stupid.

His eyes study me. Waiting for the permission he's been wanting since we met. If I want my life to change, I have to adjust my actions. I have to learn to trust people who show me they can be trusted, starting now.

"Go ahead. Ask your first question."

Cam's voice is low when he speaks. It's soothing even as his question terrifies me. "What are you running from?"

"I think I've already answered th—"

He shakes his head. "No, you didn't."

"Okay, fine." I breathe deep, resisting the urge to stand and run out the door. He moves forward. Almost like he knows what I'm thinking. "Bad things have happened to me my whole life. I'm trying to start fresh."

Cam's eyes show the pain I've felt a hundred times, and it's almost worse to see it there than in the mirror. "Second question: what kind of bad things?"

I rub at an old scar on one of my folded arms. The long slender white line is barely visible anymore, but the memory of the pain is as fresh as the day I got it.

"The Parents were terrible people. They liked to hurt us. They kept us locked in the attic and didn't tell anyone we existed."

The words gush out and I'm surprised I'm capable of speaking them. They make me ache like my old wounds have been reopened. Fresh agony covers me, but at the same time it's a bittersweet release. The scars aren't mine to carry alone anymore. I look up to see the horror in Cam's eyes and I can't face it. My eyes drop to the table where the muscle in his forearm relaxes and tightens, again and again.

Maybe I shouldn't have told him. This isn't his burden to carry. He hesitates, then reaches up and wipes a tear from my cheek that I didn't even know was there. I stare at his hand in shock. I didn't think I was capable of crying anymore. I'd learned not to—been taught not to.

"I'm so sorry." His voice drips with my pain. "You said 'us.'" Cam closes his eyes when he speaks, like he doesn't really want to know.

"My little brother and me." Anger bubbles within me, not at Cam, but at the idea of talking about Sam with anyone. He is *my* memory, the only good thing from my past life. It pierces my heart to think of exposing his life to the thoughts of others, even Cam's.

I know he can see my resistance when he nods and doesn't press me any further about it.

"Fourth question." Cam searches my face for the okay to move forward. When I incline my head he continues, "Where did Sanda come from?"

I flinch and shake my head. "I'm not sure that's my story to tell."

"She's nine and has scars, Charlotte." His eyes stray for an instant to the one on my arm, but it's so fast I almost wonder if I imagined it. "I doubt it would be a good idea to ask her about it."

I sigh. He's right. Why is he always right? "She was an orphan in another country. From what I can tell, she was kidnapped, brought here, and sold to bad people. I took her out of a situation that had too much in common with my life."

"Your *old* life."

"Huh?" I blink.

"That isn't your life anymore. No one will hurt you now." Cam seems like he wants to destroy something, but I'm not afraid. I know that emotion. I've acted on that emotion.

"Oh, right." I try to smile, but it feels false. "But I saw him again."

"Who?"

"The man from Angelo's. I think he was in the park outside my apartment last night."

His eyes flash, and they're more intense than I've ever seen them. "Did he talk to you?"

"No."

"Did you get a better look at him? Do you know who he is?"

I shake my head. "No, but he was wearing the same hat, same coat."

"What was he doing?"

"Smoking."

"How long was he there?"

"He left a few minutes after I saw him."

Cam shakes his head. "So, it was a guy wearing a hat and smoking a cigarette in the park?"

Exactly. I tap my fingertips against the tabletop. If it weren't for my stupid instincts, I'd agree with him. "I know it sounds crazy."

"No." But his face relaxes and I know he's not as worried. "After everything, it would be crazy if you weren't a little on edge."

I shrug and study the comic on the table in front of me, saying, "I hope that's all it is."

Cam shifts forward until I raise my gaze to his. "If you see him again, promise me you'll call, anytime."

The sincerity in his face sends warmth all the way to my toes. "I promise."

"Good." He keeps his eyes on mine. "Question five: how do you handle this so easily on your own after being locked in an attic your whole life?"

I sit back a bit, surprised. I didn't really think I was handling it well. "If I do, I think it's because of Nana."

He looks confused but waits for me to continue.

"My grandma came to live with us for a couple of years before I escaped."

"Wait. Your grandma knew about what was going on and didn't get you out of there?" If possible, he's even angrier now. "That's so wrong."

"No, no. You don't understand." I wait until he calms down a little before I continue. The words come fast because I'd repeated them to Sam a hundred times. "She only came to live with us because she was dying of cancer and the Parents wanted her money. She didn't know about us before. Once she got there, she was so angry, but she was also old and frail. When she called the police, the Parents convinced them she was hallucinating. Then they beat her. By the time she woke up, they'd disconnected the home phone. The nearest neighbors were miles away and it was difficult for her to even get up the stairs to the attic, let alone go for help. She couldn't fight for us anymore, so she got me ready to fight instead."

He releases a long breath. "How?"

"She would sneak up to the attic at night and bring me books. She reminded me about the outside world from before the Father put me up there, and that other people aren't like the Parents. She told us stories. It's hard to explain, but she really did help, until they found out what she was doing."

Cam closes his eyes and breathes. "What did they do to her?"

"Locked her in her room. They told us they took away her medication, food, and water." I study the table to hide the pain that overwhelms me when I think about her. Tracing the edge of one of the comics with my fingertip, I finish. "She died a week later."

"She sounds strong." He looks sad. "Like you."

I raise my eyes and blink, unsure how to respond to that.

He moves on. "Question six: what is your favorite color?"

A laugh bursts from me, so loud I cover my mouth with my hand.

Cam grins and tilts his head to one side. "Come on. I've been dying to find out."

I smile wider than I can ever remember smiling. It feels so normal to sit here with him, so nice. "I have no idea."

"None?"

"I've honestly never thought about it." I twist my lips to one side and think. "Today I'd say silver, maybe?"

"Interesting choice. Why?"

I whisper like I'm telling him a huge secret. "Does this count as one of your questions?"

His eyes twinkle behind his mock-serious expression as he considers. "Tough call, I'll be down to three."

"I know." I widen my eyes and nod. "This is a big decision. Take your time."

The way he beams when he leans back and searches my eyes melts every piece inside until I become a pile of Piper-goo. It's pathetic. I'd make fun of me if it wasn't . . . well, me.

"Okay, tell me."

"It reminds me of the moonlight." Now that I think about why, it isn't quite as funny. "I'm not used to being outside. Everything glimmers. Everything is silver in the moonlight."

Cam's smile fades but doesn't go away. I like that.

Scooting a bit closer, I lower my voice. "Can I ask you a question?"

"Depends," he says, his smile back full force. "Is it going to count as one of mine, too?"

"No." I'm surprised by the fear that comes to the surface when

I think about asking him what I've been wondering. "And if you don't want to answer, I'll understand."

Cam shakes his head. "After the questions you've answered for me, I'll answer anything you want."

I gather my courage and say it fast so it won't get caught in my throat. "You said your dad taught you what you know, how to forge documents and the computer stuff. What happened to him?"

He turns away for a few seconds before answering. "He works for the mob—you know, mafia? Organized crime stuff?" When I nod, he starts again. "Anyway, he's been with them forever. Oscar wants me to work for them, too, but I won't. And I'll keep telling them no. I've seen how they changed my dad and I won't let that happen to me."

Cam stops and stares down at the table. I know he's not done, so I wait for him to go on. "They keep giving Dad more and more responsibility. He's always been their guy when it came to providing documents and paperwork, but then they wanted more and pushed harder. Before I was born, before Mom died, he was in the navy." Cam slides back and shoves his hands in the pockets of his coat. "A couple of years ago, they decided they wanted to use him for that experience, too."

"His navy experience?" I raise an eyebrow and wait for him to clarify.

"Yeah. When I found out they had him filling in as an enforcer, I couldn't handle it. So I left and moved in with my grandparents." He seems furious and deeply sad. "I've always known what we're doing is breaking the law, but still, I believed he was a good person. A better person than one who could . . . I don't think I'll ever understand how he could kill someone. Stealing a life away takes a darkness, an evil inside. You know? It doesn't matter who they are."

His words echo and the world around me stops spinning. *Darkness. Evil.* Yes, I know about that intimately. My heart plummets and I can't stand the agony. My ears burn and I'm swallowed up in something far too familiar—an intense need to escape.

Even with his questions answered, Cam still has no idea who I am.

Jerking back from the table, I stand and I'm at the door before I hear his voice.

"Wait!"

Backing out into the street, I see him standing beside our table. The pain on his face mimics my own, and I wish I'd been smarter. I could've saved him from this. I could've saved both of us. Lily is right to think I'm bad for Cam. She's always been right about me.

"I'm so sorry." I close the door, running all the way home until I'm panting and pretending the pain in my chest is from exertion and not everything I just lost.

As I walk up the stairs, I fight to forget everything about Cam: the way he smells, the warmth of his touch, how he makes every worry fade with one look.

I've barely caught my breath when the black box in front of my door steals it away again. Scribbled on a note on the box in strange, rigid handwriting is one word:

PIPER

# 17

My hands refuse to pick the box up. My mind is whizzing through every nightmare in my life and landing on the only question that matters.

Who would know to call me Piper?

My hands shake so hard it takes me forever to open my locks. I count to ten. Breathe in, breathe out, breathe in, breathe out. My stomach, hands, and feet are blocks of ice. I force myself to move slowly. If I pretend to be calm then maybe I will be. Following my newest ritual, I walk to the window, check the park to be certain no one is watching, and close the curtains tight.

I place the box on top of my table and stare at it. No matter how calm I pretend to be, I'm still terrified to open it.

I pick it up but my fingers are numb, and when the lid pops off, the entire box slips free and lands with a thud on the cream-colored rug at my feet. It's like blood, blood everywhere, pools of red spread across the carpet before me. I stumble back and fall to my knees. Then I see it. A fully blossomed red rose sticking out of the box on the floor. Rose petals.

I gasp for breath and my head pounds from lack of oxygen. The abrupt release of tension makes me laugh as I scoop the petals into a pile and put them in the box with the now half-naked flower. My heart hurts as I think it must've been Cam, but he was with me tonight.

Who else could it have been? Maybe he had it delivered, but it's strange that he would use the name Piper. He seems too smart for that, too careful. I glance around and spot the lid on the floor beneath the table. When I bend down to retrieve it, my blood turns cold. There are four words, carved in deep gashes on the black silk inside the lid.

I KNOW YOUR SECRET

The world around me slams to a stop. Nothing about this makes sense, but there is only one thing I can think of right now and Sam and I speak her name in unison.

*Sanda.*

Tossing the box in the trash, I fumble to undo my locks and rush down the stairs. Struggling to calm my ragged breathing, I pound on Janice's door. The seconds drag on with no response—1—2—3—4—. I shove my ear against the wood and hold my breath, listening for a movement, a voice, a footstep. They are supposed to be here. I am supposed to protect her.

"Sanda!" My voice is a hoarse, desperate plea. "Janice? Are you in there?"

There is nothing.

*Find her now, Piper.*

I pace the entryway, willing my spiraling mind to settle with the rhythmic motion of my feet. They aren't here. Janice didn't mention taking them anywhere. Where could they be? Either they went out or . . .

Or whoever left my box has taken her.

The thought infects my brain like a virus, spreading fear along every nerve. It slinks down my spine and coats my feet in frost as I accept the possibility that it could be true.

The door in the entrance hall opens behind me and I rush over, hoping to see Sanda. Cam's furious eyes greet me, but when he sees my face the anger melts away.

"Did you send me a box?" I grab his arm and jerk him in through the doorway.

"What?" He shakes his head and turns around, trying to figure out what I'm talking about.

I squeeze his forearm under my fingers, but the muscles don't give much. "A box that held a red rose and said my name, my *real* name. Did you send it?"

"No, I didn't." Cam's jaw clenches, but I can't read the emotion in his expression.

"Do you have Janice's phone number?" I try to relax my grip on his arm, but my fingers don't cooperate. "The cell?"

He pulls out his phone, pushes a few buttons, and places it in my palm. Concern replaces the fire in his eyes as he watches me push the phone hard against my ear.

It takes me a moment to realize I can hear Janice's ringtone coming from nearby. Tossing the phone to Cam, I push my ear against Janice's door, but it isn't coming from there. I spin around, listening, then the door in the entrance hall opens behind Cam and Janice walks through it, digging around in her purse for the ringing phone.

"Oh, hello." She finally retrieves her phone and blinks twice at the screen before raising her eyes to Cam in surprise. "Are you calling me?"

"Yes," Cam says, and turns a hard gaze on me. "But I'm not entirely sure why."

Sanda and Rachel squeeze through the doorway behind Janice. A grin spreads wide on Sanda's face when she sees me. The breath I've been fighting for finally enters my lungs and I pull her into a tight hug.

"Oh, no," Janice says as she wrings her hands together. "I'm sorry, Charlotte. I didn't think you'd be home so soon. I took the girls to the park."

"I—it's okay. She's okay. She's okay." I brush the back of Sanda's hair with my fingers and try to get my pulse to slow to a normal rate. Janice's eyes watch me with sympathy.

"She's just worried." Cam's voice sounds drained and I'm afraid to see his face so I squeeze Sanda harder. "I'm sure you understand."

When I pull back, Sanda's eyes are full of fear and I shake my head with a small smile.

"It's fine, but I need to get your number so I can call you if this ever happens again." I dig my phone out of my pocket and put in the number Janice gives me. She says she's sorry three more times and finally goes inside.

Cam watches me, waiting, but I'm not sure for what.

"Thank you for your help." I take Sanda's hand and move toward the stairs.

"That's it?" His voice drips with disbelief. I stop, but don't turn around. "Sanda, go see if your apartment door is locked."

Her eyes shift from me to him, but she waits for me to give her the okay.

"It's open." I close my eyes tight for a moment and then release her hand. "Go ahead. I'll be up in a minute."

She nods with wide eyes and walks up the stairs to the door. I wait until it closes before I turn back to Cam. His face is a storm of emotion and I can't face the frustration I see there. My gaze drops to the floor and I wait.

He paces back and forth for at least a minute before he lets out a low growl, walks to me, and touches my face with the palm of his hand. My heart leaps in my chest and I'm not sure whether it's from panic or relief. I close my eyes but don't move.

His breath is warm on my face. The strain in his voice pains me. "Why do you always have to run?"

"Why do you still want to be around me when you know it's a bad idea?"

Pulling back, he drops his hand and watches me close. "Is it?"

"Yes."

"Why?"

I groan and move a step away, unable to think straight while so distracted by the warmth of him. Nothing is better off than it was when I left the deli. Nothing has been resolved. He'll still hate me when he finds out what I've done. "It won't work."

"I don't believe that."

"You don't have to, but I do." I turn and take the first two steps before he speaks again.

"We aren't done. You still owe me three answers."

"Fine, but not tonight." I turn back to face him and I can't hold it all in anymore. My voice cracks with emotion. "Please, Cam. It's too much. No more tonight."

I see his will to argue crumple at my words. "Get some rest." He sighs and I watch his slumped shoulders until he's out the door and gone.


Once I'm sure it's late enough, it only takes me twenty minutes to pack everything we own.

"I don't understand." Sanda follows me around, rubbing her eyes as I pick up our lives and toss them in the suitcase. The first-aid kit, the money, the electric blanket, our clothes—everything I think we might need. I shake my head, giving no further explanation as I double-check that my bolt is in my pocket. She doesn't need to understand. She only needs to be safe.

I lock all the locks and I don't realize how hard I'm breathing until the shine on one of the bolts fogs up. Tugging Sanda's hand, I rush down the stairs and out onto the street. I don't know where we're going. I'm not even sure it matters, but we have to get away. Before someone new traps us, hurts us.

The city looms over us, menacing and giving us chase. Every dark corner thwarts our escape. Buildings seem to tilt in farther with each step, threatening to collapse and bury us here—to become a city-size tomb, our forever prison.

I turn left around a corner and notice a raspy hum mingling with the clicks of my suitcase wheels. Only when I stop to see what it is do I realize the humming is me, and the rasps are the sound of Sanda's slippers on the sidewalk. Tears fall down her cheeks and shaking sobs roll through her body, but she doesn't speak. My heart shatters with each drop.

Others have been responsible for hurting her in the past, but this pain is all mine to bear and I don't know how to stop it without sacrificing her safety.

Is this the life I'm building for her? One where she walks down a dark street in the middle of the night with only slippers on? Crying right next to me and I don't notice? I'm too busy escaping to tell her to put on real shoes or not to be afraid. I'd let her believe we could have a future, that she could have friends and go to school. And then I'd let one black box rip it all away.

*You're stronger than this, Piper. Be stronger for her.*

Kneeling down, I wrap my arms around her. "I'm sorry. I'm so sorry."

Sanda curls up against me and my shirt is immediately wet with her tears. "W-we have to go?"

She deserves everything I promised her, a real life and a real home. We both do, and I'm so tired of running. Running toward safety that seems to elude me no matter how far I go. Is it even attainable or will I die still sprinting toward something that doesn't exist? Sitting on the sidewalk beside the suitcase, I pull Sanda onto my lap and let my racing heart slow. For the first time since I escaped, I let myself settle into place. Maybe I've never felt at home, but Philly is as close as I've gotten. If I want to build a life here with Sanda, I'd better start defending it.

I'll do what I should've done before Sam died. This time I will fight before it's too late, before I lose Sanda, too. I'll stay and do everything I can to protect her. I won't let anyone else hurt her. I won't let them destroy our new life, and I refuse to break the promise I made her.

I shake my head and rub my hand across her back. "No. We're staying."


"Welcome to Angelo's. Table for four?" The words flow out with ease and I don't seem to scare people as much as I used to. After seating them and giving them menus, I walk back to the host station. It's a good thing this job has gotten easier because I'm only going through the motions. My mind refuses to be present. I can only think about the box with the message, the man in the park with his cigarette, Sanda and my decision to stay.

"Hello, beautiful." The smell of smoke and alcohol assaults my senses and I take an involuntary step back. A guy a little older than me is standing in the opening to the host station. My instincts kick in when I realize he's blocking my escape and leaning toward me like he can't quite get his balance.

"I'm sorry. I didn't see you there." I try to reach around him to grab a menu, but he falls against my arm and I jerk it back. "A table for one or are you meeting someone?"

"Even if I was meeting someone, I'd drop them for you, darlin'."

His words slur together and his eyes don't quite focus on my face. I don't have the time or patience for this loser, but the last thing I need is to give Lily another reason to hate me.

"I'm working." I hold my breath and reach around him for the menu again, and this time he drops his other arm around my neck. The weight of it pulls my face toward his chest. My skin crawls and every move Cam has taught me flies into my head at once. It takes me a moment to figure out which part of him I want to injure first.

"Well, isn't this cozy?" My head jerks up at the acidity in Lily's voice and I shove my elbow against the guy's rib cage. He pulls back with a painful gasp. Gino appears from out of nowhere, grabs his elbow, and escorts him out the door into the street.

"Lily? Did you need something?" I breathe as the air clears and Gino heads back toward the kitchen. I want to thank him, but he doesn't even look my way.

"Cam is so worried about you that he called and asked me to check if you are all right." Her eyes dart from me to the door the guy just left through. "I'll be sure to let him know you're just too busy with *other things* to answer your phone."

"Lily—" I stop, unwilling to defend myself to her against something so absurd. She has to know I was trying to get the guy off me; she just thinks I'm bad for Cam and will look for any evidence she can find to prove she's right. I turn back to the menus and start organizing them, willing her to go away.

"I knew this would happen," she mutters under her breath, and laughs. The sound is biting as she walks around the host station and turns to face me. "My first impression was wrong, by the way.

Suzanna would've fit you perfectly." She saunters to the office without a glance back, her spine straight and head high—triumphant.

I grab my phone out of the cubby below the podium. Five missed calls from Cam since this morning. An elderly couple walks in. I drop my phone back into the cubby and turn to face them, plastering my best non-scary smile on.

"Table for two?"

# 18

Cam's and Lily's voices carry through the office door so well I can hear them from halfway down the hall. Of course, the fact that they're both yelling probably helps. I'd spent the last hour of my shift working up the nerve to quit and now I freeze up, unsure of whether I want to be waiting out here after their argument. Even though my instincts are leaning toward the flight side of things, I stand my ground. While I appreciate Cam getting this job for me, working with someone who hates me just isn't worth it, and after tonight's episode I don't expect it to get any better. I need to quit; I'll wait here until I get the chance.

And then I'll never come back.

"It doesn't matter what she did." Cam's voice is lower now than when I first stepped into the hall. He's trying to calm down. I'm not sure when he got here. He must've come in through the back entrance sometime during my shift. "The point is it's none of your business."

"You'll see." Lily's tone is stuck halfway between a plea and an order. "Someday soon, you'll see I'm right about her."

"Don't wish that on me, Lily." The door opens and I backpedal quickly around the corner just before I hear her speak again, this time from the hallway I'd just left.

"I tried to warn you," Lily says, as she stomps down the hall to the empty dining room.

"Lily," I say before she can make it out the front doors.

She pivots toward me, a sneer already stamped across her face.

"I quit." My voice is quiet but firm.

Lily rolls her eyes, walks out the door, and turns to lock it behind her. I can see her lips moving through the glass window and can probably guess what she's saying as she spins and stalks off into the darkness.

The front of the restaurant is quiet. We've already cleaned our sections and done our prep work for the night. I can hear the kitchen staff finishing up and the occasional *clang* of a pot or a pan being put away. Other than that, it's silent.

"What will you do with the girl?" Gino speaks from inside the closest booth and I spin to face him. I didn't realize he was here.

"What?"

"If you quit, will you give the girl away?" He stands up and walks closer until I'm backed against the wall.

My hands are damp and cold as I realize who he's talking about. My voice is quiet when I answer. "How do you know about her?"

"I told you. I pay attention." His eyes stare me down, and I can't read any emotion behind them. He's about to say more when Cam walks down the hall. Gino clamps his mouth shut and walks across the dining room to the kitchen.

I'm confused and shaken, but Cam doesn't even look at me or Gino. His eyes are still on the door, his mind still with Lily.

"I quit." I figure I might as well tell him, too.

"I can't blame you. I don't understand what's going on with her." He doesn't move, but his voice sounds sad and bewildered. "It's more than her normal protectiveness—something else. It's only been six months since Anna died. Guess she's not exactly coping well."

"She's not the only one around here acting weird." I mean Gino, but I realize he might think I'm referring to him.

He turns to me, exasperated. "Have you heard of the pot and the kettle?"

I have no clue what he's talking about, so I wait. When I don't respond, Cam pulls a chair out at the nearest table and waits for me to take it. Angling the chair so I can see the door to the kitchen, I sit, and Cam takes the one across from me. I don't think there has ever been this much tension between us. I ache with it.

"I'm ready for my last three answers," he says, and then waits expectantly for me to tell him all my darkest secrets.

"What if I'm not?" I mutter.

"You are. And I need to know why you ran." He reaches across, takes my hand in his, and squeezes gently. It's so warm, so much bigger than mine. It soothes the tension with waves of calm. Besides Sam and Sanda, I've only ever held Nana's hand. They were all small and cold. I study Cam's and run my thumb across the back of it, amazed at the difference. With my brother, I was protecting him, but with Cam, it's more like he's protecting me.

*Don't be afraid. Just say it.*

164

Drawing in a deep breath, I count to ten in my head as I let it out. As much as I have survived in my life, surely I can make it through this. Maybe I'm wrong . . . maybe he'll understand. Nana always told me I was the strong one. It's time to find that strength inside me and prove it. Curling my free hand into a tight, controllable fist, I brush my knuckles against the lump of the bolt in my pocket. I focus every piece of my energy on not letting my mind think about the things my mouth is about to say. Whatever Cam's reaction, it will be better to know it now. I need to face it before I become even more attached, before the pain from his rejection will be unbearable.

I watch, stalling, as the last few noises come from the kitchen. Then the staff turn out the lights as they leave through the back door. The lights in the dining room and the office are the only ones left on and it makes the room feel smaller and more intimate. Cam doesn't rush me or even speak. He just waits until I'm ready.

"Okay. No more counting questions," I say. "I'll just tell you what matters."

He hesitates. "As long as that includes why you ran away yesterday and why you think this won't work."

"It does."

He nods and waits. I know he'll give me as much time as I need so long as I don't run. But this is like being hurt by the Parents. All I can do is hope it's over fast and deal with the damage later.

"You remember, I told you about the Parents, the attic, and my brother?" My voice shakes so much I'm not sure how he can possibly understand it, but he nods and I see a flare of anger in his eyes.

This time when I speak, it comes out stronger, easier. "I didn't tell you everything."

I lower my gaze to the table and wrap my fingers around his in an effort to siphon some strength from them before plowing forward. "I didn't simply run away. I escaped. They'd never have let me go, not until I was dead. I'd seen that already with my brother. So, I killed them . . . before they could kill me."

The room around us is as silent as a grave. Minutes pass before he finally responds.

"You killed your parents?"

"If you can call them that, yes." Pure, stony hatred trickles from my voice and I can't miss the way Cam jerks back a little when I speak.

Get it all out now and see what happens. He has to know everything today. It's the only way. "That's not all. I had to do the same to save Sanda."

"Had to?" His voice is barely a whisper, like it doesn't have enough air to strive for anything louder.

"He tried to hurt me and I didn't let him."

Cam's hand has gone limp in mine. No longer holding, comforting—an unwilling participant in my grasp. I let go and his hand drops to the table. He doesn't move.

"I don't know what you want me to say." It doesn't even sound like Cam. His voice is low and foreign. "You're telling me you killed people. How am I supposed to respond to that?"

"You don't have to say anything. I promised to tell you everything and I have." I dredge up the courage to look in his eyes and wish I hadn't. Twin walls hide every emotion from me, everything but the pain. "Now you know why I ran when you told me about your father. I knew you'd feel the same about me."

Confusion rises to the surface for only a moment, before he shoves it back behind his carefully constructed barricade. "I don't know. I'm going to need some time."

"Don't worry. This is why I told you it wouldn't work." I hear the tremble in my voice and hate myself for showing him that weakness. I'd set aside my greatest rule for him: people can't be trusted. I shouldn't have let him get so close. Now my heart is drowning in the painful aftermath of my mistake. "If you decide to go to the police, I can't blame you, but I won't wait around for them to show up."

"I won't." His shoulders slump forward and his eyes drop back to his empty hand still resting on the wooden tabletop.

I believe him. With his hobbies, he doesn't need the police poking around in his business either. Still, it's hard to focus on anything when I'm thoroughly shattered inside.

Pulling my shoulders back, I shove my composure into place before I'm even on my feet. My voice is subzero. I'm surprised it doesn't lower the temperature of the air around me. "You won't hear from me again, but I thought, after everything, you at least deserved an explanation."

He gets to his feet but doesn't say a word as I walk to the door and let myself out into the night.

I stop on the way home and buy a new prepaid cell phone, only pausing to add in Janice's number. It's the only one from my old phone I plan to use or hear from in the future. Then I drop my old one in the garbage and keep walking.

*You are good, Piper. Don't believe someone who says you're not.*

Sam's words are more than I can take. Before I get home, before Sanda is there to see it, I stop on a quiet path between two brownstones and lean against an old brick wall for support. My fingers find the mortar cracks between the bricks. I trace them with my fingertips, using them to keep me upright. The wall still radiates warmth from the sun even though it's long past sunset. I try to soak it in, to absorb the life and strength of this city through my skin. It breathed life into me when I got here. I need it to save me again. Minutes stretch as I stand in the shadows of skyscrapers, trying to wrap my head around how small I really am . . . even when the rip through my heart seems impossibly large.

# 19

Sanda walks silently beside me. The grocery bag she carries is as big as she is, but I resist the urge to take it. Determination fills her eyes, and I know she'll be happy when she makes it home without help. A pang of guilt fills me as we walk past the street with Jessie's Studio and Sanda stares at it longingly. She shouldn't be punished for my mistakes, but I can't go back. Not now.

I'll find someone else to teach us to protect ourselves. Preferably someone more like Jessie and less like . . . I flinch at even thinking his name. It still hurts too much, but the last few days away from him have replaced a bit of the pain with a healthy dose of anger. He'd pushed, pleaded, and begged me to tell him. Even after I said it was something he didn't really want to know. It's as much his fault as mine.

As we round the corner to the apartment, the bag slips from Sanda's fingers and falls with a *thud* at her feet. I'm grateful I'd decided to let her take the bag with bread and cheese instead of anything breakable. She stands frozen, and I crouch to pick it up.

"It's fine. No big deal," I say, holding the bag out in front of her, but she is looking past me toward our building. I turn my head and see Cam sitting on our front steps. He gives a wave and Sanda's gaze rises to meet mine.

"Should we run?" She places one small hand on mine. "We can come home later."

Sanda is too perceptive. I hadn't told her anything except that I quit my job and we weren't taking lessons from Cam anymore. I must not have been hiding my emotions the last couple of days as well as I'd hoped.

"No," I say, as she takes the fallen bag from my fingertips. "He shouldn't be here."

We walk the final half a block to our house and I try to rein in my emotions.

"Hi, Sanda." Cam's smile is wide below the sunglasses hiding his eyes. "I missed you guys in class today."

Sanda looks at him and back to me, then sneaks up the stairs past him and into our building entrance without a word.

Cam sighs and his shoulders hunch forward in defeat. "Can I help with your bags?"

He shoves his glasses up onto his head, and what I see in his eyes surprises me. It's desperation, a driving need. I shake off the way my heart beats faster and step around him. "No, thank you. We've got this."

"Let me—" Cam wraps his fingers around my arm as I pass and I jerk it out of his grasp.

"I said no." Anguish radiates from the skin where his fingers touched, and it twists my soul. It hurts worse than any burn.

"I need five minutes, please." He speaks low and soft, and no matter how angry I am, I can't deny him when he sounds this upset. But I almost do when I realize how badly I want it, too.

I mumble in response, "Let me take these upstairs."

Sanda waits for me in the entryway. She watches me with growing concern as we climb the inside stairs together, go into our apartment, and put the groceries down on the counter. As I turn back toward the door, she finally speaks. "You don't have to. You told me that. You never have to."

I stand in the doorway but don't turn around. "I know."

"B-but I'm happy you are."

Looking over my shoulder, I see her studying her feet in discomfort.

"Why?"

She glances at me and the corner of her mouth curves up. "You smile with him."

I lean my head against the doorframe and try to find an argument against that. Finally, I just shrug and open the door. "I'll be right back."

Taking the stairs two at a time so I won't be tempted to turn around, slam the door, and throw my seven locks into place, I gear myself up to dive straight in and get this over with. He wants to talk? Fine, we'll talk.

He's still on the front steps when I come down and he's not even on his feet before I'm talking.

"What do you want? Why are you here?"

Cam turns to face me and his jaw is set, but his emotions are exposed in his eyes. I look away. I don't want to see what he's feeling, not anymore.

"I want to talk to you."

"So talk. We're talking." My hands are on my hips and I have to focus on relaxing my grip so I don't give myself bruises.

"Yeah, some of us are doing so rather rapidly." Cam shakes his head and steps in front of the tree I'm staring at, but I turn away and he growls under his breath. "Look at me, Piper."

The sound of his lips speaking my real name feels so intimate I flinch. We're alone and this time it isn't an accident. It's more like a secret shared between the two of us.

"No," I say.

"Why not? Are you afraid?" I recognize his taunt, but it gives my anger an outlet and I raise my chin and glare at him.

"No." I see a jumble of emotions in his expression and wonder if mine is the same. Then I really see him. Dark circles under his eyes make him appear empty and sad. His cheeks seem a little thinner.

He glares at me. "Why not? I sure as hell am."

My stomach falls to my feet and I'm surprised it isn't audible. The words to respond come slow, each one slicing on the way out. "If you're afraid of me, you shouldn't have come."

He blinks and shakes his head. "I'm not afraid of you."

"I don't understand." I slump down on the top stair. The anger drains and is replaced with pain. "Why are you here?"

"Because I don't scare as easily as you think I do." He sits beside me, but pivots so he can face me. "And you aren't answering my phone calls again. Or did you ditch the phone?"

I can't listen to him. I refuse to let this go any further. Opening myself up like that again isn't worth the pain I'm still struggling under. Remember the rule: people can't be trusted.

"You don't need to call me anyway." Raising my eyes to his, I try to convey how serious I am. "This is done. We don't need you anymore."

He flinches but doesn't turn away. "You do, but more than that, Sanda does."

This time I can't meet his eyes. "She needs *me*."

"Yes, but she needs me, too." He turns his entire body until he's leaning against the railing and watching me. "What if someone else tries to hurt her?"

"There are other places we can go."

"Where the self-defense instructor will understand what she's been through?" Cam frowns. "You going to explain her scars to anyone else?"

"Never." It comes out so fast and hard that it hurts when my teeth clamp shut after.

"Exactly." He leans forward. "If you won't let me help you, don't stop me from helping her."

My head falls forward, and I hate that he's right. It takes a full minute for me to find the ability to say it out loud. "Fine."

I turn toward him and wait until I have his full attention. "You need to know, nothing has changed. We will both come to you for lessons. Nothing else."

Cam's triumphant expression falters a little. "Charlotte—"

"No. It's a deal breaker. Remember those? The last one you forced on me ruined everything." My words come out more bitter than I intend, but I don't care.

"It did no—"

"Do you agree or not?" I get to my feet and wait. "That's all I need to know."

"Yes." He stands up and dusts off his jeans.

I nod and walk back up the stairs without another word. As the door is about to close behind me I hear him finish.

"For now."


Cam lowers his hands and rises out of a defensive position. I don't know how long he's been staring at me like that.

"What are you doing?" I drop my stance and roll my shoulders back, trying to relieve the boulder-size knot at the base of my neck.

"No. What are *you* doing?"

I shake my head. "I don't understand."

"Either you aren't paying any attention, or I'm not as good a teacher as I thought." He grabs his towel off the wall and turns with a grin. "And I know it isn't the second."

"I'm tired." Taking a drink from my water bottle, I glance over at Sanda. She's kicking and punching the bag in the corner like her life depends on it.

I can only hope it doesn't.

I've spent the last couple of nights trying to figure out who sent me the box. I've decided to stay and fight for a real life, but it's hard to fight back if you don't know your enemy. A shiver runs down my spine from thinking about it. Cam said it wasn't him. It could be Lily, but why? She must've told Gino about Sanda, what else did she tell him? Could they be trying to scare me? I ponder the message in the lid, *I know your secret.* That doesn't make much sense with Lily either. What little she knows about me isn't threatening. But besides Lily and Cam, who would call me Piper?

He taps on the bottom of my bottle until my eyes return to him. The smile is gone. "I've seen you tired. Come on. This is more than that."

I take my time with the drink, trying to come up with the right response. When I notice the water sloshing in my bottle because my hand won't stop shaking, I bring it down.

Denial. Always a solid option. "I don't know what you mean."

He lowers his chin and waits, obviously not buying it. "Yeah, right. You can talk to me. You can't want to do this by yourse—"

"Remember our deal."

He growls through gritted teeth, "You certainly won't let me forget."

I drop back into my stance and wait, refusing to be baited.

Cam follows my lead, but I can see from the muscle twitching in his cheek that he doesn't like this one bit. Too bad. He dives for my arm, but I'm out of reach in plenty of time. I come close to stomp on his foot, but he reaches around me from behind so I throw my weight into my elbow and hurl it toward his stomach as hard as I can. Seeing it coming, he releases me and jumps back before it lands.

Sweat runs down my neck, but I continue with a vengeance. This is the perfect outlet for my frustration and anger. If I don't look in Cam's eyes, I can pretend he's someone else. Someone who wants to hurt me and hurt Sanda. There is no way I'm going to let that happen.

By the time we finish I'm so tired I can barely keep my eyes open. We hurry out, ignoring Cam's request to let him walk us home. Between the last few nights of disjointed, nightmare-filled sleep and the extensive workout Cam just put me through, it takes all my energy to keep placing one foot in front of the other. Sanda walks as silent as a ghost behind me up the stairs. When we reach the landing, she grabs my hand and jerks me down toward her.

"What happened to our door?" When I see the fear in her eyes, my pulse races.

"What?" My eyes whip up. Long scratches have taken off paint along the side of the door around the lock. Some of the wood is chipped and cracked and the locks themselves are banged up.

Only one word escapes my lips.

"No."

# 20

Adrenaline pounds through my veins. I'm more awake than I've felt in days, but I take a deep breath and stay calm for Sanda. "I'm going to take you down to play with Rachel for a few minutes while I check this out, okay?"

Sanda nods, but her eyes are glued to the scratches on the door.

"Come on. Everything will be okay."

Her fingers squeeze mine. "I want to stay with you, Charlotte."

I draw her into a tight hug. "You will. It will only be a few minutes. I promise."

It seems to take forever to explain the situation to Janice.

"Oh, dear," Janice says. Her hand flutters back and forth before she places it on her chest. "You think someone broke in?"

"It looks like someone tried to, but I don't think they got inside. Have you seen anyone today?"

"No. We went school shopping for Rachel and just got home." Janice picks up a phone off the table. "Do you want me to call someone?"

"No," I say a little too quickly, and then cover it with a smile. "Like I said, I don't think they got inside. At best, they dinged up my door a little. Not worth bothering anyone about."

She inclines her head but seems troubled. I'm not sure if she meant Cam or the police, but I'm thinking Cam. From what I know about her history, Janice probably doesn't want to draw any more attention to herself than I do.

I look over and see Rachel showing Sanda some new school outfits, but Sanda's eyes are on me.

"Thanks. I'll be quick." I stare straight at Janice and whisper, "Lock the locks, just in case." And I don't move until she gives me a firm nod.

I walk up the stairs and pull out my keys, gripping them tight in my palm so they make little noise. The air feels colder up here. Unlocking each one quietly is agonizingly slow. For the first time ever, I wish there were fewer locks. Finally, the door swings open wide and I leave it that way.

If I scream this time, I want to be certain someone will hear me.

Moving into the room, I plaster my body against the wall to the left and slide along it toward the nearest shelf. Gripping a metal bookend tight in one hand, I take a deep breath as I wait for my eyes to adjust. As soon as I can see clearly, I move around the living room with swift fluidity, but find no one.

My step is soft and silent as I move, straining to hear any noise in the rooms around me. In my mind, I repeat pieces of Nana's poem.

*It will rise in perfect light . . . It will rise in perfect light; I have loved the stars too fondly to be fearful of the night.*

The street outside seems louder in the quiet. I hear nothing else. I check behind the couch, in the coat closet, and make my way down the hall to my bedroom. Then I see it. The window on the door to the fire escape is broken—still only two locks. I curse under my breath. With everything else going on, I'd forgotten to add more that couldn't be reached through the window.

Someone found it. My weakest point.

*Run.*

I tell Sam to be quiet and this time he listens. No sound comes from the bedroom. Each breath seems so loud in my head, but I know it isn't. Stealth is my ally. When I get to the end of the hall, I place my back against the wall. Drawing in a deep breath, I brace myself for what I might find and raise the bookend like a weapon.

When I peek around the corner and see no one, I release a breath. I check under the bed and in the closet. The Piper-Puppet's eyes reflect moonlight back at me like silver pools in the blackness, but there is no one else. I am alone. Whoever broke the window must be gone. Maybe they never even came in. Nothing obvious is out of place.

I walk back down the hallway and flip on the light switches. As I'm almost to the door, I see it, and the air locks up inside my chest. In the middle of the kitchen table sits another black box. Exactly like the one I'd thrown out a few nights before. I gasp and my knees go weak.

They did come in. Someone has been here, in my apartment, in the only place I've ever felt safe.

Holding my breath, I inch closer to the table until I can see the name PIPER printed on the fresh card on top.

"No," I whisper, backing away until I crumple onto the sofa across the room. "Not here."

The couch cradles me as I close my eyes and press my palms against my ears. I need a moment. Only one—to pretend that the new life I worked so hard for, killed for, isn't unraveling with me in it.

It is silent, both in my apartment and in my head. I hear nothing but the sounds of me. My breathing. My heart beating. Even the city quiets. I am endlessly alone. It reminds me of unbearable pain and unwept tears. It reminds me of the attic, when Sam was gone.

Of things I never want to go back to again.

Someone knows my old name and was determined enough to break into my apartment to leave this. It wasn't Lily. It makes no sense. I quit and I'm avoiding Cam as much as possible. I'm not her problem anymore. This is an enemy, and one that won't give up easily.

My instincts tell me to run. Every hair on my body stands on end, like they're trying to escape even while I sit still. My stomach rolls over and over. What if the danger follows me everywhere I go? What if I'm the reason Sanda is at risk? Like Sam, it's always the people around me who aren't safe. Always because of me.

No. I've already made this decision, and I refuse to be ruled by fear. Not anymore, this time I will not run.

My eyes fly open and I see the dreaded box still unopened on the table. It's sitting, waiting. I stand and walk to it.

With shaking hands, I lift the box and remove the lid. A fresh, fully bloomed rose lies inside, and the deep red petals become pools of blood in my mind again, making my stomach turn. I want so badly to close my eyes, but I remember everything I went through to get here—the beatings and the pain. Through the burns and cuts, the bruises and broken bones, so many times I had to be brave for Sam.

This time, I need to be brave for me, for me and the girl I'm trying so hard to save.

I inspect the box with trembling fingers. There, scratched out in the black silk inside the lid are three new words that explain everything that has gone so sickeningly wrong with the life I'm trying to build.

SAFETY IS ILLUSION

The next day, Janice and Rachel have more school shopping to do. Since Sanda is now registered for her first day of school next week, they had invited her to go with them. I want to be there with her, but I need to fix the window and take care of the locks on the fire escape first.

My mind hasn't stopped thinking through the message in the lid since last night. The implications make me physically ill. The Father's sneer as he said similar words hovers like a tattoo on the inside of my eyelids. Every time I blink he is there—a tormentor when he should've been my protector.

I don't want to believe he is alive. Simply thinking he might be makes me want to crawl under my blankets and cower in the cover of darkness. Even if he survived, could he have found me here? I shiver and shake my head. It has to be someone else, but who?

The Father said I could never be safe from him. Is that what the message means? Is it a warning or a threat? Could it be from someone else?

*But it said Piper.*

Sam thinks the Father has come back. The Father knew I called myself Piper, I'd been punished for it. If Sam is right—if he survived—then that man is impossible to kill. I certainly tried. Pushing aside the grim notion, I consider Brothers. He knows I'm here in the city and so, if he somehow survived the burns, he makes the most sense, but how would he know to call me Piper?

"Are you sure you want me to go?" Sanda tugs my hand, jerking me free of the troubling thoughts. Neither of us slept well, even after I'd pushed every piece of furniture in the living room against the fire escape door. She's too smart not to know something is wrong no matter how many times I assure her otherwise. I kneel before her.

"Yes. I'm going to be here doing boring stuff." Smiling, I touch the ends of her straight black hair. "Installing new locks. Making sure no one can hurt us."

Sanda's eyes fill with tears that don't quite spill over as she takes a shaky breath. Her whisper breaks me inside. "I knew we weren't safe."

"You're very smart, but now we will be," I assure her as I squeeze her small hand. "I'll find a way to keep you safe."

I drop Sanda off with Janice, leaving some money for school clothes as well. Janice's mouth drops open when I hand her the wad of cash I'd retrieved from the safe. Rather than get into a discussion about how much school clothes cost when I honestly have no idea, I tell her to return whatever she doesn't use. Rachel is bouncing up and down, ready to head out the door.

"Hi, Charlotte! Thanks for letting Sanda come!" Rachel exclaims as she walks over, throws both arms around my waist, and grins up at me. "This is going to be the best day ever."

I smile back at her exuberance. "Good, I hope so."

When she skips over to grab her small pink purse off the couch, I'm struck again by the difference between the girls. Rachel has always been cared for, never doubted that she is loved. That kind of thing makes a huge difference. Sanda stands beside the couch wringing her hands and staring at me. She'd been getting more comfortable with each day she spent with Rachel, but this new fear has set her back.

She's a sweet little girl who deserves better than the fear and pain she's used to. I *will* find a way to give her that.

I smile at Sanda until her mouth curves up and she gives me a wave before Rachel drags her into the other room to see her new clothes again. Her small sign of resilience is exactly what I needed to see.

"Thanks," I say to Janice, and she shakes her head.

"Please, she's so easy—"

"No, really," I interrupt. "I couldn't do this without you."

Janice's eyes widen for a moment, but then she nods sadly. "It seems she's much better off with you than wherever she was before. I know *exactly* how important that is." Her voice lowers to a whisper, and she checks that Sanda is no longer listening behind her. "I've seen—on her arms. I asked her. What you're doing for this girl, that's thanks enough."

I blink as she gives me an awkward hug and then shoos me out the door.

# 21

Cam is sitting on the front steps when I come home from the hardware store. I walk up and slip around him successfully without a word, but I'm halfway up the stairs before I realize he's following me. I stop and turn to face him, struggling against the happy glow in my heart that his mere presence still brings. Why are hearts such foolish things?

"Do you need something?"

"Janice called me. She said someone tried to break into your apartment last night?"

I try not to let the worry on his face get to me. "It's under control."

"Let me help you." His eyes take in the bag I'm gripping, and a slow grin spreads across his face. "Your building manager sent me after all. Consider me the handyman."

I open my mouth to argue and then close it again. He can sure think on his feet, I've got to give him that. A quiet laugh escapes my throat. It feels better than it should, so I follow it quickly with "No."

He grabs my bag out of my hand before I can react. "Sorry,

miss. I'm doing what the manager requested. If you've got a problem with that, you'll have to take it up with her."

I'm speechless and angry, trying to figure out how to get around this. I don't want to explain to Janice why I would refuse to let Cam help, and I get the impression he's stubborn enough to make me do it.

"Ugh, fine." I stomp up the stairs, and when we get to the landing I hear his footsteps stop. Turning, I see him staring at the scratches on my door.

I unlock the door and walk inside, but he stands examining the door and the locks with a grim expression. Finally, he turns to face me. "So, they tried pretty hard, but didn't get in?"

My teeth clench. I turn away and walk to the window. There's no one watching from the park; I close the curtains and take a breath. Cam always knows when I'm lying, so I'll keep my mouth shut.

He closes the door and walks to the opposite side of the room so I think he's dropped it, but when I look up, he's staring at the mountain of furniture in front of the door to the fire escape. Without a word, I start removing pieces from the pile. Blocking the door was the only thing that had made us feel safe last night, but we aren't going to do more than one night with a broken window. Someone is coming in an hour to replace the glass anyway, and before they come I'd like to get the new locks installed.

Cam's face is so pale. He stands like a statue. I don't even see the rise and fall of his shoulders for what seems like forever. By the time I've moved two chairs and a coffee table out of the way, I can't ignore him anymore.

"Cam?" Concern forces his name out, and it leaves a sweet burning sensation on my lips.

He spins to face me and his words are so soft I can barely make them out. "Why didn't you call me?"

I pull back my shoulders. "I told you. It's under control."

As Cam crosses to me, I can see his fists clenching and un-clenching at his sides. "Someone was inside your apartment. How is that 'under control'? Who did this?"

I stare into his eyes, ignoring the fear and worry I see in them as best I can. As much as I wish I could rely on him, I can't let myself take that risk again. "You can leave if it bothers you. I'll install the new locks."

He doesn't move while I lift the bag from his fingers and empty it on the table. I've never used a tool in my life, but now's as good a time as any to start. Grabbing one of the nails, I hold it against the doorframe and swing the hammer experimentally toward it. My thumb explodes with pain and the nail drops to the floor with a tiny *plink*. I force myself not to say a word as I press my throbbing thumb against my lips and hear a soft chuckle behind me.

"You're more stubborn than me, even. You know that?" His voice is warm and quiet behind my ear, but I don't respond.

Studying the diagram on the back of the lock box for a few seconds, I lift my hammer again. When I swing it toward a new nail, the hammer is snatched out of my hand. Whipping my eyes up, I see Cam smiling down at me.

"Move."

"I don't know if you noticed, but I'm kind of in the middle of something here." Stretching on my tiptoes, I still can't reach the hammer he holds over his head. He stands there, waiting for me to finish trying to steal back the only tool in my apartment.

I slump down on the couch and glare at him as he walks over, pushes the nail through the lock assembly, and knocks it into the doorframe with one blow.

"I was doing fine."

"Sure, but I think your fingers are worth preserving." He looks at me as he positions the next nail.

Holding up the thumb of my left hand, I examine the blue spreading beneath the surface of my fingernail and shrug. "It's not that bad."

I don't let myself wince as I bend it and pain shoots up my arm. *We hate bruises.*

Cam inhales and then blows it out hard like a mini explosion of air. He works for a while in silence, but for the first time since I told him everything, it isn't uncomfortable. When he's finished, he takes a step back from the door to the fire escape and hands me the hammer. "There. That should help."

*More locks are good. Check the locks to be sure.*

The three shiny new fire escape locks are positioned so they can't be reached through any broken window. I nod. It isn't enough, but it's an improvement. As I stand up and test each of the locks, Cam stands behind me. When I finish and turn around, he steps closer and brushes a piece of hair out of my eyes.

"You need to know." He doesn't move when I take a step back. "If whoever did this wants to get in bad enough, nothing you can do will stop them."

I pull in a gulp of air, suddenly needing more oxygen. "I know."

\* \* \*

I'm certain that I checked the locks at least twice before I left, but I can't stop obsessing about it. I don't want to come home to any more surprises tonight.

*Maybe we should've checked just one more time, Piper? One more check wouldn't have hurt.*

I walk into Angelo's for what I hope will be the last time. My check will be in the back office, but I keep hoping Lily won't be there.

Sneaking around the room and down the hall, I feel relief relax my tense muscles when I see the office open and empty. The box of checks is on the desk, and I dig through it until I find the name "Charlotte Thompson." I stuff my check in my pocket, hoping I can hurry out before anyone even knows I'm here.

"Wish I could say I'm surprised you showed up."

No luck. I should've known it was going too smoothly.

Anger pumps through my veins at Lily's tone. It's too much. I don't need her judgmental comments on top of everything else going on. That's why I quit in the first place. "What is your problem?" I ask.

"You." She walks in through the open door and stands next to the desk.

Taking a step closer, I lower my voice. "Well, you're becoming mine, so back off."

Lily's laugh is bitter and cold. "You think I haven't seen your kind before? Cam has too good a heart. He's been suckered in by poor girls in need—"

"I am *not* a girl in *need*." I spit out the words and the distaste that comes with them, but she barely even pauses.

She leans in, her face only a few inches from mine. "Girls like you always end up betraying him, hurting him. You're no different. Soon he'll see you for the bad-news trash that I've always known you are," she seethes.

"Lily!"

We both spin to see Cam standing in the hall outside the door. Staring hard at his cousin, he seems furious and embarrassed at the same time. His eyes don't even land on me when he speaks the name he gave me. "Charlotte, I'll walk you out. Lily, I'll deal with you later."

I storm out the door past him and he has to jog to catch up. When we get out into the fresh air, I don't slow down. The cool breeze on my face does nothing to stop the blood boiling inside me. He keeps my pace for a bit.

"Wait."

"No."

"What she said—" Cam reaches for my hand, but I pull it away like it burns me.

"I don't care. It doesn't matter." I sprint down the block, clinging to the shadows as I run, letting the city hide me from him, hold me as tight as its darkest secret. I don't slow until I've rounded several corners, until I'm certain he isn't following me.

My hand is raised to knock on Janice's door, but Sam stops me.

*Check first, Piper. Make sure it's safe. Safe for her.*

My eyes flick toward the stairs and I nod. As much as I want to see that she's okay, it's already been proven more than once that Janice's apartment is safer than mine. *Sanda has seen enough.*

When I get to my door, I release the breath I didn't realize I'd been holding. It's intact with no new scratches—a good sign.

I unlock the door, leaving it wide open again, and flip on the lights. I check the fire escape door, and everything is in place. I check on the table, under it, and behind the couch. No new surprise deliveries.

*The new locks worked. Safe is good, Piper.*

But I don't feel safe. Something is off, something is wrong. It's like a vibration centered in the marrow of my bones that tells me to keep searching. I scan the room again. This time I pick up the one difference I didn't notice at first. There's a slight lump behind a window curtain. It doesn't move, but that doesn't stop a ball of pure fear from tightening in my throat. It's far too small to be a person, even a child . . . but what is it?

Inching forward, I draw the heavy fabric aside, willing it to be a simple tangle in the curtains or something equally nonthreatening. When I see what's beneath, I fall back a few steps with a gasp. The released curtain falls against my latest surprise, leaving it swinging in midair. Sam's Piper-Puppet dangles a few feet off the ground. Her strings are wound around a nail in the wall. I struggle for breath and grip the back of my couch with both hands. Black tape has been put over her eyes to make X's.

The message is clear. She's helpless. She's dead.

Sam begins his ragged humming in my head as I realize where the puppet came from. The only place in the apartment I didn't

191

check: my bedroom, my closet . . . where the safe and any hope for my new life is hidden.

Keeping my breath quiet and even, I sneak through the kitchen and pull out the knife drawer. My whole world chills like a blizzard blew through it, leaving everything frozen and still. The drawer is empty. Every weapon I can use to defend myself, gone.

I grab the metal bookend again and sneak down the hall. A board creaks beneath my feet near the open door to the landing and I freeze, waiting—listening for any movement—but I hear nothing. I reach the end and peek in my bedroom. It's dark, too dark with my eyes adjusted to the light.

Reaching around the corner, I flip the light switch. Nothing happens. *Click, click* . . . I try again, *click, click*. The noise is so loud in the quiet that it sounds like a siren alerting everyone to my presence. My heartbeat fills my head with echoing sound. It almost drowns Sam out. I try to swallow, but my mouth is too dry to make it work.

I creep back down the hallway, flipping off every light in my apartment with trembling hands as I go, and after a few seconds my eyes adjust. I peek around the corner again. My room is dim, but with the streetlight coming in around the curtains, I can see the bed and the dresser. Nothing is out of place. Entering, I drop the bookend on my bed and reach under the pillow. My fingers close around the iron bar that helps me sleep at night. My knees hit the floor with a quiet thud and I peer into the shadows under the bed. No one is here. Only one place left to check: the closet.

I need an advantage. It's darker in the closet than in here, so I cross and quietly push open the curtains until the streetlight outside shines directly on the closet door. I inch across the room and wrap my fingers around the handle. I want to run, would give up my limited wardrobe and the safe with the money if I could never have to open the closet again. Whatever gift has been left for me this time, I'm certain I don't want it.

I yank the door open and step back in case something is going to jump out at me. Light shines into my eyes and I have to blink a few times before I realize it's a reflection of the streetlight from outside. A mirror? Why would someone put a mirror in my closet? Then I see many different reflections swaying a bit in the air.

It feels like a vacuum has been attached to my feet and the blood from my head has been sucked away. I stumble back and fight to stay upright. I recognize them, every one. More than a dozen knives of every shape and size, all from my kitchen, now hang in my closet. Each is suspended from a string with several hangers supporting them.

The words from the last box fill my mind: *Safety is illusion.*

Someone who is supposed to be dead has given me a torture closet of my own.

He's taunting me, enjoying this. And I'm not even sure who he is. Why would he give me this? A hint of what he has in store for me?

Images of Sanda tied, gagged, and blindfolded in Brothers's closet pelt my brain and I feel sick. But Brothers wasn't the only one. The Father had a closet full of his toys, too. And I'd spent half my nights tied up next to it. Memories of blinding pain send me rushing to the window. I open it and draw in a few cold breaths before my stomach agrees to calm down.

When I can finally stand upright and slow my breathing, I close the window. I turn back to the closet and realize the shining reflections aren't the only new additions. Below the knives, sitting in plain sight, is another black box. Fury bubbles inside me and I'm across the room in two strides. I grab the box, tear off the lid, and throw them both as hard as I can against the opposite wall. The rose explodes in a crimson spray across my light gray blankets and I try to regain control. I'm torn between absolute terror and a hunger to kill him for messing with me like this.

I retrieve the lid and study it in the reflected light bouncing off the blades. A sudden chill fills me from head to toe. This time the message scraped in the tight black silk of the lid is far more malicious.

NO MORE HIDING

In the silence of my room I hear it. A board in the hallway creaks. Someone is here. My heart speeds up and everything around me slows down, but not enough to save me.

*Run! Now!*

I'm cornered. There is only one place I can hide fast enough, and I wonder if I'd rather die than go in voluntarily. A footstep sounds in the hall, heavier, closer. Whoever it is, they're coming. Ducking as low as I can, I climb into the closet with the sharp points of knives scraping my arms, poking into my neck, hanging over my head. And I pull the door closed.

# 2 2

A butcher knife dangles in front of my face. Every time I move, even breathe, there is a slight clinking sound as the knives touch each other. I close my eyes for a moment and swear silently when I realize I must've dropped my iron bar on the bed.

One particularly sharp knife pokes my elbow and I feel for the string holding it. I hear another footstep, closer, in my room. In one quick motion, I grab the knife and use it to slice through its own string with a flick of my wrist. Holding the blade out in front of me, I decide I'll be better off if I catch my visitor by surprise than the other way around.

Another footstep sounds, this time close outside the closet door. If I want that advantage, I have to act now. I try to psych myself up. I can do this. What have I been taking Cam's classes for if not this? I can. I will.

Crouching below most of the knives, I explode through the door. Knocking the solid—and clearly male—figure on the other side down. I can tell from the pain and sudden warmth that I've sliced up my shoulders a bit, but I don't stop to check. Can't give him a chance to figure out what's going on. He has a hood pulled up around his face. I knee him in the stomach and hear a loud *whoosh* of air. Then I push my knife against his throat and tug back his hood.

Cam wheezes, his eyes wide. Relief and confusion extinguish the fiery adrenaline in my blood and I lean back in surprise, keeping my knife in place. He rolls, grabs my wrist, and knocks the knife out of my hand before pinning me to the ground with his strong arms and legs.

"Charlotte!" he shouts, as I immediately fight to get him off me. "Stop and I'll let you go."

One deep breath goes in and out, then another, as I calm down and my pulse slows to a normal rate. His eyes search mine and I glare back, trying to figure out why he would be sneaking around my apartment in the dark. I blow my hair out of my face and glare at him. "I stopped."

He backs off and sits on the ground beside me. Now that I'm not fighting him, I watch him look in the closet and see the knives hanging there. His eyes go from the closet to the explosion of rose petals on my bed and the bloody cuts on my shoulders. Then he reaches over and picks up the lid of the box, reading the words inside.

Cam raises his eyes to mine, his voice only a strained whisper. "What in the hell is going on?"

Pulling myself to a sitting position, I examine the damage. Most of the cuts are shallow and superficial. Only a few will need attention. "Why does it matter?"

He gestures toward the closet incredulously. "How can you not think this matters?"

I lower my chin. "Let me rephrase. Why does it matter *to you?*"

"How many times do I have to tell you I care about you before it sinks in?"

His angry tone only makes me want to fight back, to lash out. "How many times do I have to tell you to leave me alone before you listen?"

He stares hard at me, and the fire in his eyes feels like the only heat left in the apartment. "Always once more . . . until you make me believe you mean it."

I'm too confused, too upset, to even attempt to understand what he's saying right now, so I focus on my latest injury. "Why are you here anyway?" I press a piece of my shirt against one of the deeper cuts, trying to stop the bleeding. "And you showed up at Angelo's. Are you following me?"

He grabs a towel out of a basket of folded laundry in the corner and pushes it against my shoulder. "Yes."

"Wha—why?" I scowl and try to take the towel from him, but the glare he gives me is so obstinate that I stop fighting.

"Let's see. Maybe because a psychopath keeps breaking into your apartment? Oh, and what was that other thing?" He leans in until his face fills my vision and then lowers his voice, but not the intensity. "That's right—and because I *care about you.*"

His breath comes in short angry bursts and the heat from it warms my face. I don't have the right words to answer that, not right now anyway. Without any response, I grab hold of the towel, get to my feet, and walk to the living room. He stays right behind me, flipping on the light switch with a good deal of force as we pass. I walk to the window and search the park across the street for a shadowy figure, a lit cigarette, any sign of life. Is he still here? Watching? Waiting? There is nothing. When I shove the apartment door shut and slump down on the couch, Cam sits beside me.

His expression is pained when he meets my eyes. "Can we declare a truce for at least a few minutes?"

I watch him. Half of me wants to disagree, to tell him again and again that I don't need him or his truce. The other half is still cowering in the closet with the knives and knows I might be in over my head here. My compromise is to say nothing.

"You may not need my help. I don't know because you won't tell me anything." Cam closes his eyes and rubs his hand against his forehead. "But I need to know what's going on. You blasted, bleeding, from a closet full of knives and attacked me. Please give me the courtesy of an explanation."

*You don't have to fight alone anymore, Piper.*

I retrieve my first-aid kit from the bathroom and bring it back to the couch. "All right, but we talk while I patch myself up. What do you want to know?"

"How did he get in this time?"

I shake my head. The main door was untouched, same with the fire escape. "I have no idea."

"The card on the box says 'Piper.'" Cam has the same focused expression I've seen on his face while he forges documents. He lowers his chin, takes one of the bandages from the kit, and examines a long cut on my other arm. "Who else knows that name?"

"No one here really. You, Lily, Sanda." I wince as he cleans out one of my deeper wounds. "Which is another reason this doesn't make sense."

"How many boxes have you received?"

"Three."

"At different times?"

"Yes."

He grinds his teeth and presses a bandage against my skin a little harder than necessary. "Do they all have that sweet message written inside the lid?"

"No." I shudder as I pack the first-aid kit. I focus on Cam's questions and my answers. Solve the problem—don't let the fear take hold.

He takes the box from my hands and sets it on the ground by his feet, then turns to face me, his expression grim. "Tell me."

I rest my head against the back of the couch, my eyes on the ceiling above me. "They said: 'I know your secret,' 'Safety is illusion,' and 'No more hiding.'"

Speaking the words makes me nauseated. Am I done hiding or is he? I can't face the possibility that it could be the Father, even if my name and one of the messages sound like it could be him. If this is Brothers, I took away Sanda and left him to burn—and now he wants me to pay. Exhaustion and defeat overwhelm me. What this person did in my closet took time. How long must he have been here in my home, touching my things?

Placing my arm over my eyes, I try to block out my life. This is nothing like the new life I've fought for. No, it's far too much like the life I've always known. Maybe I deserve it. Maybe I'm a magnet for bad people.

"What do you think it means?" Cam leans the side of his head against the couch next to mine.

"Maybe he's not dead." My voice shakes and I don't even try to hide it. I turn toward Cam and he's only inches away. I don't understand why, but his presence lends me strength. "And he knows who I am, where I live . . . everything."

"Who?"

My answer comes out low and quiet. "I'm not sure yet. None of it makes sense." Now I close my eyes, unable to face him anymore. I know how he feels about what I've done. I don't want to see his judgment and disappointment again.

Cam slips the ends of his fingers beneath mine but doesn't make any further move. "Look at me, please."

Opening my eyes, I watch him and wait.

"I promise, whatever is going on, I'm here. I know *you*. I don't care what you've done, you don't deserve this. I'm not going anywhere—no matter what." He waits. His eyes are turbulent pools of emotion before he speaks. "Tell me."

"I can't." I pull my hand back, but he grabs my other one.

"Why not?" He raises his voice enough to set me off.

I yell back at him. "You already know."

"Then this should be easy." His voice softens. "Who is doing this?"

I raise my eyes to meet his. "Probably one of the people I killed."

Cam doesn't seem horrified, turn away, or take his eyes from my face. He doesn't run or get angry. He does none of the things I expect. Instead, he steps forward and speaks.

"If so, your methods of killing are seriously ineffective."

Now I blink, and the corner of his mouth lifts a little. I can't help but laugh, and when I do, it feels so good. He laughs, too, and we're both laughing. The irony hits me and I'm clutching my stomach because I can't stop. We're sitting in my apartment with a closet full of knives, my shoulder is bleeding, I almost stabbed Cam, some psycho is stalking me, and we can't stop laughing. It's so inappropriate—so twisted and dark and beautiful.

A full minute passes before we can breathe again. When the laughter is gone, I can see in Cam's eyes what is left—pure fear. Reaching out, he pulls me to his chest and wraps his arms around me. They crush me against him so hard it almost hurts and at once makes me whole in a way I've never been. It's like his embrace is the only thing holding me together. Without his arms, I'd shatter. The tension in me unwinds like a spring kept tight for way too long. Part of me wants to hold as tight to him as he is to me, the other part wants to push him away and escape. I do neither. Instead I focus my energy on trying to understand his reaction.

Could it be possible? After everything he knows, he doesn't think I'm a monster? The idea is as sweet as the sunlight on my first day out of the attic—surreal. But that's the point. It isn't real. Right now, when he's afraid for me, he can see past it. But on a different day, with no danger lurking around the corner, he couldn't. And I can't see past that.

"I am so sorry for everything." Cam presses his lips against my hair, and I know if I don't push him away now I'll never bring myself to do it. Pulling my hands in, I press gently against his chest until he leans back, and I change the subject.

"When I found Sanda here in the city, the man who had her kept her locked in a cabinet under the stairs and had an entire closet of weapons he used to torture her."

Cam winces and his fists clench so tight I can see the veins stand out on his forearms. "So you think it's him? And that's why he did that to your closet?"

I shrug. "Not necessarily. Maybe this is common for psychos like him. The Father had one, too. I mean, they aren't going to leave it all spread out everywhere. Plus, I don't even know how her captor would find me. Let alone know my name is—was Piper."

*You'll always be Piper.*

Cam walks to the window and peers through the small gap in the curtains. His expression is like he's fighting a war in his head. When he speaks, he doesn't move. "Can I ask you a question?"

I ignore my first reaction to build up a few more barriers between us for good measure. He pretty much knows all my secrets now anyway. When my response comes, it sounds tentative. "Okay."

He keeps his eyes on the world outside. "How many more have you . . . ?"

I'm dismayed, realizing it's really not an unfair question. "No, no more. That's all. I swear it."

"Was there another way?" His eyes come to mine and the street-light reflects off them. There is a hope and misery in his expression that throws me off balance and I don't answer right away. "Did you have to kill him?"

"I didn't go there intending to hurt him." His eyes are so penetrating I can't face the intensity there. I study the swirls in the wooden boards beneath my feet. "He came back when I was inside, trying to save her."

"Wow." He lets out a long, low whistle. He scrutinizes me until

I become so uncomfortable I have to turn away. "So what? You're some kind of vigilante? Save those in need? Avenge them?"

"No." I whisper my answer too fast.

*Maybe.*

"No," I repeat, louder this time, and Cam tilts his head to one side. "I was only trying to help her. He came after me and I defended myself. He dropped his cigarette when I knocked him out and it started the fire."

*He deserved to die.*

A bitter growl escapes my throat. "It'd sure be nice to know if he did right about now."

"If he did what?"

"Oh." I shake my head, willing Sam to be quiet for a minute. I need to get a grip, no more talking to myself. I gesture toward the bedroom and the chaos we left in there. "If he died."

Cam turns from the window with a nod and a purposeful stride toward the bedroom. "I think I can help you with that."

"You can?" My eyes widen and I start to get to my feet, but then he freezes and pivots toward me.

"Before we get to that, we should narrow our options," he says. I can see in his face that he's formulating a plan. "Could it be anyone else? Friends or family of his who might know what you've done?" Cam asks.

"No. I don't think I've ever met anyone that he knows," I say, shaking my head and bending over to retrieve the first-aid kit before getting to my feet.

"Excuse me for asking this, but how did you kill your parents?" When I whirl back to face him in shock, he continues. "Sanda's guy—if someone came to help, the fire wasn't that bad, or he wasn't out for long—he could've made it out alive. Was there any way your parents might have survived?"

I swallow hard, and the image of the bloody knife flashes through my mind. One they'd used on me a hundred times, but the blood I see isn't my own. The word slips out between my teeth. "Unlikely."

"You didn't say impossible."

The air leaves me in a gush and I flop back on the couch. "Nothing's impossible when it comes to them."

"Okay. Then we'll start tomorrow." He sits back down beside me and throws his arm across the back of the couch.

"Start?"

"Figuring out who this psycho is."

Without hesitation, I shake my head. "No. This is my problem, not yours. I don't need help."

"Right." He nods. "And I'm sleeping on your couch until we figure it out."

"No," I protest. Standing, I turn toward the door to escort him out, but he gets there first, puts his hand on it and stops me.

"If not for you, let me do this for Sanda." His eyes are pleading and kind. "She deserves a chance at a normal life. You saved her already. Let me be the hero for her this time."

The sound that comes from me is a half sigh, half groan, but he knows he's won. With a grin, he leans against the door and reaches out to touch the tips of my fingers with his.

"Fine," I mutter, and jerk my hand away with a shake of my head. His grin falters a little, but not much, and I see that familiar glint of determination in his eye. I'd been keeping him at a very safe distance, and somehow in one night he'd knocked down most of the barriers I'd built to protect myself. I refuse to be left completely unguarded though, and I'm keeping that last one up with all my strength. It is the only protection I have left. "Help me clean up, then I'll go get Sanda."

As I dump the rest of the rose petals in the garbage, I hear Cam moving in my room and a scraping of metal on metal. We haven't spoken since I agreed to let him stay, both of us working to clean up the nightmare in grim silence. I can't face the closet again, not right now. I sit on the couch with the Piper-Puppet in my lap. Closing my eyes, I wait. After a few minutes, he sits down and rests his arm next to mine. Not touching, but close enough for me to sense his presence even with my eyes closed.

"We'll stop him. I don't know how, but we will."

I swallow and press my head back harder into the soft couch cushion, wishing I could sink down inside it and disappear from this madness forever. I want to hide from the new horrors in my apartment and my life, but as the message said, I can't hide from them anymore.

In fact, I'm certain I'm the only one who can stop them.

# 23

Letting Cam sleep on the couch was the best idea ever. I don't think I've slept this well since I first saw Sanda in the park. Feeling safe is a wonderful thing, an unfamiliar sensation. With my new stalker I'm probably less safe than I've been since I escaped the Parents, but with Cam it doesn't seem that way. I just hope letting him stay isn't putting him in danger, too. Not that he'd leave even if I begged him, because I tried.

Cam ran home for a shower and to see Jessie while I dropped Sanda off with Janice. He'd called his aunt last night to tell her he was staying with a friend, but from the fact that she'd already called three times this morning, I'm pretty sure she suspects something is off. When I step out the front door, he's waiting in fresh clothes. His hair is damp. Before I can say a word, he gets to his feet and takes off walking.

Without a glance over his shoulder he says, "You coming?"

I watch his back for a moment before hurrying after him. It feels backward. Usually it's him trying to catch me, not the other way around.

"Wait, where are you going?"

"We have a lot to do." Cam turns and walks backward so he can face me as I jog toward him.

"Like what?"

"I thought we'd start with the Free Library."

I swallow and try really hard to focus on the plan. No getting excited. A real library? I've only read about them in books . . . ironic, I know. I've wanted to find one since I arrived in the city, but with Sanda, I've never had the time. "But why?"

He doesn't slow down. "We're going to check up on your parents and find out if Sanda's villain survived your little bonfire."

I freeze in my tracks. "They'll have that information in the library?"

A sad smile crosses his face. He stops and walks the few feet back to me. "They have computers. We can search news reports. I'd offer to do it at my place, but after I didn't come home last night, I think it might be awkward to bring you with me. Aunt Jessie didn't give me enough room to take a breath while I was there, so the library is our best option. Lucky for you, I'm a sucker for cute girls with serious problems." He stops a foot in front of me and leans forward, his voice lowering to a whisper. "I'm happy to help you."

"Thank you. I need a good *friend*." I can see from his expression that he caught my not so subtle hint, but he nods without comment. Pushing back the confusion that fills me when he stands so close, I step to the side and walk next to him. I can't afford to sort through my emotions right now, but he's a good guy, and as much as I hate to admit it, I do need his help.

* * *

The Free Library at Rittenhouse Square is smaller than I expect. It takes up the bottom two floors of a high-rise apartment building, which explains how I haven't realized it was here. Still, I love every inch of it. Each level is packed with shelf upon shelf of books. The entire place smells like books. I love it. I want to move in and live here with all the other worlds I used to escape into.

Cam walks straight to the computers without a second glance at the shelves. I'm sure computers are useful, but next to all these warm, beautiful books they seem so cold and clinical.

The moment Cam starts clicking away at the keyboard, I remember what he said those cold machines could tell us. I move to his side and study the screen. Before I can even begin to wonder what on earth a "Google" is, he starts firing off whispered questions like an extremely quiet machine gun.

"Where did your parents live? State? Address? Anything you can give me will help."

I swallow hard. "Wyoming. The closest town was named Greenville."

His gaze is on me even as his fingers fly across the keyboard. "How long ago?"

"May of last year."

"Can you tell me their names?"

"Douglas and Betty Nelson." I speak the names I've never uttered and stare at the floor with unseeing eyes. The only reason I even know their names is because Nana told me. I try to ignore the fear that seeps through my marrow. They shouldn't still have this power over me. I won't let them.

"Betty is dead."

I don't look up, but the tightness in my chest eases a bit. "How?"

He doesn't answer, and I wonder if he's as afraid to tell me as I am to hear it. "Haven't found any details yet. I'm still checking."

"And him?"

Cam's hands stop. His shoulders tense as he bends closer. I glance up at the screen and everything slows to a halt—my breathing, my blood, my heart, my brain. Every piece of me the Father tried to control. His ice-cold eyes watch me. The image dated only a month ago. He sneers at my belief that I could ever survive him. He mocks my attempt at escape.

Sam hums so loud in my head it drowns out all sound. His scared voice echoes in my skull as it did in the attic. We are alone, Sam and I. The Father is here and no one will protect us . . . just as I failed to protect Sam.

"Charlotte?" Cam's voice sounds distant and panicked. His arm drops around my shoulders and I don't even flinch. I'm back in the attic and everything I've worked for seems so unattainable, so far away. His voice is a whisper on the wind, drawing me toward him through the miles and states between us even as his warm breath moves across my ear. "Please, you have to breathe."

His fingers brush my chin as he turns my face toward him. His hazel eyes replace the Father's blue ones. The warmth and concern I see there pull me back as the edges of my vision begin to dim. I gasp in a deep breath and blink a few times as he crushes me in his arms.

"Thank God," Cam whispers against my forehead.

The air in my lungs is like a portal back to the present and I can't get enough. I'm here now, in the living, breathing city of Philadelphia, not the barren woods and empty trails of Wyoming. I am free and this is my home.

I pull my bolt out of my pocket and wrap it tight in my palm. Gathering the strength to stand on my own, I pull myself from under Cam's arm and step toward the computer screen. Forcing my voice not to shake, I face this new truth. This new world seems darker and more dangerous now because I know the Father lives somewhere in it.

"He's alive," I say.

"Yes," Cam answers. He stands behind me like a support beam inside a wall. I can't see or feel him, but somehow his presence keeps me upright. "But he isn't here. This isn't him."

I turn from the screen, but I still shiver from the Father's eyes on my back. "How can you know?"

"Because he's in jail." Cam bends his knees slightly until I raise my eyes to his. "He's on trial for his wife's murder."

I shake my head. Nothing seems to make sense anymore. I have my fingertips on all the puzzle pieces, but I can't turn them into the full picture. "But he didn't . . ."

"You can't know that." Cam shrugs. "The details of her death aren't public yet. Maybe they both survived and he killed her in anger after you escaped. Either way, it answers our question."

I can see in Cam's eyes how much he wants that possibility to be the truth, but I don't. Deep down I need it to have been me. As terrible as it sounds, I want the end of her cruelty to have been by my hands. After everything she did, after she didn't care that I was starving, after she took me to live with him and let him lock me in an attic—after everything the Father did and how she even supported it. She chose drugs over me and then the Father over me. Time after time, she proved that her needs, her addictions meant more to her than I did. Then—after what she let him do to Sam— I, her shield, turned into a weapon. I want to be the one that stole her life to make up for everything she'd stolen from me.

A girl walks from the rows of shelves on one side of the room to the other. I'm suddenly very aware that we're not alone. People quietly move up and down the aisles, studying books, typing on keyboards. They make me feel exposed. I want them to go away so I can sort all this new information into something logical, something I can understand or control.

Only one fact matters right now—the Father may still be alive, but he's become the prisoner I used to be. He can't come for me, can't hurt me and the people I care about, not anymore. And if the Father isn't breaking into my apartment and leaving me black presents with dark messages, then who is?

I whisper, "Check the man who had Sanda."

Cam gives me a grim nod. With two clicks the Father's face disappears from the screen and I can breathe easier.

"What can you tell me?"

"It was on Clarion Street."

"Okay, and what was the date?"

"Maybe five weeks ago?" I try to piece together the timing of the last few weeks for more specifics, but my brain refuses to cooperate and I come up empty. "His name is Steve Brothers, if that helps."

He types for a few moments in the computer. "Nothing under that name, but that doesn't mean anything. Let me adjust these dates a bit."

After about a hundred more clicks he stops. "Is this it?"

A black-and-white photo of Brothers's charred building is right there on the screen. It is even creepier with the color stripped out. "Yes."

Cam skips through the article. I skim the words as fast as my eyes can read them, but as hard as I've tried to teach myself how to read quickly I still can't keep up with Cam. I only catch a few words here and there as he flies down the page. Then suddenly the little arrow on the screen freezes over a single paragraph.

> In a stroke of luck, the fire happened during the middle of the day when none of the tenants of the building's three apartments were home. No injuries or fatalities were reported.

Clenching my hands by my sides, I read it again and again. Each time hoping it will say something different than the last, hoping it will say he's dead. I remember the dark thrill in his eyes when he saw me in the mirror at his apartment. He's alive and in the city, and that alone makes him the prime suspect.

Cam lowers his chin and meets my eyes. I realize from his expression that he's been speaking. I didn't hear a thing, nothing but my heart plummeting through to the floor of the library basement below us and landing with a sickening thump at the bottom.

"What did you say?" I ask.

"This is a lot of information to process at once." His brow furrows and he brushes his knuckles against my forearm. "You're freezing. Are you okay?"

"No. Do you expect me to be?"

Cam shrugs out of his light jacket and drapes it across my shoulders. It's filled with his warmth, and the smell of him. Tugging it tight around me makes me feel significantly better.

So many things about this don't add up. How would he know my real name or find out where I live? "Are you sure this is right? Any chance they didn't see him in there?"

Sam's whimpering fills my head with images from Brothers's apartment. He doesn't want to admit the possibility any more than I do.

Cam shakes his head and gives me a rueful grin. "No. Missing dead bodies in a burned-down apartment is kind of frowned upon. I'm sure they were thorough."

My fingers tug the jacket tighter against my neck. It's still filled with Cam's heat. He's warm and I'm cold, inside and out.

"Wow, I'm kind of terrible at killing people," I mutter, low enough that even Cam has to strain to hear.

"I'm not sure that's a bad thing," he says, and laughs.

"It's not looking so great right now." When my hands tremble on the buttons of the jacket his grin fades, and he moves my hands aside and buttons it for me before turning back to the computer.

"Let me check a couple of other things." He glances around to make sure no one is watching and pulls a small black square out of his pocket. He pushes it into one of the holes on the front of the computer below the desk.

"What is that?" I ask.

"It's a flash drive." At my blank look, he continues, "It has some programs that help me dig deeper than a normal person can for information."

Within a few seconds, a bunch of new boxes pop up on the screen and he is flying through them so fast it makes me dizzy. Half of them are filled with some other language that doesn't even seem to use complete words.

After about a minute, I stop watching the screen and watch Cam's expression. The way his scowl keeps deepening fills me with a sense of dread. Finally he steps back, hits a few keys, and the picture returns to the one we started on. The flash drive disappears back into his pocket and he shakes his head.

"Steve Brothers doesn't exist."

My breath catches in my throat. "So he *is* dead?"

"No. He never lived. At least not the Steve Brothers that was receiving mail at that address."

I can't quite get my throat to release air, and my words are a whisper. "I don't understand."

"I checked back through every record that exists on him: no credit cards, no cell phone contracts. The police are looking for him since they found some 'articles of interest' when cleaning up the fire, but everything leads to a dead end. It's a fresh identity—a sloppy one, definitely fake. Steve Brothers is even less real than Charlotte Thompson."

"Then who is he?" My voice is a whisper as the implications fall into place. Who knows how long he's been doing this under different names in different places? How many other kids has he hurt or killed? Kids like Sanda. Kids like Sam. I slip the bolt back in my pocket as anger lends me strength in its place.

"I don't know and neither do the cops." He rubs a palm against his eye. "But I guess we've figured out who's leaving you presents."

"Fine. So it's Brothers or the guy who calls himself that. He knows where I live. He's b-been in my home." Staring down, I avoid Cam's eyes. I don't think I can take them reaching into me right now. Filled with fresh fire, I remove his jacket and hand it to him. I straighten my spine and head toward the library doors. "Now it's time to make sure he won't come back."

# 24

"Will you be able to find him?" Cam asks. "He's obviously comfortable in hiding," he adds, his long legs easily matching my fastest stride as we round the corner toward our destination.

"I don't know," I answer, without raising my eyes. I'm afraid he'll try to stop me if he sees me preparing to fight. Even my voice sounds grim. "But I have a good idea of where to start."

I can only think of one way to stop Brothers, and that's to turn him from the hunter into the prey. It'll at least make it a lot harder to spend so much time breaking into my apartment if he's watching over his shoulder all the time. But none of it will matter if I can't discover where he's been hiding out.

"Are you sure you want to be a part of this?" I don't stop walking, but I'm ready in case Cam does. He should turn back now. It's the right thing—the smart thing—to do. "I'll understand if you don't."

Cam doesn't respond and I shiver, afraid of what he'll say when he does. But his warm jacket drapes back around me again and I have my answer.

* * *

The bar is nearly empty. I guess it isn't exactly a Sunday afternoon hot spot. Other than the bartender, there is one guy passed out on a nearby table and another playing pool by himself in the back.

When I walk up, the bartender's bloodshot eyes go from me to Cam. He shrugs and presents us with two highly questionable glasses. A tag with the name JIM printed in large black letters hangs diagonally off the front of his shirt. "What'll ya have?"

"I need to know about one of your customers. His last name is Brothers and he's been in here more than once, sometimes with a young girl." I keep my voice low, leaning across the bar so he can hear me.

I swear I see a flicker of recognition in his eyes at the name, but he turns away and rubs his grimy towel over a couple of glasses. "If you ain't payin', you need to leave."

Digging in my pocket, I bring out a hundred-dollar bill and slap it on the bar. "Now do you remember him?"

The money disappears into Jim's pocket before I can blink, and he leans a little closer. His breath smells like he drinks more liquor than he pours for customers, and I fight the urge to take two big steps backward. "Yeah, I know him. That it?"

"No." A dark thrill of anticipation sweeps through me. "Have you seen him recently?"

"Yeah, he comes in pretty regular." Jim stuffs the corner of the towel into the waistband of his jeans, and I'm glad I didn't order anything to drink. "Don't talk to him more'n I have to though. We get some twisted customers in here."

217

I hear a low chuckle from Cam behind me and he mutters, "No freakin' kidding."

"He moved a little over a month ago and I'm trying to track him down. Any clue where he's living now?" I ask.

Jim shakes his head and his jowls keep moving when his face stops. "Nah. But come back with more money tomorrow and I'll introduce you to his buddy. He's always here on weekdays."

I bend closer, pretend I can still breathe and my throat isn't threatening to close up just from being near him, and smile. Jim grins back and I see a couple of missing teeth on each side. "I want to surprise him. You don't mind keeping our chat a secret, do you, Jim?" I pull out another hundred and tap his chest with the corner.

"Nope. I'm good with secrets."

"I bet you are."


My mind is a jumbled mess as we walk back to my apartment. What we'd discovered at the library, plus Jim and the bar, made me want to take a hundred scalding hot showers. Even with Cam sleeping on the couch, my nightmares plague me. I'd awoken this morning, screaming, from a world filled with hanging knives, the Father, Brothers, and blood—so much blood. Sanda cowered in the corner as Cam tried to hold me, but I'd pushed him away. That's the answer. It's the only way to stay safe from the pain.

Only I'm not sure I want to be safe if pushing him away again and again is what it takes.

As he walks beside me, I can't meet his eyes. I'm pretty sure he'll find mine empty, haunted. I don't want him to pity me. I'm stronger than that.

"I'm confused." The truth comes without thought. My brain is too overwhelmed to battle with honesty.

"I know." Cam doesn't need me to clarify. This has been hanging between us like a dark cloud. He knows exactly what I'm referring to. "I was wrong. I don't know that I would've done anything different in those situations. You did the best you could with what you had and there is nothing wrong with that. I'm sorry."

My relief on hearing his words isn't nearly as sweet as it should be. So many things have been poisoned between us. If I'd never told him about my past, if Sanda and I had never been in danger . . . There are so many ifs, and at the end of each is something I wish I could take from him right now. Something I've never asked for from anyone: a moment of solace, a moment of protection, of safety in his arms. I wish I could take it now with no consequence to either of us, but I know I can't. Ours is a world where the choices have already been made and we can't go back without risking us both.

Yet, even with me fighting him every step of the way, he's still here beside me, climbing the stairs to my apartment.

I only speak two words before I walk through the door he's holding open for me.

"Thank you."

One fact remains after everything else settles. I will not let Cam or Sanda become collateral damage in the carnage of my life.

\* \* \*

Sanda and Rachel skip ahead of us the entire way to school. I've never seen Sanda this happy. Cam went home to get some fresh clothes as long as I promised to stop by the studio and pick him up as soon as I'm done.

I lied.

"It's my first day. My real first day! Can you believe it?" Sanda comes back, squeezes my hand, and giggles.

"Yep. It's real." I smile, and Janice laughs next to me as Sanda skips up to link arms with Rachel.

Rachel's excited squeal can probably be heard a block in any direction. "I'm so excited! First days are the best."

"I want to walk home with you," Sanda yells back to me. "You'll be there to pick me up from school, right?"

"Right." My hands shake and my fingers slip as I struggle to bring the envelope out of my pocket and hold it in front of me. I'd mulled this over all night. Inside, it holds everything Janice will need if I ever stop coming home. The combination to my safe, a letter to Sanda, and instructions on what is in the safe and what to do with it. It's a just-in-case plan, and I hope she never has to use it. Reaching out, I press the envelope into Janice's hand.

"What's this?" She turns the envelope over, but it's blank on both sides.

"It's for you. If anything ever happens to me, please open it." I plaster a grin across my face when Sanda looks back at me again.

"What do you mean 'if anything happens to you'?" Taking her cues from me, Janice keeps smiling, too, but she grips the envelope anxiously.

"The person who hurt Sanda is back. I'm going to find a way to stop him." I hope this is enough explanation for Janice, because it's the only one I am comfortable giving.

There are a million reasons to go after Brothers. I'd been running and hiding since I left the attic. I don't know if I can go back to that or force Sanda to live that way without losing the pieces of myself—the sanity, the security, the hope I've fought so hard to regain. On top of that is an intense desire to stop being a victim . . . to fight. Even if it's the last thing I do, I must make certain the man who has spent the last year hurting Sanda will never have the chance to put those scars on any other child.

Janice stares at me, biting her lip. She glances at the backs of the girls giggling in front of us. "Are you sure you don't need help?"

I shake my head, and my jaw tightens. "I don't trust the police, and I'm afraid if I go to them and give them enough information to put him away they could take Sanda. We have too many secrets they could uncover, and this life would tumble down around us. Besides, you said it yourself, she's better off with me. But I promise I won't let him get to any of you. No matter what."

Janice stuffs the envelope in her massive purse but doesn't speak again until we're almost to the school. "Okay, but please be safe. She needs you more than you know."

"I promise."


Child mayhem is the only way to describe the grassy area in front of the school. Kids are everywhere, running, playing, and giggling—so much joy. A boy with blond hair that hangs in his big blue eyes runs straight into my legs and I fight for control of my emotions.

He grins up at me, and everything about him is so much like Sam, except the smile. Sam never smiled that wide. He never had a reason to.

"Oops, sorry." And then he's gone, sprinting off after another boy toward the front doors of the school.

Sanda tugs on my hand, and I remember why I'm here. I crouch down. Her fear is back as she watches all the other kids and flinches when one runs too close. "What if I'm scared now?"

"It's okay to be scared." I remember something Nana used to whisper in my ear when she came to visit us in the attic. "You're strong enough to be brave anyway. If you can do that, you can do anything."

Sanda looks around again and nods, but she's still trembling. I reach in my pocket and pull out the bolt. I take one of her small hands and press the black metal against her palm. Her eyes get huge and she shakes her head.

"No. This is—"

I nod and gently squeeze her fingers shut. "It gave me what I needed already. When you're afraid, squeeze it or rub it and remember everything we've survived. You are strong, Sanda. Don't forget."

Her dark eyes blink up at me a few times before she sticks the bolt into her pocket. Then a shy smile spreads on her face. "I won't. Thank you, Charlotte."

"Good." I give her a quick hug. "Now, try to remember everything that happens. I want to hear every detail after school."

"I'll do my best." She nods and yanks her purple backpack up on her shoulders.

A small redheaded boy runs up to his mother on the sidewalk a few feet away and I hear her say, "Remember, don't talk to strangers."

I *know* I'll never have to remind Sanda of that.

"One more thing," I say, and her muscles tense as she waits, poised to sprint back home if I say the word. "Have fun, okay?"

"We're going to have the mostest fun ever!" Rachel yells as she comes over and grabs Sanda's hand.

They grin at each other for a moment and then Sanda turns to me. "I promise."

The bell rings and kids everywhere rush toward the front doors. Sanda waits as several run past her, but then she waves at me and follows Rachel toward the entrance. "Bye, Charlotte! See you after school!"

# 25

There are a few more people in the bar this time, but the moment Jim sees me, he grins and walks over.

"Welcome back. Your friend beat you here. He's in the arcade."

My eyes whip up and I see the "arcade" is a small area in the back with two nasty, beat-up games. Leaning against the wall in front of them is Cam. He is angrier than I've ever seen him when I cross the room and say with a sigh, "Why did you come?"

"You promised you wouldn't do this." His arms are crossed over his chest, and he keeps squeezing his left forearm with his right hand like he desperately needs to crush something.

"I lied." I step closer because I see one guy at the nearest table who seems to find us more interesting than the soccer game he had been watching. "Please go home. I don't want you here."

He doesn't move a muscle but his smile is so dark it's almost scary. "I am *not* letting you do this alone."

As much as I want him to go, to be safe, I can see that arguing this point isn't getting me anywhere.

"Okay." I poke him in the chest with my finger. "But if you get hurt, I'm going to kill you."

His face breaks into a twisted grin and he nods. "Ditto."

As we walk back over to Jim, my eyes do a quick sweep of the room. The soccer fans in the back, three guys sitting alone at the bar, the same guy still passed out on the table in the corner—I'm beginning to wonder if he's dead. "Is he here?"

"Not sure." Jim shrugs and begins wiping some water off the bar with a nearby towel. "Did you bring our friend Benjamin?"

Pulling out the money, I place it on the bar with my hand over it and wait for Jim to answer my question.

"Yeah, over there." He inclines his head toward a guy with a white shirt and blue tie sitting at the other end of the bar. BRADY's LOCK & KEY is embroidered in red on the pocket. He's staring at the brown liquid in his glass with slightly bloodshot eyes, but still, he's the last guy I would've picked as Brothers's friend.

"Name?" I don't take my hand off the money.

"Sean Brady."

"Thanks." I stick my hands in my pockets and move down the bar.

"Don't be a stranger." Jim doesn't even glance at us as he slips the new bill into his pocket and walks over to wipe down the tables on the opposite end of the room.

"I think we have a mutual friend," I say, as I slide into the chair beside Brady and Cam stands behind us.

"Doubt it," Brady answers. As drunk as he appears, his response is swift, his tone aware. There's also a hint of an accent to his voice, but I can't place it.

"I can make it worth your while to tell me where he's been hiding and keep our visit between us."

"Doubt that, too." He still hasn't lifted his eyes from his glass. Back and forth, he swirls the ice in the cup one way and then swirls it the opposite direction.

I turn toward Cam and he raises one eyebrow at me. When I nod, he sticks one finger inside the back of Brady's tie and yanks it with one hand while pushing between the man's shoulder blades with his other. I can tell immediately that Cam's been holding out on me in our classes. He's much stronger than I knew. Brady's eyes bulge and he sputters at the sudden lack of oxygen. I check around the bar, but the only person paying attention is Jim, and when he sees me pivot to face him he quickly focuses his attention on the tabletop in front of him.

"Are you sure you don't want to help her?" Cam's voice is low and calm. Brady's face reddens as he struggles to loosen the tie currently standing between himself and the rest of his life. Then Cam releases him. Brady coughs a few times before taking a swig of his drink.

"Okay, okay. I don't want trouble." He spins on his barstool, seeming uncomfortable at having Cam where he can't see him. "He didn't mention your bodyguard, sheesh."

His words slow down time as I meet Cam's eyes and see his teeth grind together. I close my eyelids tight before asking, "Who didn't mention?"

"Steve Brothers." He watches me carefully when I reopen my eyes, a strange expression on his face—something between fear and satisfaction.

"He knew I would come." My words are almost a whisper as the implications sink in. Brothers is so much like the Father. Too smart, too much enjoyment drawn from my fear and pain.

Cam frowns, picks up the end of Brady's tie, and pinches it between two fingers. The man jerks it free and holds up his hands, cowering behind them.

"I'm only the messenger." Brady waits for Cam to lower his hands back to his sides before reaching in his pocket and pulling out a phone. "He asked me to give you this."

Cam extends a hand, but Brady tucks the phone against his chest. "No. He said it's for her."

I try to read the intentions behind the bloodshot eyes, but the only thing I can tell for sure is that focusing on me is a struggle. "Why would I want to take that phone?"

"I don't know. You said you were looking for him. Maybe this is how you do it." He swallows and his gaze darts between us. "Brothers is nothing to me. And you can bet I won't be doing him any more favors."

I feel unsteady and unsure. Brothers keeps outmaneuvering me. Toying with me, pulling my strings like the puppet in my closet. Each move he makes twists me up further, binding me until he feels like playing again. There are so many things wrong with this, but I might have to play along for a while. Holding out my hand, I wait as Brady places the phone in my palm and releases a breath thick with the smell of alcohol.

"Now, why don't you two go away so I can enjoy my drink in peace?" Brady sags over his cup and begins swirling it back and forth without another look in our direction.

Cam and I walk in silence halfway back to the apartment. My mind is going over and over every box Brothers left, every message, trying to make any sense of it. "I know your secret." "Safety is illusion." "No more hiding." And then he builds me a torture closet and leaves me a phone. One grim fact is undeniable: he knew I had come to the bar before. He's obviously been watching even closer than I thought.

Why doesn't he corner me, kill me, take Sanda and get his revenge? I know the answer even if I wish I didn't. He wants something more from me. Something I won't give him, but I don't think he'll leave me alone until he gets it. Brothers has proven he's nothing if not persistent.

"I think you should give it to me." Cam's voice is strained.

"You weren't even supposed to be there."

"I might be able to get some information from it. See if he's made any calls on it. Stuff like that."

I flip open the phone and go to call history. Even I've spent enough time with my phone to understand the basic menu. When I tuck it in my pocket, it's like an anchor dragging me down, one more string tying me to Brothers. "Nothing. And I'm keeping the phone."

His jaw flexes and he stares hard into my eyes. "Fine. Then after I grab some extra clothes, I'm staying at your apartment indefinitely. Until that phone rings I'm not leaving your side."

I can see it's useless to fight him on this. Besides, for right now, we're probably both safer together. "Fine."

* * *

Cam ran to Jessie's in total frustration when I refused to go with him. I'd watched him jog down the street from my window, even his stride looking angry. I wish he'd stay away, stay safe, but at the same time I'm glad he's hurrying. I hate being this powerless and alone. Brothers has me cornered. My only idea to find him didn't exactly play out the way I'd hoped. I can't seem to get warm and no matter where I stand in the apartment, it seems like Brothers's phone is watching me.

I wrap up in my heating blanket in the hopes that it will stop my shivering. As I finally start to feel normal, the new phone rings and I'm cold again. All the way down through my bones. I lift it off the dresser with shaking hands. Opening it, I can't think of any greeting that I want to say, so I just listen. Slow breathing and a soft chuckle come through the line before he speaks.

"I'm glad you got my gift." The voice is so slick it almost sounds wet.

"What do you want?"

"So direct. One of the things I like most about you." He speaks each word slowly, almost lazily. It makes me want to scream. "You always get right to the point."

"Answer my question." I force in deep slow breaths.

"I want you to pay, Piper. Or is it pay *the* piper? So confusing," he says with a laugh.

My whole body tightens, but I fight to remain calm. I breathe slowly in and back out. I can't let him know how much he scares me. "Why do you call me that?"

"Because it's your name."

"I know it's my name. How do *you* know it's my name?" I wait, but the only response is silence. "Fine, but I want something, too."

"Do tell." He breathes heavily into the receiver and I'm nauseated.

"I want you to leave Sanda alone."

"Okay."

I sit down on the edge of the bed, my mind struggling to piece together whatever I'm missing. I repeat, "Okay?"

"I'll leave you both alone. *If* we get together and have a little conversation first."

"Why would I meet you?" My pitch goes up and I try to regain control.

He's silent for a moment before he says, "I like what you did with her hair."

"No." I'm on my feet. I grip the phone hard so it won't slip from my grasp. "You don't have her."

"I don't." He sounds confident. "Not yet, but I could. Or I could tell the police that you suddenly have a girl living with you. I've seen the scars and I'm a concerned citizen, you know. I wonder what they'd find when they start checking your past. I wonder if they'd let her stay with you after that."

*We have to stop him. No more hurting. No more pain.*

Closing my eyes, I sit back down on the bed in defeat. I've already taken everything from him so I'm the only one with something to lose—Sanda. My fingers itch to reach out through the phone, to hurt him, to kill him.

When he continues, his tone has lost any warmth. "Either way, you won't be there to protect her."

"Where do you want to meet?"

He gives me an address in Camden. I'm so shaken I have to repeat it three times to make sure I have the numbers right.

"Meet me now." I tuck the paper in my pocket, trying to figure out what weapons I might be able to hide somewhere on my body. Cam and Sanda aren't here. They're safe and I need them to stay that way. Whether I survive our conversation or not, I will make sure Brothers can't hurt them anymore. "I want this to be over."

"Always in such a hurry. You need to learn how to appreciate the little things. I can teach you that."

I don't respond. I don't even want to think about what he could mean. All I know is that I need to be sure that by the time Sanda gets out of school, Brothers won't be there to hide in the shadows, waiting to grab her or hurt her.

If I get my way, he'll never creep out of the shadows again.

"See you soon."

Closing the phone from Brothers, I stick it in one pocket and shove my phone in the other. I pull on a loose shirt over my tank top, grab the iron bar from under my pillow and stick it in the waistband at the back of my jeans. Rushing into the kitchen, I don't let myself slow down or even think. If I think, I know the fear will overtake me, and I can't let that happen. Not right now. I grab the smallest knife, wrap a thin washcloth around it, and tuck it in my sock.

When I reach the door, I skid to a halt. Every bolt is unlocked. Had I left them that way and not noticed? I was always so careful about it. I check around the apartment, but it's empty. I'm alone. Shaking off my confusion, I lock up and go out.

The only thing that matters now is figuring out how to survive a conversation with a madman.

# 26

I've never been to Camden and I wish I didn't have to go. I stand in the subway station hoping I can overcome my fear and climb on board when my train comes. We're underground, enclosed, and I'm supposed to climb on a train with so many strangers. What if we get stuck? Being trapped underground sounds worse than being locked in an attic. At least I could see the night sky. At least I knew there were only walls keeping me in, not walls *and* twenty-five feet of smothering earth.

My anxiety makes it hard to breathe, and for an instant I regret giving my bolt to Sanda. But the thought is like the trains going through this station, gone almost as soon as it appears. I don't need it anymore, she does. It's time to be strong without it. My hands tighten by my sides as my train pulls to a stop. The doors open. It waits for me. I close my eyes and try to picture my life here with Brothers gone, a future where Sanda and Cam are safe, a future without fear. When I open my eyes, my nerves have settled and I climb on the train. I'm relieved to see it isn't too full or too empty, and shortly after we leave the station the train moves aboveground as we cross the Delaware River. Coming out into the daylight helps me breathe easier.

When I reach the address he gave me, I stand in stunned silence. This building is worse than Brothers's old apartment. If that is the venom in my new life, this is the rotting, festering bite. The building is like those surrounding it: old and smelling of garbage and decay. Its once white bricks are yellowing like a smoker's teeth. Littered papers cover the flower bed that, like the building, has long been void of life.

Even in the sunlight, I'm freezing cold from a chill that sinks deeper than the heat of the sun can touch. I hurry past the boarded windows and up the stairs into the entrance before I get a chance to change my mind. In the lobby, a directory lists office numbers and old tenants who have moved on. With one glance at it, my steps slow, and then stop. There are way more X's on the directory than there should be. He's removed every vowel and replaced each with an uppercase X. The way they are placed, and the image in my head of the Piper-Puppet, makes my skin crawl. It's like dozens of dead eyes are staring out at me from within the wall. It's a message to tell me he's here.

He's waiting.

I walk through the lobby and turn down the second hall on the left. No matter how careful I am, each footstep echoes around me, announcing my presence. The world seems to slow as I inch down the hall. My mind searches for another answer even though I know this is my only chance to end this. To face him alone . . . and win. It's the only way to end this without hurting someone I care about.

At the end, I reach a door labeled STORAGE, exactly as he'd said. This is the place.

As I raise my fingers to try the knob, I hear muffled voices inside. Brothers isn't alone. I drop my hand and back up a step. Even with everything Cam has taught me, how can I possibly take on more than one person?

Every hair on my body is standing on end, like they're smarter than me, like they know better and are trying to escape what is coming. I can't tell if it's fear or knowing I'm so close to Brothers. Either way, something bothers me. I wish I could run. No part of me wants to be here doing this. But I have no other option. So far, Brothers has only been trying to scare me into doing what he wants, but he'll tire of that sooner or later, and I will not let him decide to take Sanda back as the next step in his game.

The voices inside stop, and I wish I could've made out any words. I study the door. There are a few bolt locks, each locking from the outside. My heart races, pounding hard against the wall of my chest.

This door isn't designed to keep people out. It's meant to keep someone in. A glimmer of hope flickers in my mind.

*It's an attic for him. Lock him in forever.*

My mind whirls through the implications. This may not solve anything. It's a storage room, but there could still be a window. Even more important, he's not alone. Can I leave someone—*anyone*—trapped in a room with Brothers until they kill each other or die of dehydration? What if it's another child?

I sigh and lean my forehead against the wall. It would be so easy, but still I can't do it for so many reasons. I can't leave anything to chance. I have to know for sure. This time, I will make certain he can't ever come after us again.

I draw in a silent breath and check out the doorknob. Everything is unlocked. If I can catch them by surprise, that might be my best chance.

Pulling the iron bar out of the back of my jeans, I put my other hand on the knob. With three quick breaths I turn it, throw my weight against the door, and crash into the room.

The lighting was already dim, but as soon as I enter, a dark figure scrambles to one side and flips the light off. The lack of windows makes it pitch-black inside, like a crypt. The darkness is reaching out, striving to draw me in. The room is much bigger than I expected. I can't make out the back wall from where I'm standing. Aside from the metal racks stacked with overflowing storage boxes directly inside the door, I can't see anything. I do the only thing I can, kick the door closed, duck behind the storage rack, and wait for Brothers to turn the light back on.

The darkness is silent, but also very loud. I hear rapid breathing that is close—too close. Water drips through pipes in the wall behind me. It falls erratically, each unexpected drop setting me on edge. I slide up against the wall, trying to protect myself the best I can in the utter blackness. The wall is covered with grime beneath my fingertips, but I do my best to ignore it. Sam whimpers in my head.

*This is bad. We shouldn't have come.*

"This really isn't what I had in mind." Brothers's voice comes from a few feet to my right and I spin toward it. Bending my knees,

I inch forward, lifting the bar over my head again. One more word, one loud breath, and I will have him. My heartbeat pounds in my ears. I'm primed and ready to attack. Then I hear a *click* and duck back behind the rack as the darkness is driven away.

Blinking in the light of the single dim bulb that sways overhead, I tighten my fingers around the cold metal bar. I wait for any words or noise, but I hear nothing. Peeking out between two boxes, I see Brothers's dirty-brown eyes staring straight at me. I can see the burn scars on his neck even from here.

"You should drop that before somebody gets hurt."

"That's kind of the idea," I growl, and try to decide the best way to get around the metal rack between us.

"It won't be me"—Brothers gives me a dark smile and it makes me squirm—"or you." He raises his wrist and I see the black metal barrel of a gun. My arms tremble so hard I almost drop the bar. I hate guns.

But it's not pointed at me. It's pointed at the wall opposite us. I take a step back, my breath catching in my throat as I peer around the other end of the rack. I'm overcome with gratitude that I'd decided not to lock the door and walk away. Cam is sitting against the far wall. A dirty cloth has been stuffed in his mouth. His wrists are red and raw from struggling against the ropes that bind them. His hazel eyes are wide as he stares at me and waits.

Sliding out from behind the rack, I step between Cam and Brothers. The monster moves his eyes and gun to me but doesn't speak. His free hand hangs at his side, tightening into a fist and then relaxing and tightening again. I see the corner of a bandage poking out below the cuff of his sleeve. He definitely didn't escape

237

the fire unscathed. One vein at his temple is pulsing and his cheeks are flushed. He seems upset and frustrated. Not confident and in control like he'd sounded on the phone.

I'm not sure what to expect. His anger confuses me. My movements are sure, the hand holding the bar steady, but my voice wobbles when I speak. "Did you bring him here?"

Brothers glares at me like I've just said the stupidest words ever uttered. "No. I wanted you, not him."

Behind me, I hear Cam's quick breaths matching my own and the realization hits me. My unlocked apartment door—he must've come back and overheard the phone call. A small groan escapes my lips. "You're impossible."

Cam frowns, but I guess it's hard to argue with a gag in your mouth. I wish more than anything that this time he'd stayed out of my business. He'd probably be worried, but he'd be at home. He would be safe.

I chew on my bottom lip. It doesn't matter, he's here now. Watching out for me got him into this. I should've fought him harder. I should've refused his help at the library and refused to talk to Brady with him there, something or anything. If he'd never met me, he'd be hanging out with Lily or his aunt at the studio. I know better. It's dangerous to let people get close to me.

They always die.

"Why don't we let him go, then?" I lower my iron bar so it dangles at my side. It won't protect me against a gun anyway. "And we can have the conversation you wanted."

"He wasn't supposed to be here." Brothers's voice is louder than before. He keeps his gun pointed in our general direction and starts pacing back and forth along the opposite wall. I notice a limp that definitely wasn't there before the fire. His eyes shift between us, wild and angry. This man is nothing like the Father. Cold, calculating, and cruel, the Father never lost control or acted without knowing the full plan and every contingency. When Nana called the police, it certainly hadn't been expected, but he'd been ready for it. Nana was drugged beyond recognition in front of us, then Sam and I were bound, gagged, and tossed in the attic. The Father was back downstairs, relaxing and watching some muffled TV show that I could hear through the vents before the cops even pulled in the driveway. He was always too smart, too calm—too inescapable.

With Brothers, things haven't gone as planned and he doesn't know how to handle it. He's smart when he gets to move everyone around like pieces on a chessboard, but when the pieces don't play by his rules, he loses control and he doesn't know how to recover. He's panicking. He's not logical, he's unstable.

And in some ways, he's even more dangerous.

He limps back and forth, back and forth, like some sort of caged animal. Every time he takes a step, the gun bounces in his hand and I hear a clicking sound. I'm afraid it might go off.

*Click—click—click—click—*

My mind scrambles to find a way to focus his energy, to calm him down. "Okay, let's pretend he isn't here. What did you want to talk about?"

Brothers stops and turns back to face me. His eyes clear a bit and he wipes the palm of his free hand against his leg. "I wanted to show you."

"Show me what?" I keep my face blank, knowing he needs to feel in control again or none of us will get out of here alive.

"It's hard to be alone. And you took the girl." He's speaking to me like I should understand. Waves of ice and heat take turns slamming through my body as he continues. "Now I need a replacement, and you—you have scars."

I don't answer, but I nod and wait for him to continue.

"I need it. You understand. And no one should judge me. They're small and I'm so large. I do things they can't imagine." His eyes are wide and he keeps bobbing his head up and down, like he is willing me to agree with him. "I've heard of people like you—girls who like it. Some have told me before and I understand. We have different hungers and different needs, but it isn't wrong. Who the hell gets to decide what is wrong?"

*Don't listen to him, Piper. He doesn't know you.*

"You think I-I choose this?" I ask. My voice wavers as I peek down at one of the scars on my arm.

"I know you do. You must." Brothers looks satisfied and superior . . . almost *certain*. "The ones who don't like it, they die so fast."

My head echoes with the words of the Father saying the same thing, again and again. *You won't give up. That's how I know you must like it. I can see it in your eyes.* His blue eyes pierce my spirit as he ties me down and grabs his favorite blade. The image burns against the backs of my eyes like someone is branding it there for eternity. No matter whether he is dead or in prison, he will always be there in my head—haunting me, taunting me. He always said the part of me that was like him was what kept me strong, what kept me alive. Of the various ways he tortured me, it was those words that sliced the deepest.

I'd rather die than be like him—but is it that madness that kept me alive?

"No no no," I hear my voice moan over and over without my consent. Wrapping my arms around my waist, I drop the bar and curl in on myself as I battle away the memories, the nightmares that ricochet around my world. Cam taps his foot against my shoe, trying to get my attention. But I am stone, no longer capable of motion. Deep down inside, where it's so dark I don't dare to look— could that be what I hide? That in some ways I share their madness? I scoot back toward the corner with a firm shake of my head. The need to escape from his words and these thoughts overpowers me. "No, you're wrong. I don't like it."

His grin fades. "Yes, you do. You must not realize how much. You don't let yourself. I will show you," he continues, his voice turning desperate as he steps closer, towering over me. "After we get rid of him."

"No!" I shout, and force my body to obey as I climb slowly to my feet. I hear that familiar humming and I don't know if it's coming from Sam or me.

Brothers's face tightens and he speaks through gritted teeth. "Untie him."

I blink at him in confusion, dreading Brothers's intentions. His words have shattered me inside in a way I haven't felt for a long time. Even as broken as I feel, I recognize that no matter what, our chances of surviving this are better with Cam free. Crouching, I do as ordered without a word.

"You okay?" Cam asks as he rubs his wrists together. His eyes speak to me, begging me to cling to the truth I *know*, but I can barely see him through the haze of my own fear for his life—and mine.

"No." My voice is low, lost amid the dreadful memories in my head.

He bends his knees, his eyes searching mine, and I see my own fear reflected there. "Me neither."

His eyes are so kind. He's so strong. My skin prickles with fire and ice. I don't know what Brothers wants now and I don't care. I just have to find a way to get Cam out of here, but my mind is a soup of confusion and denial. I can't focus enough to find a way around the gun barrel pointed straight at my chest.

"I untied him and we had a conversation," I say. Brothers is pacing again and I'm not sure he even hears me speak. "Are we done?"

*Click—click—click—click—*

Brothers skids to a stop in front of one of the shelves and mutters under his breath. It's like he's forgotten we're here, but when Cam shifts his weight, the gun is pointing straight at him before I can blink. The dark smile playing around the corners of Brothers's mouth fills me with dread. He reaches in the box closest to him and draws out a dusty old mason jar. A few spiderwebs remain inside, but other than that it looks empty.

He lifts it toward us and his lips split into a full grin. "We'll see which role you play, but one of you will have to pay."

"Rhymes now?" He has clearly developed a new plan and the panic is gone, but for some reason I feel dread instead of relief. Swallowing hard, I meet Cam's gaze before speaking again. "What do you mean?"

242

"You refuse to see yourself clearly, so I guess I have to prove it to you." He sounds like he's barely holding back laughter, and my stomach rolls as understanding dawns. I've rarely wanted to hurt someone this bad in my life—and that's really saying something. "I can see the knife sticking out of your sock. Now use it. Fill it to the top."

"Sick psychopath," Cam mutters under his breath.

"I'm going to let you choose. You cut him"—Brothers glances from me to Cam—"or he cuts you."

# 27

Brothers's laughter echoes through the room as Cam and I stare at each other.

My voice comes out low and foreign. "Not going to happen."

"If you want out, if you want me to leave you alone like you say, this is the first step to make it happen." All hint of humor is gone now. His voice is loud in the cold room, and my head vibrates with his words as he turns the gun to Cam, then back to me. "Make her bleed or I will."

I press my fingers against my forehead. There has to be an answer. There's always an escape somehow. I've gotten out of worse situations than this—well, worse is debatable, but similar.

My brain whirls through the possibilities. Cam blinks at the gun, his skin paling. I'm more likely to survive being cut than being shot. I try to think it through.

"And no little slices." Brothers's voice is lilting, almost singsong. He places the mason jar on the floor and rolls it into my foot. A tiny spider skitters out across the floor. "Fill the jar."

"This guy is seriously twisted," Cam whispers to me. His eyes are still glued to the barrel of the gun in Brothers's hand.

"What do you know about the human body?" I grab Cam's chin in my hand and turn his face until his eyes finally come to rest on mine. "Focus. We need to get out of here."

"Are you seriously considering it?" He frowns. "You can't believe he'll actually live up to his part of the bargain."

"I don't know. Maybe, maybe not, but I'm not seeing any other way out that doesn't include one or both of us getting shot. Are you?" No windows, no large vents, no other doors. The only way out is through Brothers and his gun. "I have to do something."

*Nowhere to hide. Always nowhere to hide.*

"Not helping, Sam," I mutter, and press both fists against my temples.

"Sam?" Cam speaks his name and I clamp my jaw shut. Now is really not the time.

I shake my head. "Nothing."

We have to fill it with blood to get out. The jar seems bigger every second. Can a person lose that much blood without dying? Brothers watches us silently. He has regained control and it shows. His hands are steady, his gun level . . . he waits.

"If we each filled it halfway, would we still have enough blood to stay alive?"

Cam nods. "Yes, it's not that much if we split it."

"No!" Brothers bellows, and then continues more quietly. "One of you only."

I glare at him. "You're asking us to kill each other."

"Not necessarily." He shrugs, seeming bored by my statement. "Depends how fast you bleed, how deep you cut. Too shallow and it loses its fun, too deep and it's over too quick. You have to learn how to make it last."

I freeze and stare at the floor between my feet. There really is no other option and I know it. Still, my brain and my body refuse to respond. All I can see is blood, so much blood—my world is stained red. That jar is so big—too much for only one of us.

"Charlotte."

Always blood. I hate it.

"Piper." Cam grabs my arm and squeezes gently until I look up.

"He's a monster. People are monsters," I say, as I blink and blink, but my eyes won't focus on him.

"Not everyone . . . I promise. It's okay. One of us can do it and survive, *if* the other one calls an ambulance as soon as we're out."

"Ticktock, Piper. I don't have all day. Are you going to cut your boyfriend, wait for him to cut you, or should I shoot you both for entertainment?"

"You said you're good with first aid . . ." I remind Cam of his claims from when my side was bleeding at his studio. My hands are damp with just the thought of what I'm about to do. "I hope that was the truth."

A thousand tiny bolts of electric fear go from my spine to every finger as I reach down, pull the knife out of my sock, and slip it out of the washcloth. I raise it to my arm and take a breath. It's just one more cut, like hundreds before it. Just one more slice, just one more scar. I can do this. I *will* do this—for Cam. Before I can press it against my skin, Cam has his hands clamped around both of my wrists, holding them apart.

His hazel eyes are panicked and desperate. "Stop! What are you doing?"

"I'm giving him what he wants." I push against his grip, but he's too strong for me. "We need to get out of here."

Cam bends his knees until his eyes are at my level and waits until I stop struggling. His expression changes abruptly, becoming grim and decided. It confuses me. "You're sure this is our only option?"

The hopelessness bubbling up inside spills out in my voice, and it cracks. "I won't watch him shoot you."

"Okay, but be quick." Cam twists my hands in his and before I realize what he's doing it's too late. "I won't have much time."

"No! Stop, Cam!" Holding my wrist so tight it hurts, he takes my hand with the blade and presses it down hard—too hard—against his opposite forearm. The blood comes immediately. He trembles a little before releasing me and holding his hand over the jar.

"Why did you do that? This is my fault." I reach out for the jar and his arm, wanting to make it stop, to make him take it back. But I can't. I pull my hands back in and squeeze them across my stomach. The now-bloody knife clatters to the floor, forgotten. "Why would you do that?"

"No!" Brothers bellows and the wild rage is back in his eyes more than ever. He steps closer, shaking his gun at me as I step in front of Cam. "That isn't what I said. Why can't you do as I say? You ruined everything!"

"Shut up! We did what you asked!" I yell at him, and turn back to Cam. I can't fix this. It's wrong. The only thing I can think about is that the knife was in *my* hand when it cut him—mine. I can't shake the image. There is so much blood in the jar already. The cut is too deep, much too deep.

"Be logical. It makes the most sense. It could never be you. I'm much bigger so I can lose more blood than you and be okay." Cam leans against the wall, and when I rush over he presses his forehead against mine. "And he's wrong about you. You *hate* everything about what was done to you. And I knew you'd never cut me."

The jar is filling so quickly it makes me dizzy. So much blood. How can he lose that much blood? I hold his elbow with one hand. "I think you should sit down."

"G-good plan." He slides down the wall until he's in a sitting position. I kneel beside him. Already, his skin is paler. It terrifies me. Brothers is pacing and muttering again, but I don't care. I'm too scared to take my eyes off Cam. What if when I look back, he's gone?

"You need to stay safe, you and Sanda." Cam's words slur a little and I'm submerged in a sea of dread.

"We will. I'll keep you both safe." I hesitate, then take a deep breath and intertwine my fingers with those of his uninjured hand. The warmth in them helps clear the haze of panic in my brain. I ignore the sound of Brothers's gun clicking as he continues to pace by the door.

"A girl I knew, she died." Cam's eyes meet mine, and he appears clear for a moment. I wonder if he's talking about Lily's little sister. "You can't. Promise me you won't."

"I'm not the one bleeding. It's going to be okay. Just hang on." His breathing sounds different, more ragged. My brain strives to focus and think of a way out. Every idea is tarnished by blood.

Memories of my brother plague me. His body couldn't recover. He hadn't survived it. Can Cam?

I shudder and focus on hard logic. I can't lose touch with reality right now. The facts comfort me as I remind myself of the differences between them. Cam is healthy and strong. Sam's body was never as strong as Cam's. There is still a chance. "Does it hurt?"

"At first, not anymore."

Another flash of my past fills my mind, and I know the pain going away isn't a good thing. One time the Father went too far with a knife. There was no pain toward the end, but I also didn't wake up for three days.

I glance over at the jar. It's not quite full but I don't know how much more of this he can take. "That's enough."

Pulling my left arm into my shirt, I rip the red sleeve above the elbow. Then I take the bottom few inches of Cam's shirt and yank on it until it rips. I use one pad to absorb and stanch the bleeding, the longer piece to hold it tight, slow down the blood, and keep the bandage in place. Not as good as a tourniquet, but it will slow the bleeding and there is less of a chance he will lose his arm.

He winces, but then releases a deep, shaky breath. "Thank you."

I shake my head, my entire body one huge ball of dread, confusion, and fear. "Do *not* thank me for this."

First aid saves the day again . . . I hope.

I turn back to Brothers. "You need to let us out *now*. I have to get him to a hospital."

"No." He stops pacing, backs up, and throws his arm out, knocking one of the metal racks against the wall with a *clang* that echoes endlessly around us. His eyes don't focus on me when he turns and yells, "You'll never know. With him you'll never learn."

I flinch away. Even with the Parents, I'd never seen such madness.

His wild eyes settle on mine and he shakes his head, his voice lowering to a whimper. "You keep disappointing me."

"Please, he can't—" Finishing the sentence is impossible. I can't say the word out loud. It's silent for too long before Brothers responds, and I want to rip my hair out or hit someone. I can't sit here and watch Cam die. Already the blood is seeping through the bandage. It won't hold for long.

"If you want another chance, you have to earn it. I've tried to help you enough." Brothers backs toward the door. "Or you can both rot in here. It's your choice."

"No!" I get to my feet and run toward him as he puts his hand on the knob, but I'm brought up short by the cold metal of his gun pressed against my forehead.

"You have so much potential." He speaks softly, his mouth not far from my ear. "Don't disappoint me again."

A hunger rises from a dark place inside me as I rage in silence, kept at bay only by the slender tube of black metal. It's more than a want, more than a need. The only way to satiate it is to bring Brothers pain, to knock his gun out of his hand and squeeze the life out of his throat. Nothing could feel as good right now as the satisfying *thud* of slamming a bat into Brothers's head again and again. I must hurt him the way it hurts me every time I look at Cam. Every hope, every dream he's ever had must be demolished in my wake—exactly like he's doing to me.

"Please, Piper, don't." Cam's voice welds my feet to the floor. It keeps me from acting, from doing something that would kill me and almost certainly him as well.

Brothers slips out the door and I hear the locks on the other side click into place with the finality of a stone over a tomb.

# 28

"Brothers, wait!" I pound on the door with both fists. It's made of solid wood, sturdy, not rotting like half the wood in this building. Without a key, we're never getting through it. My mind scrambles over anything to make him return and release us. But already it's too late. His footsteps are gone and I hear nothing but silence.

*It's just another attic, Piper. Another prison.*

My mind sorts through any other way out, but there are no windows. I run my hand down the side of the door, dusting off some dirt. Under the grime, the wood is brand-new. Even the knob shines under the swaying light.

A block of ice settles in my chest where my heart used to be. He'd planned for the possibility that he might be locking me in. I walked right into his trap and I brought Cam with me.

Pacing the room, I examine everything and search for any escape. The metal storage racks tower over my head. I could climb them, but the ceiling is solid. It would get me nowhere. The vents are too small for even me to fit through, let alone Cam. No way out but the door.

Reaching in my pocket, I withdraw my phone, but when I open it there is only a black X where the signal bars should be. I check the phone Brothers gave me as well—nothing.

"Do you have your phone?" Keeping my voice low and level is so hard I'm afraid I might break. Cam fumbles in his pocket and the phone falls to the floor. I grab it, but he doesn't have a signal either.

"He must be using a jammer or the walls are thicker than they seem." Wincing, Cam leans his head back and closes his eyes. His normally olive skin has turned almost transparent. The cloth on his arm is soaked through and starting to drip circles of red on the floor beside him. Like the rose petals—another present from Brothers.

I can't breathe right. My own lungs match each of his shallow gasps. I yearn to see the hazel of his eyes, to see his skin return to the healthy warm color I'm used to.

But it won't, not now, probably never again.

His life is fading away before me and I'm powerless to stop it . . . like Nana, like Sam. Like Sam—he looks more and more like my dead little brother every moment. Like Sam with his paper-white skin and the wound and all the blood. For a moment I can't remember whether I'm in the storage room or standing under Sam's tree. The peeling linoleum beneath my feet becomes dirt and I can smell tobacco on the Father's breath as he tells me to "bury the Boy." I can't breathe and I can't think and I want everything to stop. Before Cam is gone like my brother, before I'm alone again.

"No. No more." I run to the door and throw myself against it. Pound on it with both fists and scream until my throat is raw. "Please, anyone! Help! Please, let us out!" I'll do anything—anything, but there is no response. Not a sound from the other side of the door, or the streets, or the city. The world around us holds its breath and watches me again lose someone I care about. Like always, no one is here to save us. No one but me, and this time I have no answers.

"Piper?" Cam's voice is so weak I almost miss it. I come back to his side and wrap his hand in both of mine. "Stay with me."

"Why did you do this? Why did you even come?" My voice cracks as I lift his hand up to my face, pressing it tight against my cheek. The same touch I used to fear and avoid, I now yearn for. I want to take all the warmth from my body and pour it into his, to pour my life into his. He could do so much more with it than I have.

"For you. Haven't you figured that out yet?" His eyes open and land on mine, his lips curving into a weak shadow of the smile I long to see. "I love you, all of you—Charlotte and Piper."

I close my eyes and clasp his hand tighter. Tears fall down my cheeks and across his fingers. No one has ever said they love me, not Sam or Nana. Of course, Sam and I did love each other but we never spoke the words. It was never something we thought to do. Maybe Nana didn't feel those words or simply wasn't the kind to say them. Each word she gave us was stolen and secret.

Yet here we are, in this room, under these circumstances, and this guy who drives me crazy as often as he makes me laugh has said those words. He loves me. Cam loves all of me. With that simple understanding, everything I used to keep him at a distance comes tumbling down. The pieces bury me in dreams of what could have been if I hadn't been so stubborn, if I'd seen what we could be sooner.

I lower his hand into my lap, wrapping my fingers around his and holding tight to the only thing that can make me forget about Brothers and my past. Forget about everything that threatens to shred the ship of my life and drown me in the depths of a bottomless sea.

Whether I've wanted him to or not, he's always anchored me and calmed the storm. And now I'm losing him, too. "It should've been me. It should be me."

"No," Cam says, as firm as he can. "You are the only one who can stop him. We both know that. Not me."

When I release his hand, it falls limply to his lap and my heart drops with it. I lean forward, fear and desperation fighting through every inch of my body. Tentatively, I press my lips against his nose, his cheeks, his forehead. The warmth that is already fleeing from his fingers still remains in his face and I need to feel it—to know I haven't lost him yet.

"I'm so sorry, Cam. This is my fault." Being able to say the words is good, like a burden is lifted. I never got to say them to Sam. I never had a chance to save him. My face is wet with tears for everyone I've lost, for the life that has never really been mine.

"Never say that again. Promise me." Cam raises his uninjured hand and brushes his fingertips across my cheek and neck. When I don't respond, he enfolds my hand in his, and I'm stunned by how cold his fingers are. How much I wish it were me instead of him. Suddenly his hand is not enough. I need more of him. Tugging my hand free of his, I see pain flicker in his eyes before I ease it by stretching both my arms around his neck and pulling him tight against me. I bury my face in his chest, cradling his heartbeat against my head like somehow I can keep it going if I hold him close enough.

He kisses my cheek and nose, burying his face in my hair. I drag him ever closer. Cam moves his lips to mine and kisses me, slow and soft. My breath catches in my throat. I'd never expected it to be so good, so right. With one kiss he heals damaged pieces of me no one else has been able to reach. I kiss him back. He returns my panicked, frantic kisses with slow, sweet ones, calming my lips and my soul with his. I don't know what I'm doing, but it doesn't matter. Neither of us cares. His lips are the only thing about him that remain warm with life and I want to hold on to that life. As if keeping them warm will make him okay. I'm flooded with instant regret for every time I've been with him and not wrapped my arms around him or held his hand in mine. It all seems like a tragic waste now.

He leans back against the wall and his lips curve up into a sly grin. "I'm sorry."

I rest against his shoulder and gaze up at him. "For what?"

"For not doing that sooner." He winks at me before his eyes flutter closed and he goes still.

Visions of burying Sam's cold body swamp me, only now it is Cam that I see cold and pale in the shallow grave. Now it's Cam's body that I must cover with dirt even as I mourn him with every piece of me. Knowing I'll never see his smile again, never hear his laugh or feel the warmth from his hand enfolding mine. I choke back a sob and battle the images away.

"No, no. Cam?" I squeeze his hand, but he only moans in response. He's going to leave me like everyone else. Like Nana and

Sam. My eyes fill with tears again and I kiss his lips, but they're so cold already they only fill me with fear. Suddenly, I can't breathe. I don't want him to go, not yet. We didn't have enough time.

*Then don't let him go.*

How? I don't have an answer. There is no way out.

*Piper never gives up.*

As long as Cam's still breathing, I have to keep trying. I will not stop. Ripping off another piece of his shirt, I tie a tourniquet around his upper arm. Losing a limb isn't a concern anymore. If I don't find a way out soon, he'll lose much more than that. I drag myself to my feet and pace the room. There has to be something. With one shaking hand, I tug my phone out of my pocket. There is still no signal, but I keep pacing. Maybe there's a spot I missed, maybe one minuscule spot where I can get a signal. If I don't focus on trying to find it, I'll start screaming. That won't help Cam. How can I help him? Back and forth, diagonally across the room, and corner to corner—I pace in silence. With every breath, he sounds weaker and the overwhelming dread piles on, burying me, shovelful upon shovelful.

Tossing the phone onto the floor, I drag down box after box from the racks. I dump them into a massive pile in the corner. Nothing seems useful. Most are empty or have cleaning supplies in them. I keep telling myself to keep searching. If I give up, I'll just sit and watch Cam die.

I cannot do that. I will not do that.

There has to be something, anything, that can help him. When I bend to pick up another box, I see it. Tucked beneath the nearest rack is a large toolbox.

Throwing myself to the floor, I pull it out, and my fingers fumble with the latch. The top shelf contains screws, nails, washers, and bolts. I lift the shelf, shoving aside screwdrivers and a hammer. In the darkness below, I see hope in my own reflection. The silvery distorted image of my own face on the head of a shining ax. Yanking it out of its hiding place, I run to the door, haul back and slam it into the wood with all my strength. At first nothing happens. I see Cam's still form in the corner of my vision and keep swinging. I have to. Then the door splinters away, piece by piece, as I keep swinging. Minutes drag like hours, my arms go numb, but finally I've done it. I've cut a hole big enough to drag Cam through.

He's still leaning against the wall, still breathing, his eyes closed even with all the noise I'm making. Is it safe to move him? Maybe not yet. I run out into the hall and finally get a signal at the opposite end of the building. Thinking fast, I dial 911 and give her the nearest cross-street address before the girl even gets out her first word.

I hear her fingers clicking on a keyboard. "And what is your emergency?"

"There is a guy here. His arm is cut and he's lost a lot of blood. Please, we need an ambulance."

"Is he alert and able to speak?"

"No. Please hurry."

"I'm sending help now. Stay on the li—" I close the phone and check my watch. Sanda will be out of school in ten minutes. There is only one person I trust to get her. I don't hesitate to dial the number and she answers on the first ring.

"Hello?"

"Janice, I need your help."

"Charlotte?" Her voice is a blend of concern and surprise, but I don't have time for questions.

"Can you please pick up Sanda when you get Rachel from school? I've had some trouble, and with only ten minutes until school gets out I can't possibly get there in time."

"Of course. It's no problem." There is a slight pause on the line and then she asks, "Are you all right?"

My throat tightens with emotion and tears roll down my cheeks. I really can't answer that question, not right now. "Thank you, Janice." I take a deep breath. "I'll meet you at the apartment as soon as I can."

It's silent for a moment. "Okay. Be safe."

I close the phone and run back down the hall to Cam. He lies so still, I'm almost afraid to move closer. A dozen images of Sam flood my senses, and I fight to keep myself upright. This isn't him. He isn't dead, not yet.

I see Cam's chest struggle to rise with another breath and I rush to his side. Easing him down onto his back, I grab the shoulders of his shirt and slide him as gently as possible toward the doorway. Kicking the last remaining pieces of wood out of the way, I drag him into the hall and toward the front doors. By the time we get there, I hear the ambulance coming.

"What are you doing?" Cam's voice is barely a whisper.

I reach down and touch his hair. "It's okay. I got us out and help is coming."

"You should go." His eyes refuse to stay open.

"No. I can't leave you."

"Go get Sanda. Make sure she's safe." He presses his head against my hand. "Don't let him get her again."

The ambulance stops in front of the building and I rush out onto the steps to flag them down. Two paramedics with the names MARK and ALVIN stitched on their uniforms hurry in with a stretcher.

"What happened?" Mark waits for me to answer.

Cam groans as they move him and I twist my fingers together trying to find the right response. "He cut himself. I t-tried to tie it off."

Alvin examines my makeshift bandage and nods. "If he survives it will be because of you."

All I can think is if he dies it will be because of me, too.

"He cut himself? What's his name?" Alvin turns to me with a hint of suspicion.

Before I can answer, Cam speaks, and both paramedics immediately lean over him to listen. "I don't know her. She found me. I'm Cam. Take me to Penn Hospital, please."

He gave me an out. I know what he's thinking. He wants me to run.

"Thank you for your help then, young lady. You did the right thing by calling." Alvin's suspicion is gone, but I can't meet his eyes. A police car parks behind the ambulance. "The officer will be right over to get your statement."

The cop walks past the ambulance and asks the paramedics something as they wheel the stretcher along the sidewalk. My muscles twitch with the urge to run. Cam is right: the last thing I need right now is a nice long chat with the police.

I whisper under my breath, "Please be okay." Then I sprint to hide behind the corner of the building before the officer finishes talking to the paramedics. Crouching in the shadows between buildings, I rip the back off both phones, remove the sim cards, break them in half like Cam taught me, and throw everything over the fence.

"Where did she go?" Alvin's voice sounds more confused than anything else.

"I don't know, but he's lost consciousness. We need to get him to the hospital right away if he's going to have any chance," Mark responds, before slamming the doors closed. With sirens blaring, they drive away.

I wait until I hear the officer enter the building looking for me before I walk out from my hiding spot. Tugging off the remnants of my torn shirt, I'm left shivering in the sunlight in only the tank top I was wearing beneath. I throw the bloodstained tatters in a Dumpster a block away.

As I hail a cab just past the first corner, I take one last glance at the front of the building where Brothers tried to make us kill each other. My hands are raw and splintered from swinging the ax. My soul is raw from pain. All I want is to hurt Brothers, make him stop the pain forever.

And all I feel is alone.

# 29

Numb fear fills every shadow, every doorway, every street around me as my taxi drops me off a block from home. My mind is tied to Cam at the hospital. He has to be okay—he has to be okay. I'll get Sanda and we'll go to the hospital to see him. Then, I will find a place for Sanda to be safe and turn myself in to the police. I will give up the future I'd hoped for to make sure the people I care about don't get hurt anymore. Sanda has to be better off with an unknown family than running from a psychopath, even if running meant she could stay at my side. I will tell the police about everything. About the Parents and Brothers. I am willing to be punished for what I've done, as long as Brothers gets locked away, too.

It's the only way and it is worth it.

Unable to wait any longer, I stop at an ancient-looking pay phone to call the hospital. It takes me a minute to figure it out and I curse loudly when I realize the bill reader is broken and it only takes coins—coins that I don't know how to count and refuse to carry. A guy plays his guitar on a nearby corner. I can see coins in his open case glinting in the sunlight. I hurry over.

"I need your help."

He barely looks up. "I—uh—try to stay out of other . . ."

I tug a twenty out of my pocket. "I'll give you this if you give me the right amount of change to make a call on that pay phone."

His gaze goes from the twenty to my face and back again before he reaches down and gathers a few coins from the case. I can hear him muttering under his breath, but I don't even care enough to try to make out his words. I'm watching the coins. These coins that could help me find out if Cam is still breathing.

I throw the twenty down as soon as he hands me the change, and I run back to the phone. I dial the number labeled "Information" on a tattered directory sticker and they connect me to the hospital. It only takes a moment to get directed to the emergency room.

"ER nurse, how can I help you?" She sounds bored.

"I'm trying to find out about a patient," I tell her.

"Are you a relative?"

"No, he's a friend, but—"

She doesn't let me finish. "Sorry, we don't give out information unless you're a family member. Please contact his family and they'll be able to update you."

"Oh, okay," I say, frustrated, but there is no point in arguing with her. I pull the phone away from my face, and my hand trembles as I place it back on the cradle. I can't breathe right until I know if Cam is okay. I can feel the guy with the guitar watching me as I walk to the corner and hurry out of sight.

I know something is wrong from the moment I turn onto our street. Janice is pacing in front of our building and Rachel sits on

263

the stairs, staring across at the kids in the park. I can't see Sanda anywhere.

My dread is buried by blinding fear, as I realize that deep down I knew he might get to her first.

When Janice sees me sprinting down the street toward her, she jogs out to meet me.

"Where is she?" I ask.

"She wasn't there," Janice says. Her hair is even fuzzier than normal, like she's been tugging on it. Her hands are clamped together when I approach, like they're frozen in prayer. "I tried to call you, but I kept getting your voice mail. I considered calling the police, but you said they'd take her away and . . . and I didn't know what to do."

My phone. I hadn't thought about Janice trying to call me when I'd ripped it apart. "It's okay. Tell me what you know."

Rachel stares up at me, her eyes wide and full of tears. "We were waiting by the sidewalk for you and Grams and it was my turn for the game. I counted and my eyes were closed and then she was gone. She disappeared."

"It's okay, Rachel. I'll find her. I promise." I pat Rachel on the shoulder as Janice hugs her. My mind is still in shock over Cam. It skips past fear and straight into solution mode. It flies through all the details, trying to figure out where Brothers would've taken her.

I meet Janice's worried eyes. "You and Rachel go inside. I'll let you know if I need help."

"Be careful." She chokes on emotion and nods before putting on a brave smile for her granddaughter and heading inside.

Lily rounds the corner and I can see the dark lines of mascara-tinted tears on her cheeks from here. Her black jacket only hangs over one shoulder and the rest falls behind her like a dark tail. I've never seen her so disheveled. "I've been calling. You got rid of your phone?"

"Yes. What's wrong?"

"Have you seen Cam? I can't find him anywhere and . . ." Her eyes are wild with worry.

My heart aches inside when I say the words. "He got hurt, Lily. He's at Penn Hospital."

"No." Her whisper is horrified. "It can't be true."

"What can't? What's going on?"

"I didn't know. I believed it was you, I swear. I didn't know." Lily doubles over onto the apartment stairs, her body shaking with sobs. Grabbing her elbow tighter than necessary, I jerk it until she raises her face.

"What are you talking about? You believed what was me?"

"He has her, doesn't he?"

A chill runs down my spine, but I make myself ask the question to which I'm afraid I already know the answer. "Who?"

"Steve."

I blink and whisper, "Steve who?"

My whole body waits for her to answer. My heart is not beating, my lungs are not working, even my brain is caught in a thoughtless void while I wait for her to utter the name I'm dreading.

"Steve Brothers."

Everything feels like it's in slow motion. He's always ahead of me, five steps—ten even. Cam is the only one who has been able to surprise him. Brothers knows what I'll do and acts first. He knew where to get Sanda and he'd been there waiting. He's taking away everything I'm willing to fight for, trying to bend me, break me. Now Cam is in the hospital fighting for his life and Brothers has Sanda.

"How do you know he has her?"

Lily curls into a ball of misery, and I almost pity her until she answers me. "Because I've been helping him."

"You what?" My head fills with images of Cam's paling skin, of Sanda tied up in Brothers's closet . . . of everyone left in the world that I care about. They're both at risk because Lily has been helping a lunatic.

I leap for her, white-hot fury driving me forward. One hand is in her hair, pulling, the other at her throat, and it takes every ounce of self-control I possess to stop myself from squeezing. From stealing her last remaining breaths the way Brothers has stolen everyone I love.

Lily whimpers but doesn't fight back. She doesn't even push me away. Her warm tears drip from her cheeks onto my forearm, and I slowly relax my grip on her windpipe.

"You helped him?" My voice is weak and pained. Drawing in a deep breath, I release her. "Tell me what you know."

Her wide eyes blink a few times before she starts talking so fast I can barely keep up. "He told me Sanda was his niece and you took her from her home. You kidnap kids, make them think you're going to take care of them so they don't give you any trouble, and then sell them off to slave markets in other countries. He told me that's how you got your money. He even told me about the accident where she got the scar on her left hand."

"Because he gave her that scar and it was no accident." I sit on the step next to her and rub my palm over my pocket, where I wish so badly I had my bolt right now. "You're an idiot."

Her cheeks flush like she might argue, but then her eyes turn to the sidewalk before us. Everything about her deflates and she shrinks visibly before me. "It was all a lie?"

"Yes. He held Sanda captive and tortured her. I took her to save her life."

Her shoulders slump and she takes a weak shaky breath. "And Cam?"

"It's a long story, but Brothers had us trapped. Cam was cut and lost a lot of blood." I close my eyes tight and make myself say the words that I hope to God aren't true. "I'm not sure if the ambulance came in time."

Lily's wide brown eyes are red from crying. She digs into her bag with shaking hands and produces another black box—Brothers's calling card.

"He left this at the restaurant. The card said your name, but I didn't know why Steve would leave you a gift after everything he said you did. When I asked, he said, 'People get hurt when you call the police. Don't make that mistake.' Which didn't make any sense until I took off the lid and then Cam didn't come back and . . ." At the end she's just mumbling. My hand aches to smack her. Instead, I pull off the lid.

Inside I see the words that turn my blood to ice.

NOW YOU'LL ALL PAY

I press my fingers against my eyelids, trying to make sure my hammering heartbeat doesn't make my eyeballs burst from my head. "How exactly have you been helping him?"

"I told him everything I knew about you. Your old name, where you live." She touches my shoulder and I flinch away. "I'm so sorry, Charlotte. I didn't know—I was only trying to protect Cam."

Fiery anger boils in my stomach, and I pick up the black box and throw it at the ground. The red rose inside explodes against the cement. It feels destructive, a fitting release. The streets of this city should run red with blood after today. "Great job protecting him, Lily! Now he's in the hospital and Sanda has been taken by a lunatic who likes to play with knives."

Lily glares at me, but she appears more sad and humiliated than angry. "Do you know where he might have her?"

"I don't even know where to start." I stand, fold my arms across my chest, and kick the naked rose across the ground toward her. "Why did you do this? Can't you mind your own business? Why are you so possessive of Cam?"

"I thought you were like her."

I turn back to face her and wait. I'm tired of asking her for explanations.

"The first girl Cam helped two years ago—like he helped you. He's always been a sucker for the hopeless cases," Lily says, and rests her head on her knees. "He fell hard and she screwed him over. Stole his money, half his equipment, and then she ended up floating in the bay a month later anyway."

I slide down against the railing and sit on the step. For the first time since I met her, Lily makes sense. I remember Cam mentioning the girl who died. He'd lost more than Lily's sister. Cam has more painful secrets than I realized.

"I didn't want to see him destroyed like that again, you know? He's like my brother. Since my sister died, he's all I have left." Her big brown eyes fill with tears again. "And now—"

"How did your sister die?" I interrupt.

"Anna was hit last year by a drunk driver. It was the second time he killed someone while driving drunk."

A million conversations with Lily spin through my head and something finally clicks into place. The only response I can choke out is, "I'm sorry."

We have more in common than I knew. We share pain and loss.

"We need to work together now. You've been helping him. Any idea how we can find Sanda?" I ask as I rub my face in my hands and try not to panic. "Think, Lily. Did Brothers say anything else?"

"No." She wipes her tears and watches me. "I've been over it a thousand times since I realized Cam hadn't come home."

Then something in my head clicks into place. This is Brothers. I've spent most of my life in the shadow of the Father, and for once that might actually be useful to me. Brothers has the same twisted tastes as him. He won't kill her—not yet. It wouldn't be as fun for him without me there to watch.

He wants me to find her.

Scooting forward, I pick up the box and the decimated rose

from the ground and find what I'd hoped would be there: his message, a clue. There is a strip of white paper twisted around the stem. Careful not to rip it, I gently tug the paper loose.

SHE WILL DIE WHERE YOU WERE CREATED

Blood surges through my veins and I jump to my feet. I'm halfway down the street before Lily catches me.

"Wait. What does it say? Where are you going?"

"She will die where I was created."

Lily frowns but tugs her purse up on her shoulder and keeps walking with me. "Oh no, I told him about that. I'm coming with you."

I don't even stop to argue. "No. You need to go to Cam."

"I can't do anything there." She pulls on my arm and I whirl to face her. Her voice is pleading, frantic. "I can't do that again. I stood in the room for hours waiting for my sister to wake up and she never did. After everything I've screwed up, I have to help you now. Please let me help you."

I can tell from her expression that it's useless to argue, but still I hesitate.

Her eyes dart from side to side before she continues. "I might be of more help than you think." She opens her bag and gestures for me to peek inside.

There, among makeup, gum, and a wallet, I see the gleaming black metal of the gun from the safe at Angelo's. I draw in a quick breath.

"Why are you walking around with a gun in your purse?" I hiss.

"After I read the message on the lid I was scared." Lily snaps her bag closed and finishes: "Having it makes me less afraid."

Guns never make me feel safe, but being in a rush has gotten me into trouble with Brothers more than once. Maybe I need to come prepared this time.

I force my voice to stay level as I respond. There is no room for doubting myself anymore, not when Sanda needs me. "Fine, but I get the gun. Don't get in my way."

# 30

The old barbershop is more ominous when I know what might be hiding inside. The chipped candy-cane-style pole is like a symbol of lost days and happier times. I shiver as the evening sun descends toward the horizon. The world knows this place should be hidden in darkness right now, not bathed in sunlight. The fact that there's a heavy metal gun tucked in Lily's bag reassures me. I hate that I need it, but at the same time feel better that it's here. With Brothers's fondness for knives, plus the gun he had with him at the warehouse, this might be my only chance to finally get on an even footing with him.

I glance over at Lily. Her eyes are glued to the barbershop. In spite of everything, I'm glad she's with me. I don't want to go into this alone, but it hurts when I can't help wishing Cam were here with me instead. He always knows the right thing to do, the right thing to say.

"So, are you sure we shouldn't call the police?" Her voice is fragile and thin.

"Yes." I know Brothers well enough to be certain he'll make

good on his threat. "The second he hears sirens getting close she'll be dead . . . and he'll be gone. You have to trust me on this one."

I hear her gasp and she gives a jerky nod. "Yeah, yeah, okay."

"Ready?"

She doesn't respond, so I start walking. It only takes about five feet before she catches up with me.

"How can anyone be ready for this?" she asks. Her hands tremble as she straightens her jacket.

I shrug and open the door.

Everything inside is dark. The door closes silently behind us, and the only thing I can hear is Lily's rapid breathing. Gesturing for her to hold still, I reach in her bag and remove the gun, pointing it at the floor. I keep telling myself it's simple, just point and pull the trigger. It doesn't matter that I've never used a gun in my life. They aren't designed to be difficult. It's the easiest way in the world to kill someone—so distant, almost clinical. It's nothing like the intimacy of a knife, where you have to be close enough to see the terror in their eyes.

I suppress a shudder and walk silently, keeping my eyes on every shadow and dark corner. Lily grabs my left elbow with one hand and her skin is cold and clammy.

But there is no one. The barbershop is empty. My shoulders slump forward in frustration. I'd been so sure this was the place the note described. Although, this is where Charlotte was created—not Piper. Could I have been wrong?

Lily lifts one shaking hand and points toward a hall at the back of the room. That's right. I'd almost forgotten there are more rooms here. Just as we move toward the hall, I hear him.

"You brought a friend. That's good. You seem to be losing too many today." His laugh echoes down the hallway, low and amused.

Lily whimpers beside me, and my heart aches at his implication, but I'm not afraid. The only emotion pumping through me right now is fury. He's gone too far, done too much. I won't let him hurt anyone else that I love. I can't.

Pointing the gun at the darkness down the hall with both hands, I take deep breaths and force my arms not to shake. Even in the barber's area, the windows have long been boarded up with plywood and the lighting is dim. There aren't any lights or even windows in the hallway. My finger feels dangerous on the trigger. Even though I know I brought it to protect me, it seems more like I'm carrying live explosives. The thing in my hand could as easily kill Sanda as Brothers in these dark rooms.

We inch past Cam's empty tech room to the only remaining doorway in the hall. The storage area in the back is bigger than I expect and the only light in the room is from slivers of fading sunlight streaming in around the tiny, dust-covered windows high up on the wall. I squint, trying to find him.

"Hello, Piper." Brothers's voice comes from ten feet to my left. I spin to face him and he flips on a single bulb right in front of me. Blinking my eyes rapidly, I take two steps back. I center on the direction of his voice, trying to focus on the dark figure sitting in a chair. I almost squeeze the trigger before recognizing it's Sanda. She's taller because he's strapped her to some kind of box. Her hands are bound in front of her. She's blindfolded, with a thin rope keeping a piece of fabric in her mouth.

My heart pounds loud in my ears as I realize what I could have done. Sanda's head is tilted to one side and a thin trickle of blood runs down her cheek. I'm frozen as I watch her chest, waiting for the rise and fall of breathing. When her chest moves with a full deep breath, I release the one I'm holding.

My eyes finally adjust, and I see a slight movement in the shadows behind her before Brothers limps forward and points a gun at the back of Sanda's head.

"See? We're more alike than you think."

I keep my gun trained on him and try to figure out my next move, and two after that.

*See? Guns are bad, like him. I hate guns,* Sam whimpers in my head.

"Shh," I whisper as Lily steps forward and stands beside me. She's shaking but trying to be brave anyway. My anger toward her begins to fade.

"You don't know how to use a gun, Piper. I can tell from the way you're holding it." Brothers speaks slowly and it only irritates me more, but seeing his gun pressing into Sanda's hair is like having a bucket of ice water dumped over the flames of my anger. I'm left sputtering as I strive to draw out the fire again.

Anger is a more useful emotion than fear.

I squint one eye and stare down at him. "I know where the trigger is. That's all that should matter to you."

"Very good." His tone mocks me, but I need to keep him talking. Buy a few more minutes to figure out a plan. "One thing though: the trigger can just as easily hurt my little toy here as me. In fact, much more likely her, since if your shot doesn't kill me immediately, she still dies."

Brothers steps into a sliver of dust-packed fading sunlight, and I notice a new limp when he puts his weight on his other leg. I wonder what caused it until he steps again and the movement is extremely familiar. It has to be from Sanda. One of the moves Cam worked with her on the most involved stomping on an opponent's foot and then going for the kneecaps. One lesson, she hit Cam harder than either of them expected and he walked like that for the rest of the day. I see a long scratch down his cheek that is seeping blood, but it's too big to have been made by Sanda's tiny nails. My bolt. She'd attacked him with the only thing she had. She'd definitely used it for something better than I had. It fills me with a strange pride to know she fought him like I'd hoped.

"Oh no," Lily gasps from a few feet to my right. Her voice is miserable and I slide over to see what upset her. From this angle I can see Sanda's back is bare and fresh blood seeps from two new slices on her skin. Rage flares and I want to shoot him so badly that I actually lift my finger off the trigger for an instant to make sure I don't.

"You bastard." The only words I can find.

He snickers, deep and soft. "Yes, I got bored waiting for you so we had some fun."

"What do you want?" I spit out each word, now beyond the point of reason.

"You stole something that belonged to me. I took it back."

"Not something," I reply. Taking a breath, I struggle to control the storm inside me. "Someone."

"It's my favorite toy." He grins, truly enjoying himself.

"She is *not* a toy."

"I have it back now, and our new friend, Lily," Brothers says. His eyes twinkle as he leans forward and thrusts his gun hard against Sanda's head. She doesn't move, but I hear a small moan escape past the gag. "This time you should listen when I give instructions, Piper. Or even more people will die."

The fury inside me rages and I want to let it out. To squeeze the trigger a million times until he's covered in his own blood. I want to kill him, to destroy him. The only thing that brings me any sense is Nana. Somewhere in a corner of my mind, a memory of her comes rushing back. She'd told me that I was stronger than the Parents because I could control the anger inside me.

*"Better to be the calm than the storm, Piper. The calm knows where it begins and ends, and controls what happens in between."*

The calm. I will be the calm.

Brothers has the power here. I have to figure out how to take it away. He wants to feel strong, smart, and in control. He's so like the Father, but I'd seen in the storage room the ways he isn't like him. Brothers needs something from me in a way that the Father never did. He's lonely. He misses Sanda because she's vulnerable and he needs someone he can control. I squeeze my eyes shut for an instant and know what I have to do. Brothers has a weakness.

And I will use it against him.

Drawing another breath, I trust my instincts and lower my gun. "We both know this isn't what you want."

For the first time, Brothers seems surprised. "What do you mean?"

"You don't like guns. People die too quick." I try to keep my face neutral, but I'm afraid it comes out more like a grimace.

Brothers nods but doesn't lower his weapon.

"I'm sure you brought something you'll find more interesting." I raise my eyebrows and ignore Lily's confused expression as I wait for him to respond.

He relaxes his grip and I know I've won this round. He doesn't want to use it. "You put yours down first."

I lower mine to the ground, release it, and stand back up. It only gave me an advantage if he didn't have one anyway. The moment it is out of my hand, Brothers tucks his into the back of his pants. He looks happier with his hands free.

I inch a few steps closer, wanting to force him to take the lead in the conversation. "I got your last box. You wanted me here. I'm here. Now what?"

He retreats to a table a few feet back that I now see is covered with knives, spikes, and rope. Anticipation oozes from his voice as he brushes his fingers across them. "Depends which game you want to play."

The moment his focus shifts, I sprint as silent and quick as I can toward him. Another weapon in his hands will seriously cramp my plan. I'm almost there when he hears me, grabs the nearest thing—a hammer—and spins to face me.

"No sneaking up on me this time, Piper."

"I didn't sneak up on you in your apartment. You knew I was there. You saw me." I keep the focus of our chat on his power over me. Moving out of reach, I wait, watching for overconfidence, for an opening. I remember all the things Cam taught me—eyes, nose, ears, neck, groin, knees, and legs. If you're going to hurt him, make it count. It's easiest to distract and then destroy. "Speaking of which, I never found out how you managed to survive the fire."

"You were hesitant." He smirks and holds the hammer with both hands. "Didn't hit me hard enough. Rookie mistake. I wasn't out for long and woke up in time to crawl out of the house with a few burns."

I slump my shoulders a bit, watching every breath he takes, every shift of weight—searching for his weakness. "You're right. I am a rookie."

He nods, looking very pleased that I'm showing him more respect. My stomach churns in distaste.

"How did you get in my apartment after we installed the new locks?" I take a few hesitant steps around him, slowly and patiently.

"It pays to know a locksmith." He grins.

I falter a step as his meaning hits me. "Your friend from the bar—Brady."

"He thinks you look like your puppet, too," Brothers says.

I take a deep breath. They both broke into my apartment. I wonder for an instant what other interests they might share, and the thought makes me sick. "You're very smart," I say.

"Your classes might have helped you here if I wasn't so prepared." Brothers reaches behind him and grabs the butt of a long knife with his free hand. "Too bad your teacher won't be around to teach any more lessons."

My hands tighten into fists and I almost lose control when he mentions Cam. I notice a movement to the side and realize Lily is untying the ropes binding Sanda to her chair. I can't let Brothers see them.

"Cam is going to be fine." I don't have to force the tremble in my voice, and my face tightens with the hope that my words are true.

"Stupid girl." Brothers shakes his head and pivots to face me as I step to one side, angling to keep him turned away from Sanda and Lily. "You didn't follow the rules. You ruined the game."

"It's hard to follow the rules when you don't tell me all of them." My voice comes out small behind my gritted teeth.

"You're not the best listener." Brothers's jaw tightens and he grimaces. "Besides, the boy was a distraction. Now that he's gone, I have plans to keep you busy."

I need to buy them a few more minutes. As much as I hate everything I know about Brothers and the Parents, I have to tap into that even more—push this even further—if I'm going to get us out of here. Swallowing a fresh wave of disgust, I lower my arms to my sides. I try to appear nervous and small, like I am no threat to him.

"I'm starting to feel like I might be outmatched here. Please don't hurt me."

Brothers freezes, his eyes squinting, trying to read my plan.

"Wh-what do you want from me?" I stutter, and let my voice quaver. The corner of his mouth turns up, but he doesn't speak.

"I've already seen what you can do," I continue. I thrust aside all the fear, revulsion, loathing, and try to think like him, to understand him, and then feed into his hunger—make him let his guard down. The lies come easily and the fear in my voice makes them sound true even to me. "Sanda's scars are w-worse than mine. You're stronger than the one who gave me mine."

A glint of pleasure that is almost nostalgic comes over his face and he lowers his hammer. "You're asking me not to hurt you?"

I cower and take a half step back. When I glance up at him, he's practically drooling.

"Please?" I ask, watching him from behind lowered eyelids, flinching when he shifts his weight, knowing he needs the fear, to feel the sick power.

He relaxes his stance, but he keeps himself between me and the weapons on the table. I have to let him think he's still pulling the strings until I can get in the right position to wrap my hands around his throat.

The blades glint before me. I see fresh blood on one and know he used it to cut Sanda. My hands clench into fists so tight my nails slice into my palms, so I stuff them in my pockets and take another shuffling step backward. I'm strong enough to do this, I have to be. If I keep repeating that then maybe I won't fall apart. Maybe my disgust and horror won't shatter me to pieces. Brothers is much bigger than I am. Hand to hand, he'll win, but I'm quick. If he loosens his grip on the blade, he's dead.

And this time, I'll be sure it's for real.

"I know your name isn't Brothers. We both have to hide who we really are," I whisper, finding common ground. He nods and his fingers begin to relax on the knife. "It's hard to be alone. No one understands."

"But you do?" He takes one step toward me.

I inch back in the hopes that he'll step with me away from the weapons. "You're dangerous."

"I can be." His eyes shine back at me in the darkness.

The chair Sanda is sitting on shifts and makes a noise. Brothers whips his head around. Grabbing for his knife, my fingers only manage to knock it out of his hand. I pounce, but his guard is up again and he responds faster than I expect.

"You're trying to fool me?" he roars, and steps back.

"No!" I scramble to one side, trying to get close enough to reach his throat. "I'm trying to kill you!"

He swings and I duck, kicking low, going for the groin. My leg isn't as long as his arms and I connect with his thigh instead. He grunts, but it wasn't the impact I'd been looking for. I step close, stomping on his foot and reaching up for his throat exactly like Cam taught me.

But he reacts too fast. The side of his hammer slams down on the top of my head and I fall to the floor like discarded trash. I can't hear, can't see, can't think. Every sense is eclipsed as an explosion of pain drenches me in a vibrating wave of nothingness.

# 31

I force my eyes open, knowing I can't black out, not now. In the dim light, I see hazy images of Brothers chasing Lily around a table across the room. Sanda has fallen from the chair, but her arms and legs are still bound and I hear her crying as she tries to roll away from the sound of their struggle. Lily is fast, but it's clear this fight will be over quickly.

Adrenaline helps me turn over, and I manage to silence my groan when the ground tilts oddly to one side. My eyes settle on the only thing that might save us now—the gun from Angelo's, still sitting on the ground where I placed it. It's halfway across the room, but it's something. I crawl toward it, keeping my eyes on Brothers's back. Lily scurries one way and then another, keeping the table between herself and Brothers. She decides to make a run for it and dashes toward the table with the knives. She almost gets one in her hand when Brothers slams his arm into her back and sends her crashing across the floor and into the nearest wall. He grabs a long, lethal-looking knife from the table and spins toward Sanda.

I freeze, knowing I can't keep moving without Brothers seeing me, but I can't reach the gun yet either. It doesn't matter. When Brothers takes his first step in Sanda's direction, his eyes land squarely on me. The eagerness I'd seen before is gone; all that remains now is wild fury and a lust for blood.

With a dark chuckle, he stumbles toward me, but Lily staggers to her feet with tears and blood streaming down her cheeks. She grabs a knife with one trembling hand. I can see his thoughts stamped across his face. I'd attacked him with my bare hands while she ran. She is clearly weaker, less of a threat. When he dismisses her and turns on me, I hear her voice shatter the silence.

"No! Stop. I-I won't let you hurt her," Lily says, as she steps closer but doesn't strike. Even from here, I can see she is terrified. Keeping me in sight, he shifts his feet until he can see us both. I watch him sizing her up: the shaking knife, trembling shoulders, blood- and dirt-streaked face—not exactly intimidating.

"You *won't let* me?" He laughs, shakes his head, and turns away from her. "Don't worry, little mouse. You'll be next. First, I have to handle the snake."

My eyes take in every detail in the room. Realizing I can't get to the gun in time, I scoot to the right, hoping to get under the nearest table for a little protection. He's almost made it to me when he slows. His eyes widen as he sputters and turns. I see Lily right behind him and her knife sticking out of the lower left side of his back.

"I s-said to stop." She's no longer crying, and she stands over him as he falls to his knees. I can see it in her eyes, the emotions fighting. Horror, fear, and triumph—I've felt them. I wish I could've saved her from this.

She'll never be the same again.

As Brothers leans forward, the gun tucked in his waistband comes loose and falls to the floor in front of me. I see the muscles on his back flex and realize what he's doing.

"Lily, run!" I shout. My voice echoes as time screeches to a halt. I grab the gun, point, and pull the trigger back so far I'm afraid I've done it wrong before it finally shoots, and I'm not prepared for the blast of sound or the way it jerks my forearm up. My ears ring so I know it went off, but he's still moving, still going for her, so I raise my other hand to brace it and stare down at the center of Brothers's back. My heartbeat is concussive against my eardrums. It is like someone replaced my heart with a block of dry ice, and with each beat, frigid smoke rolls through my veins. I squeeze the trigger twice more, this time prepared for the recoil, before he finally begins to fall. The air settles and a burnt metallic scent fills my nose. I'm struck by the mechanical distance of it, nothing like a knife going through flesh—I don't even have any blood on me. When he hits the ground, I see I was too late. Once again, too late to save someone.

The knife is already buried to the hilt in Lily's stomach. Her back hunches as she falls to the floor, and I'm by her side in an instant. I grab her hand in one of mine and use the other to reach into her pocket and grab her phone.

"It's okay, Lily. I'm calling for help." I can barely make out my own words through my still-ringing ears as I dial 911 with shaking fingers.

Lily reaches out and takes the phone before I can speak. "I was kidnapped and stabbed. I'm bleeding . . . s-so much. Please come help."

I listen, helpless, as she gives them the address. She's right. There is so much blood; hers and Brothers's mingle on the floor between them. The image feels so wrong.

Trying to reassure myself, I do the only thing that seems right at the moment. I check for a pulse on Brothers's still form—nothing. I can see all three bullet holes, but the first one only grazed his shoulder. The last two got the job done. I think about moving him. He doesn't deserve to be near Lily, even in death.

Sanda whimpers, and the room only spins a little as I rush to her side. I can hear Lily talking to the 911 operator as I undo the ropes on Sanda's hands and untie the blindfold. The moment I remove her gag, she throws both arms around me and sobs against my shirt. I'm careful not to touch any of her new cuts as I bring her over by Lily.

"He found us, Charlotte. We're never safe. We've never been safe," Sanda chokes out between sobs. "I'm sorry."

"It's not your fault," I tell her. I want to make everyone stop hurting, but I can't. No one has that kind of power. "He can't come for you ever again. He's dead."

"It's not enough," Sanda mutters, and cries harder. I rub her cold arms and hold her tight, knowing there is nothing else I can do to make her feel better, not here.

Lily closes the phone even though I can still hear the operator talking.

"Please help me, Charlotte." Her voice is frantic but weakening. "It won't stop bleeding. Should we pull out the knife?" She closes her eyes and lays her head back against the cement.

"No." I grab a scarf from her bag and place it around the knife and against the wound. She flinches, her skin pale. "Don't touch it. It will bleed worse if you take it out now."

"Charlotte?" Lily's voice is softer, and we lean forward to hear her. "I was wrong about you. I'm so sorry."

"No, Lily. You don't have to be sorry, ever." My eyes are wet as I stroke her hair.

"You'll regret saying that someday." Her voice holds a feeble hint of humor that gives me hope.

I grin. "I'll hold you to that."

I lift Sanda onto my lap. She lays her head against my chest and her crying eases a little.

The ambulance siren blares in the distance, and Lily blinks her eyes slowly. "Take care of Cam. Make sure he's okay."

"I will, and so will you." I reach down to squeeze her hand. "You keep breathing. That's all I want."

She nods slowly, and then her eyes fly to Sanda and back to me. Her gasps grow more ragged with every word and she closes her eyes. "You need to get her out of here, police coming."

"Stop, Lily. You hold on. No more talking now." I shake my head.

"Wipe the gun off on your shirt and then p-put it in my hand." Her voice shakes, but she's adamant.

"What?"

"Hurry. Now."

When I do as she asks, she fires two shots into the wooden table nearby. Sanda's crying grows louder. Lily winces, drops the gun, and closes her eyes.

"What are you doing?" I ask. My question comes out more like a yell, my ears haven't stopped ringing yet.

"Gun powder residue," she whispers when I lean close to hear. "I just killed him. It should be on my hands."

An icy shiver runs through my body and I shake my head. "No, Lily. I can't let you do that."

"Relax. Look around you. It's clearly self-defense." I take in the state of the room and realize she's right. With her injury, the table of weapons, and the obvious struggle, it's pretty clear what happened here. At least in a TV show it would be. I hope the shows get it right.

The sirens sound like they're almost on top of us.

"You both have to run, now. Sanda is no safer with the police than you are."

Her words snap me into action. Of course she's right. I get to my feet and head for the hallway as we hear the sirens come to a stop just outside.

"Go through Cam's tech room. There's a back exit there. No one will see you." Lily strains to get out the last few words and I can see the pain in her face.

"Thank you." They are the only words I can come up with as I race out of the room with Sanda's hand tucked safely in mine.

# 32

We go home to shower, bandage ourselves up, and change before we head to Penn Hospital. Neither of us speaks a word.

Janice knocks on my door, and when I open it her eyes widen so much I'm afraid they might fall out. I can't even begin to answer the millions of concerned questions she throws at me.

"I'm sorry, but we're alive, we're exhausted, and we need to get to the hospital to check on Cam. Can we please come by and chat tomorrow?"

"Of course, but please let me know if I can do anything. Okay?" After I nod, she gives us each a hug and closes the door after casting me a sad glance on her way out.

Every few minutes, Sanda starts crying again. If I wasn't so drained and empty of emotion, I'd do the same. I can't find tears to match the pain that oozes from every piece of me. Judging from the throbbing headache and occasional moments of nausea, I'm fairly certain I have a concussion, but it's a mild one and nothing compared to Cam's and Lily's injuries.

Everyone I care about was in danger today. Some still might not make it. Each person who dies takes a piece of me with them that I'll never get back. With so much of me gone, how can I be anything more than a shell without them?

We walk through the hospital doors with Sanda's hand in mine. I can't be certain which of us is trembling harder. When we find the ER desk, I freeze up, terrified to step forward and ask the question I've been dodging for hours. Did Cam make it?

I jump when a crash sounds from a room down the hall, and then Cam's voice yells, "What do you mean hospital policy? You can't keep me here."

His shouting voice is the best thing I've heard in a long time. A grin spreads on my face as my fears are replaced with a sense of peace. It's as though someone took my city this morning and shook it up like the massive snow globes I saw in gas stations and souvenir shops on my way across the country. All day, I've been careening around inside, trying to make sense of the chaos. Just hearing Cam's voice returns gravity to my world, sense to my city. Everything is going to be all right again. Sanda stares toward Cam's doorway with wide eyes. Her tears have calmed now. Even if she seems afraid to speak, I'm proud of her for being so brave.

We walk to his room and I can hear the doctor speaking. "The best thing for you now is rest. Please lie down before we're forced to sedate you."

Cam is sitting on the edge of his bed and one of the nurses is holding a bag of clothes out of his reach. I see another nurse picking up a tray from the floor. That must've been the crash we heard.

He hasn't noticed us yet, and I study his face. His skin is still pale, but nothing like earlier. A frantic craving to see the warmth in the green-brown swirls of his eyes again fills me. I have to see his familiar grin before I'll believe I succeeded in saving him when I couldn't save Sam. We step inside the room and everyone turns to face us.

One of the nurses looks like she's about to say something to me, but when Cam waves at us, she closes her mouth and waits.

"Hey," Cam says, but his eyes say so much more. A million emotions I'm feeling but would never know how to express reflect back at me through his eyes. He tries to stand up, but wobbles, and the nurse presses him back on the bed.

"Hey." I step closer, still afraid that at any moment he could be stolen away again. I'm engulfed by a tidal wave of relief with each breath I see him take. He'll be okay. He's really going to be okay. A huge weight evaporates from my shoulders, and suddenly the tears come. I wipe my cheek with the back of my hand and smile. "I'm so glad you're okay."

Cam grins back and reaches out for my hand, wrapping his fingers around mine. They are warm again, and the warmth seeps up my arm and fills my chest with an unfamiliar heat. I'm suddenly ultra-aware of the three nurses and the doctor in the room watching us.

"Tell them you're going to be good and get some rest now," I whisper, and he nods, sliding back in his bed until he's leaning against his pillow with his legs tucked under the blankets.

"I've understood the error of my ways." His face might crack if he grins any wider, but I can see the exhaustion behind his eyes. "No sedatives necessary."

The doctor and nurses give him a few wary glances and shuffle out of the room, closing the door behind them.

"Where were you going?" I squeeze his fingers. "Big plans this evening?"

"I was sure trying." His eyes drop to Sanda and his relief is obvious. "She's safe."

"Yeah." I nod, knowing the rest of the story can wait until later. "We're both safe."

Sanda walks over to the bed, kisses her hand, and then rests it gently on Cam's bandaged arm.

"The first time is the worst," she states simply.

"There won't be any more times, Sanda." Cam covers her hand with his and stares her straight in the eye. "Not for any of us. I promise."

She looks doubtful but doesn't argue. It will take time to adjust to such a strange and wonderful idea, for both of us. But with Cam here and safe, it's hard to believe there is anything that's impossible.

I grab two chairs and pull them over next to Cam's bed. Sanda curls up in one and rests her head on my lap. In under a minute her eyes flutter closed.

"You look like you've been through hell." His eyes scrutinize me even though he seems more tired by the second.

My laughter comes out light and airy. "You're one to talk."

"I'm so glad you're here and that you're okay." His eyes shine wet, but no tears fall. "I was so worried."

"*You* were worried?" The awe in my tone brings a smile to his face. "Are you kidding? Last time I saw you . . . last time I saw you . . ." My voice chokes up and I can't finish.

He chuckles and it's low and sweet to my ears. "I'm fine. You saved me."

I'm shaking my head before he even finishes, but he places one finger against my lips until I stop. Then he pleads, "This one time, don't argue, please? I'd be—I wouldn't have made it without you."

*He's right, you know.*

Maybe partly, but I couldn't save you, Sam. The agonizing truth crawls from the pit deep inside me and brings with it that same raw pain.

*Did you expect me to save you?*

Of course not.

*Good, because I couldn't, and neither could you. But you saved Cam, Sanda, and Lily when you could. That's what matters.*

The gaping pit crumbles a little at the words, and shrinks even smaller as I watch the color returning to Cam's cheeks. I may have gotten him into trouble, but I got him out of it, too. That minuscule slice of redemption is like a beam of sunlight coming from inside my chest.

"An ambulance brought Lily in. She had surgery and Jessie is with her now. There was some damage to her spine, but we won't know how much for a while." His eyes turn cold and hard as he glares at the wall across from him. "Was it Brothers?"

I give him a grim nod. "Yes. I told her not to come, but she wouldn't listen."

Cam rubs his fingers gently across the back of my hand, but I can't miss the strain in his expression when he asks, "Did you get him?"

I nod. "He's dead. The rest of the story can wait for later."

He sighs heavily, lifts my hand to his lips, and kisses the back of it. "Later sounds good."

"Do you think Lily will be okay?" My voice is soft, and I hear Sanda whimper in her sleep.

"She's a fighter. I guess you saw that tonight." He lifts his eyes to mine, and it hurts to see the sorrow there.

"More than you know." My mind absorbs how truly messed up his life has become since I came into it, and I wish I could fix it all. "I'm so sorry, Cam. For everything." The words are so insufficient to make up for the way I've broken everything he knows. They feel feeble in my mouth.

"Stop." He brushes his thumb across my lips and I lean my cheek against his hand. It's quiet for a few minutes, and I don't want to break the spell. Cam said he loves me. He knows I killed Brothers tonight and he's not looking at me like I'm a monster. Sanda is alive and sleeping here next to me. There is even hope that Lily will be all right. I may have been living with people who were supposed to be my family before, but this is my real family.

I wish for the millionth time that Sam had lived to escape with me, that he could've met them. We both could've belonged here. For the first time I can remember, peace descends over me like a warm blanket. I've survived so much horror that a little peace is long overdue. But that's the point, isn't it? I did survive.

Maybe Nana was right. Maybe I am the strong one.

*You'll always be Piper. You'll always be strong.*

Sam's words echo in my head and I'm filled with a sudden emptiness. I know it was never really him, that he was never there, but it seems he's talking less and less. Maybe a time is coming when I won't need to hear his voice to get me through the day, but there will never come a day when I won't miss him. The ache in my chest is so strong it steals my breath away as Sam's face flashes in my mind. His blond hair, blue eyes, crooked smile, and the dimple in only one cheek—I'm glad I can still see him so clearly. I have no pictures of him to refresh my memory. I take a slow breath but leave the stray tears on my cheek. Sam deserves to be remembered, to be wept for.

No. I still don't regret what I've done.

"I need to know." Cam's voice pulls me from my thoughts. His expression is full of hesitation. "When I said I was sorry, I meant it. Do you think you can forgive me? Because I'm crazy about you, and I can't imagine spending another day with you running away from me."

Without a word, I slip out from under Sanda, resting her head gently on the cushioned chair. I wrap my arms around Cam's neck and bury my face in his chest. His uninjured arm encircles me instantly and he rubs my back with his right hand. This is what I've needed all along. I needed someone to see who I am in spite of what I've done. Cam can see me, all of me, and he still loves me. It's the best feeling in the world.

His arms set my world aright again, and I lean my face against his neck. The heat of his skin is surreal and so strong. I tighten my arms and drag him closer, enjoying the way he eases the ache in my heart.

I press my lips against his and only pull back to whisper the words I've never said to another living soul. "I love you, too. And I'm done running."

# ACKNOWLEDGMENTS

I've heard other authors refer to certain books as the "book of my heart," and I think Piper's story is mine. I have a few people to thank that *Cut Me Free* is finally out in the world.

First, I need to thank my family. To my mom and Krista, thank you for your feedback and for loving Piper enough to push me to keep working on it, even when it was a struggle. Thank you to Bill, Eric, Amanda, and Matt for reading and supporting me on this crazy path I've chosen. And to my husband, Ande, and our boys, Cameron and Parker, thank you for blessing my every day with laughter and love. Because you've given me such a wonderful life, Piper has the will to fight for something more.

To my girls: Thank you, L. T. Elliot, for being the first to see the beauty in Piper's story. And thank you to Michelle Argyle, Natalie Whipple, Kasie West, Sara Raasch, Renee Collins, Candice Kennington, and Bree Despain. You helped me through the madness that is publishing. I'm the luckiest girl in the world to have found friends like you!

Huge thanks to my kindred authors from all over: Nichole

Giles, Jessica Brody, Jennifer Bosworth, Morgan Matson, Michelle Gagnon, Jessica Khoury, Marie Lu, Brodi Ashton, Emmy Laybourne, Jennifer Lynn Barnes, J. Scott Savage, Leigh Bardugo, Kendare Blake, Gretchen McNeil, Jennifer L. Armentrout, James Dashner, and Julie Berry. Whether at conferences, retreats, or just online, you've made this trip so much better by being a part of it. Love you all!

I've been lucky enough to be a part of some fabulous author groups that have been so good to me. Thank you to all the Lucky 13s for being so supportive and making the debut road easier to navigate. Thank you to the Friday the Thirteeners (Natalie Whipple, Kasie West, Ellen Oh, Erin Bowman, April Tucholke, Elsie Chapman, Shannon Messenger, Megan Shepherd, Mindy McGinnis, Alexandra Duncan, Brandy Colbert, and Renee Collins) for taking me in and feeling like a safe place in a scary time. And thank you to the YA Scream Queens (Lindsay Currie, Lauren Roy, Sarah Jude, Courtney Alameda, Trisha Leaver, Dawn Kurtagich, Hillary Monahan, and Catherine Scully) for making what I write feel so freaking cool.

To my agent, Kathleen Rushall, you're my friend and advocate. Thank you for fighting my battles and celebrating my victories. You're the best!

To my fantastic readers, I know your lives are busy and I am so glad you take time out of them to read my stories. Every e-mail I get from you brightens my day, and I'm so grateful you keep reading!

And of course, to my brilliant editor, Janine O'Malley, thank you for helping me polish this story until the truth of it could shine through. I'm so thrilled to be working with you! Thank you to

Simon Boughton and Joy Peskin for always making me feel wonderfully welcome. To Angie Chen, thank you for putting up with my crazy questions and always having all the answers! Thank you to Andrew Arnold for capturing perfection in this brilliant cover and having the absolute coolest chair in the office (someday I hope to inherit the cover lock from you!). To Nicole Banholzer, Katie Fee, and Caitlin Sweeny, thank you so much for helping readers find Piper and her story. And to the rest of the *Cut Me Free* team at FSG, thank you for bringing Piper into the world. I am forever grateful for all you've done and continue to do.